INITIATED

A reverse harem bully romance

STEFFANIE HOLMES

Copyright © 2019 by Steffanie Holmes

All rights reserved.

No part of this book may be reproduced in any form or by any electronic or mechanical means, including information storage and retrieval systems, without written permission from the author, except for the use of brief quotations in a book review.

Cover design: Amanda Rose

ISBN: 978-0-9951302-0-3

❋ Created with Vellum

INITIATED

They were my tormenters. Now, they're all that stands between me and my nightmares.

Trey, Quinn, and Ayaz—the king, the joker, and the enigma.
Three guys who've flipped my life upside down,
set my heart on fire,
and shown me that nothing is as it seems.

Last quarter, they broke me. I thought that was the worst it could
get at Miskatonic Prep.

I was wrong.

Twenty years ago, a tragedy changed this school forever.
Arrogance turned this place of learning into a house of horrors.
Greed awoke *something* from the deep.

And that something waits, dead but dreaming, beneath the
gymnasium.
Waiting for its next target.

Waiting for me.

I want to trust the guys.
I want their friendship.
I want *so much more*.
And right now, I need their help. But after what they did to me,
how can I let them in?

Secrets. Lies. Sacrifice.
Welcome to my nightmare.

Welcome to Miskatonic Prep.

HP Lovecraft meets *Cruel Intentions* in book 2 of this dark
paranormal reverse harem bully romance. Warning: Not for the
faint of heart – this story of three broken bad boys and the girl
who stood her ground contains dark themes, crazed cultists,
books bound in human skin, high-school drama, swoon-worthy
sex, and potential triggers.

Can't wait to find out what happens next? Grab book 3 – *Possessed!*

JOIN THE NEWSLETTER FOR UPDATES

Get bonus scenes and additional material in *Cabinet of Curiosities*, a Steffanie Holmes compendium of short stories and bonus scenes. To get this collection, all you need to do is sign up for updates with the Steffanie Holmes newsletter.

www.steffanieholmes.com/newsletter

Every week in my newsletter I talk about the true-life hauntings, strange happenings, crumbling ruins, and creepy facts that inspire my stories. You'll also get newsletter-exclusive bonus scenes and updates. I love to talk to my readers, so come join me for some spooky fun :)

A NOTE ON DARK CONTENT

This series goes to some dark places.

I'm writing this note because I want you a heads up about some of the content in this book. Reading should be fun, so I want to make sure you don't get any nasty surprises. If you're cool with anything and you don't want spoilers, then skip this note and dive in.

Keep reading if you like a bit of warning about what to expect in a dark series.

- There is some intense bullying in the first couple of books, but our heroine holds her own. Our heroes have been born into cruelty and they'll need to redeem themselves.

- This series deals with themes of inequality and cycles of violence – there may be times where this is tough to read, especially if it hits too close to your lived reality.

- This is a reverse harem series, which means that in the end our heroine, Hazel, will have at least three heroes. She does not have to choose, and sometimes her heroes like to share. Although this book is set in high school, I'd call it R18 for sexual content.

- Subsequent books contain violence, threat of sexual violence (that doesn't succeed), and cruel and capricious cosmic deities.

Hazel and her friends are deep in a cruel, bloodthirsty world. It's not pretty, but I promise there will be suspense, hot sex, occult mysteries, and beautiful retribution. If that's not your jam, that's totally cool. I suggest you pick up my Nevermore Bookshop Mysteries series – all of the mystery without the gore and trauma and violence.

Enjoy, you beautiful depraved human, you :) Steff

To James,
Who didn't just stand up for me,
but taught me how to stand up for myself

"The most merciful thing in the world, I think, is the inability of the human mind to correlate all its contents. We live on a placid island of ignorance in the midst of black seas of infinity, and it was not meant that we should voyage far."

– HP Lovecraft, *The Call of Cthulhu* (1926)

CHAPTER ONE

"You saw the stones," Ayaz said. "You know that Quinn, Trey, and I are dead. We're all dead."

In my hand, the lantern flared. Flames licked the edge of my hand. Heat stabbed my skin like a knife, sending me back to another time and another fire that tore my world apart.

I screamed and dropped the lantern. It rolled against the headstone, and the fire flickered out. Darkness consumed me, making the looming trees and the three guys standing around me all the more menacing.

"Hazy, are you okay?" Quinn's boots crunched over dead leaves. His hand reached through the gloom and brushed my arm. A hand that was very much alive, very much skin and bone and vein and sinew. The same hand that had touched my face so tenderly in the grotto, that had pulled me closer as he'd kissed me like a fire starved of oxygen...

I should be terrified. I should be running as fast as I can away from these psychopaths.

Instead, I was angry as *fuck*.

I leapt to my feet and planted my hands on Quinn's chest. He reached for my wrists, probably thinking I was clinging to him in some terrified stupor. Instead, I shoved him. Hard. Quinn grunted as he stumbled over his own gravestone and landed on his ass in a pile of leaves.

"What the *hell* are you guys playing at?" I screamed. "You have been nothing but cruel to me since I arrived at this school. Now you drag me out here in the middle of the night, try to drown me in the ocean, and then you tell me this fucking bullshit story that the teachers are trying to hurt me and that you're all dead? I'm done with this. It ends tonight."

"Keep your voice down," Trey hissed. My eyes had begun to adjust to the darkness, and I could just make out the outline of his head. An owl hooted in the trees. Trey spun toward it, his shoulders rigid. *He's scared.*

But why? I'm the one who should be afraid.

"I'm done taking commands from you, Trey fucking Bloomberg." I shuffled backward, shifting my weight on my back leg, preparing to run. "The shit you've orchestrated goes beyond bullying... it's fucking *assault*. I don't care who your parents are or what you say about me being in danger. I'm in danger from *you*. I'm going back to Derleth, and I'm reporting all of you. And if Headmistress West doesn't do anything about it, I'm calling the police."

"Hazy, *please*." Quinn's voice ached with emotion. He didn't move from his pile of leaves. "We can explain everything. But you have to be quiet. They're probably out looking for you by now. If they catch you here, you're dead, too."

"You can't possibly expect me to trust you." Another step back. Moonlight pooled through gaps in the trees. I could make out the lumps of stone on the ground, the rough slope of the hill above. Ayaz shuffled out to the side, trying to close around me. But if I went the other way, I had a clear run toward the gate.

"She's right," Ayaz's voice cracked. "Of course she can't trust us. This whole thing was fucking *pointless*."

"What whole thing? You mean the whole, 'oh, we're so sorry,

Hazel. We'll make you think we're remorseful, that maybe there was some fucked-up reason we put you through all of this. And then we'll drag you outside in the middle of the night to humiliate you in front of the entire school because really, we're a bunch of dick-weasels.'"

"I mean the whole thing where we tried to protect you. We tried to save you from ending up like us." Ayaz's voice sliced the darkness like a razor. "Now it's too late. It's always too late—"

I sprung into action, flinging my body along a row of graves. So many graves. This cemetery was a lot larger than I expected. My chest burned as I wove between the stones, my feet catching on loose sticks and branches. I stumbled, came down hard on my knee, pulled myself up, kept on running.

Let's see you catch me, bully boys. I'd outran gangs, drunk fondlers, and creepy dudes outside Mom's club. Dante and I once ran twelve blocks without stopping to lose a meth-head with a knife. *You live in the Badlands, you get fucking good at running—*

Trey stepped in front of me, his broad chest blocking my exit. *Damn lacrosse players. I guess he's good at running, too.* Although he wasn't breathing heavy, like me. "We'll explain everything," he said.

"Get out of my way," I growled, lunging forward.

To my surprise, Trey stepped back, raising his hands in surrender. I shoved past him, sprinting toward the iron fence. A bitter breeze blew up from the ocean below, tossing dead leaves against my legs. Shoes crunched in brittle foliage as the guys followed me.

"Why'd you let her go?" Quinn wailed, but I didn't stick around to find out the answer. I flung open the gate and jogged out of the trees.

Pale moonlight cast an eerie glow over the pleasure garden – the trees bent in the wind, their shadows dancing over the ancient statues, making their features dance and twist. I looked out to my right, toward the top of the cliffs where the edge of the school grounds met the ocean. Flashlight beams swung through the trees. Teachers out looking for someone. For me.

We're dead, Hazel. Ayaz's words repeated in my head.

We're all dead.

I tried to push aside the memories of the horrible things those guys did to me and focus on the weird things I'd seen during my first quarter at Derleth Academy – things I couldn't explain but that hadn't held my attention like the immediate threat from the monarchs. The teachers checking the students were *out* of their dorms so they could sneak down to the gymnasium in black robes. The total lockdown against any kind of internet connection or transmitting device. Loretta's disappearance and return. The article I found about the old school – Miskatonic Prep. The shadows that attacked me in the gym. The rats in the walls. All the things Trey, Ayaz, and Quinn spoke when they thought I couldn't hear, about not being able to protect me anymore, and about someone called Zehra.

I knew that even if I couldn't trust them, I couldn't trust Ms. West and the faculty, either. But I needed answers, and I wasn't going to get them from my three bullies. I shoved down all the conflicting feelings I had for them – the warmth of Quinn's arms when he saved me from the gym, the ferocity of Trey's convictions and the hunger in his kiss, the searching darkness behind Ayaz's eyes, and the giddy feeling in my stomach when I was near them.

I squared my shoulders and set off up the path at a jog, scrambling around the edge of the grotto where Quinn had convinced me to swim with him in my underwear, where his kiss had melted something frozen inside me...

Don't think about it now. You need all your wits about you if you're going to survive this night.

I deliberately avoided looking at the ledge where I'd sat with Quinn as I scooted around the edge of the pool. Behind the grotto, a set of narrow steps cut into the rock, leading up into the woods that surrounded Derleth Academy. It was how most of the students accessed the pleasure garden – those who didn't know about the secret passage.

Without the lantern to hold, I had both hands free to steady myself as I scrambled up the rocks, pressing my body into the side of the cliff. My legs trembled with vertigo as I climbed above the grotto. The moon reflected in the pool below – a lidless eye watching me from the deep. It made me think of the horrible dreams I'd been having about the malignant *thing* hiding in the hole in the middle of that shadowy cavern. But dreams couldn't hurt me, and I *knew* whoever was searching the forest for me didn't have my best interests at heart.

"Hazel, Hazel, don't go up there!"

The boys ran through the pleasure garden, faces tilted up at me, moonlight catching on their handsome features. But they didn't follow me up the steps. Trey sounded so panicked, it spurred me on.

It's about time Trey Bloomberg learned what it's like to be afraid.

My nails scraped against stone as I scrambled over the top. The boys disappeared from sight. The steps gave way to a rocky path that circled through the trees on the edge of the cliff. I clambered around the rocks, heading in the direction of the lights but trying to stay low and not step directly into the beams. I had to know for certain it was me they were looking for – that I really *was* in danger from all sides. The trees grew thicker and stood straighter as they sloped up toward the school. Lights bobbed and ducked through the trunks, and voices called out to each other. They weren't worried about being quiet. On the surface, this was every bit a concerted effort from the faculty to search for a missing student.

To search for me.

I'd locked the door to my room behind me. There was no late-night inspection at Derleth (supposedly), and students frequently flouted the 'no sleeping over in other dorms' rule. Ayaz and I had come to the pleasure garden via the secret passage, so they had no way of knowing I was out of the school. So why did every staff member seem to be out here, hunting through the woods? Why did they care where I was? They'd never cared before.

A beam swept across the path only twenty feet in front of me. I dived into the trees, my heart thudding in my chest. At least two people were nearby, talking in hushed voices. Footsteps crunched in the dead leaves. A branch snapped.

Keeping low and stepping on the twisted roots where I'd be less likely to make a sound, I darted between the trees, trying to get close enough to hear their conversation. A vein of rock jutted up from the dirt, bending the trees outward as if they shied away from it. Ancient stratigraphy pushed up from below to form a low shelf and a scattering of large, cone-shaped rocks, like the towering dolmans of a Neolithic temple.

I made my way toward the formation, letting the smooth stone beneath my feet muffle my footsteps. I crouched low behind one of the craggy stones, listening. In the still night, even their whispers rang clear.

"We've checked the entire eastern wing, Headmistress," Professor Atwood said. "Hazel's not there."

"She can't have gotten far," Headmistress West snapped. Flashlight beams bounced across the grounds. "Alert the maintenance staff. Send them down the peninsula to guard the road. That girl cannot be allowed to leave the grounds alive."

Her words were a shard of ice, thawing the fire inside me.

That girl cannot be allowed to leave the grounds alive.

If I'd wanted evidence, I had it now. But what could I do? Where could I go? For the first time, the helplessness of my situation washed over me. There was no one I could trust at this school. I had no family, no one to call for help. Even if I did make it down to the town of Arkham, what good would it do? The police wouldn't believe anything I told them. "The teachers are trying to kill me, Officer." Yeah, right. I hardly believed it myself.

Something brushed my ankle. I spun around, my heart leaping into my throat. Quinn's face peeked out from between the rocks. He held out a hand to me, fingers reaching, grasping at air.

"Trust me," he mouthed.

Trust me.

Something invisible reached through the air between us – a flare of heat that sizzled against my skin. I flashed back to the gymnasium, where Quinn dragged me to safety before those shadowed things got to me. In a surge of heat, my body remembered the brush of his lips against mine and the times he'd let his guard down around me and had been more than Quinn the tormentor, Quinn the trickster.

The beam of a flashlight flickered across the rocks, just above my head. The voices drew closer. It wouldn't be long until they were right on top of me.

Whatever Trey, Ayaz, and Quinn are involved in, they're trying to help me.

I think.

Maybe.

I hope.

It was all I had to go on. But it was better than being caught by Headmistress West.

I reached out and took Quinn's hand. A pulse of heat flared up my arm. I allowed Quinn to pull me under the ledge. We slithered through a narrow gap and dropped down into a pitch-black cave. My ass cracked against wet rock as I slid and skidded down a steeply sloping rock face. Just as my feet slammed into flat rock and I wrenched myself upright, a flashlight beam passed over the entrance several feet above my head, flickering through the space without penetrating it.

"I've got her," Quinn whispered, one hand circling my wrist, the other resting protectively against my hip, radiating warmth through my clammy skin.

A match struck. A moment later, a lantern burst into flame,

illuminating Trey's face. He appeared stricken. Dirt smudged along his cheek, humanizing his too-perfect, too-pretty features.

"Hey, Meat," he said, his voice barely above a whisper. "You've decided to trust us."

"Don't make me regret it," I growled. "Where am I?"

Trey swept the lantern around him, casting the warm glow of the flame against unyielding stone. Unlike the secret tunnel connecting the storage room on my floor to the pleasure garden, this cave was rough – not hollowed out by humans or machines, but formed from water being forced up from somewhere deep underground, reshaping the rock, bedding planes and fractures in the immovable chunks and creating a giant's staircase of abutting shelves leading down into an oppressive black hole. Stalactites hung from the underside of the rock shelf above our heads – a hundred tiny swords of Damocles just waiting to drop on me.

I noticed a row of lanterns and a waterproof box resting on a low shelf behind Trey. A symbol had been scrawled into the wall – the same runic symbol I'd seen tattooed on the guys' wrists. Someone had definitely been hanging out in this cave.

Something slapped against the wet floor. I whirled around and stared at that dark hole. Trey thrust out his arm. The lantern illuminated the muscled slope of Ayaz's shoulders as he straightened up on one of the lower shelves.

"They're heading back to the cavern," he called up to us. "We have to hurry."

"Hurry where?" I demanded.

"To the place where you'll get your answers." Ayaz sounded exasperated, as though this was obvious.

"Why can't I get my answers here?" I wrenched my hip away from Quinn and folded my arms across my chest.

"We can't explain, Hazy. You won't believe us."

"Try me."

"There's no point. The whole thing is so fucking unbelievable, I barely accept it, and I'm living it." There was a hint of a smile in

Quinn's voice. He couldn't take *anything* seriously. "Perhaps 'living' is the wrong word."

"Quinn, shut up," Trey snapped. He tried to grab my arm, but I jerked it away. "We have to go."

"I don't see why I should go anywhere with you," I shot back.

"Fine. Go back to school and report us." Trey gestured to the mouth of the cave above our heads. When I didn't budge, he added, "Or, come with us and find out what's actually going on."

The lantern caught a glint in Trey's eye – a hint of his usual arrogance. As much as I hated Trey for all the times he'd burrowed into my weaknesses and exposed them, he *knew* me. We were bitter enemies because something inside us recognized an affinity with the other – an equal capacity for cruelty, a duplicitous desire to control, to know everything. I hated that Trey knew me without my permission, but neither of us could take back what he'd done now.

Trey knew that if he turned away from me and started clambering down into that darkness, toward the answers, I'd follow him.

Damn him, he was right.

CHAPTER TWO

About fifty feet down the slippery rocks, I decided I wasn't going to follow any longer. My limbs were already jelly, Ayaz's damp t-shirt clung to my body, and my leggings were slick with sticky mud. My teeth chattered. My knee burned with pain from where I'd cracked it against one of the gravestones. Tired, scared, pissed off – something inside me shut down and I couldn't budge.

We're dead, Hazel. We're all dead.

What did that even *mean?*

Quinn tugged my arm. "Come on, Hazy. It's not much further."

"Where are we going?" I demanded, folding my arms across my chest. "I'm done with this cryptic shit. I need to know things before I move another inch."

Quinn leaned against me, wrapping his arms around me. "You're freezing."

"Duh. Ayaz pulled me out of bed in the middle of the night." I yanked the hem of my hoodie over my knees. "I didn't exactly dress for a spelunking adventure."

"Here." Quinn shrugged off his ski jacket and wrapped it around my shoulders. I felt mildly warmer, but by now the cold had seeped into my bones. He knelt down in front of me. The lantern-light danced over his emerald eyes – they no longer appeared like smooth pools of water, but were laced with tiny shards, like shattered crystal. "Okay, Hazy, you want answers. We laid some heavy-ass shit on you tonight. Everything we told you in the cemetery was true, and if you hadn't run we could have shown you more... but I get why you ran."

Quinn ran his hand through his shoulder-length surfer hair, biting his lower lip in a way that made my heart flip. Which was dumb, because I didn't trust him, and I such as fuck didn't want to kiss him now in the middle of this freezing cold cave, even if my body felt drawn to him and his jacket smelled like coconut and sugarcane. Probably the cold was doing things to my mind – first I lost feeling in my fingers, then I wanted to jump Quinn's bones, then I keeled over like a Hazel Popsicle.

"What we're about to show you... it's messed up." Ayaz's silky voice penetrated the gloom. "In the library, I told you about Thomas Parris. Do you remember? How he built the house and grounds around sacred geometry to honor his pagan gods, and he enlarged the natural caves to form tunnels and caverns where he held his rituals?"

I nodded, my lips too cold to form words.

"Parris dug too deep. He awoke something that has lain beneath the rocks, dead but dreaming, for millennia. This is a being without form, without a face, a being that shapes reality and devours stars, and it now exerts its malevolent force over this school. Parris was able to trap this entity, preventing it from being unleashed upon the world. Only instead of destroying it, he worshipped it as a god and dedicated himself and his cult to doing its bidding. You remember those shadows that came after you in the gymnasium?"

I nodded.

"Well, you're about to get up close and personal with their master."

I swallowed hard. Ayaz's words should be ridiculous to me, and yet... those shadows... I thought at first they were the rats in the walls, but they were too large, too human-like. No human could move like that, floating with silent footsteps, black cloaks billowing around them like a tornado formed of darkness...

"How?" I managed to croak out. "How are you all dead?"

Quinn squeezed my hand. "You found that newspaper article about the old school that used to be here – Miskatonic Prep. It was shut down twenty years ago after a tragic fire killed 245 students."

I nodded.

"This *is* Miskatonic Prep. Everyone here – the students, some of the staff and maintenance crew – we all died in that fire." Quinn's voice was swallowed by the darkness. "Our parents buried us in the cemetery beyond the pleasure garden. We woke up inside our coffins, and had to dig ourselves out. Now we don't age, we can't be killed, and we can't leave the grounds of the school."

I snorted. "You're not a zombie, Quinn. You've done many evil things to me, but you haven't yet tried to eat my brain."

"We're not zombies," Trey snapped. "We're... I was never allowed to watch horror films. Not cultured enough for my parents. I don't know the proper term."

"Revenants," Quinn added. "I always liked 'revenants.' It has a biblical ring to it, like I'm going to enter a paradise of nubile virgins at the end of all this nonsense."

"In Turkey, we talk of the *edimmu* of ancient Mesopotamia," said Ayaz. "They are the souls of the dead who are not properly buried. They rise from their graves to seek vengeance on the living."

"Edimmu sounds like a kind of cheese," Quinn shot back. "I don't want to be a cheese zombie unless they get the best virgins."

I rubbed my temples, smearing cold mud across my face. "You're not explaining anything."

"You don't need us to explain anything to you," Trey muttered.

"You're clever enough to know it all already. You just don't want to see it. If you want proof, then just look at the cave walls."

"I don't see anything except rocks and... oh yeah, rocks."

"Try not to look. Then you'll see."

I opened my mouth to say that made no sense, but I swallowed the retort as I realized Trey was right. When I tried to study his face for a sign this was all some cruel joke, slivers of sickly light pulsed through the rocks in the places where my eyes couldn't focus. Long veins of that otherworldly substance I'd seen in my dreams wove through the stone, projecting a sliver of light in a color that didn't seem to match anything on our spectrum.

Yeah, okay. That's weird. The cold is making me hallucinate.

I dug around inside myself, storing all this nonsense about star-killing deities and shadow children in the section of my brain reserved for stuff about Derleth that didn't make sense (it was a large swath of real estate, rapidly expanding), and pulled strength from some nebulous place inside me so we could continue. I grabbed Quinn's arm and let him pull me to my feet. Down, down, down we climbed. Each step on the rock jolted through my body. The temperature dropped so low that even with Quinn's jacket tight around my shoulders, my whole body trembled. The cold rattled in my chest, and I kept slipping on the rocks as my depth perception wavered. The mineral veins pulsed along the walls, disappearing every time I tried to focus on them.

I pressed my fingers into the scar on my wrist and tried to think of warm things – hot chocolate, pumpkin soup, a blazing fire...

The guys slipped down a rock shelf and stopped on the edge of a body of water. While Trey rolled up his school slacks, Quinn hoisted me onto his shoulders. The three of them splashed along the edge of a dark pool of unseen depth. I could tell from the movement of air that we were in some large cavern. The flickering light of Trey's lantern was swallowed by the stygian gloom.

On the other side of the pool, Quinn set me down. Trey and

Ayaz moved further up the slope, grunting as they pushed at a large slab of rock covered with an etching of lines and dots that were definitely not caused by dripping water. Quinn turned to me, tucking a strand of my short hair behind my ear.

"You'll find your answers on the other side of that rock." He flashed me his Quinn smile, but it was all lopsided and forced. "I hope you're ready for this, Hazy."

I could barely get any words out, my teeth were chattering so badly. "Why are we in these caves? Why couldn't I get answers back in your room, where it's *warm*?"

"You want to go back to my room?" Quinn cocked an eyebrow.

"I'd slap you if I could move my arms," I muttered.

Quinn swept an arm over his head, indicating the cavern. "There are caves like this all through the peninsula. We've been exploring them for twenty years, and we're barely scratched the surface of what's down here. We're about to walk to one of Parris' caves – it leads directly under the gym."

I didn't think it was possible for my body to feel even colder, but at the mention of the gym, a bitter chill ran up my spine.

Trey ran back to us, holding up the lantern so I could see his face and clothes streaked with filth, less King of the school and more unfathomable creature of the deep. He held out his dirt-streaked hand.

"I'm not going to lie to you," he said. "On the other side of this rock are your answers, but it could also be your doom."

"She's scared enough as it is," Quinn glared at Trey. "Keep talking like that and she's going to assume we're leading her into a trap."

"I'm not convinced we aren't." Trey's voice was hard, devoid of emotion. "I gave her my points so she wouldn't have to face this, but here we fucking are."

"I'm starting to think we shouldn't have brought her here," Quinn muttered.

"Jesus H Christ," I snapped, steadying myself against a stone as I struggled to my feet. "I'm not scared. I'm freezing cold and grumpy. I don't care if I'm walking into a trap anymore. Anything is better than sitting here getting colder while you lot argue over what you think is best for me. Could we just get on with this?"

"Wait," Ayaz grabbed my hand, snapping my body against his. Fire flared through my body where we pressed together. "There's something we have to do first."

"For fuck's sake, *what?*"

Ayaz's hand stroked my cheek. His fingers seared my skin – a heat that burned through my body and right down to my toes, replacing the frightful numbness inside me with a delicious glow.

"Those two have had the pleasure of a kiss." Ayaz's breath caressed my lips, melting away the numbness. "If we all end up destroyed in there tonight, I think we should have ours, too."

Wait, I could die in there? I—

Ayaz brought his lips toward me, and all rational thought fled my head. A trail of heat stretched between us – drawing us together like a moth to a flame. But who was the flame, and who was the moth? Who would burn up in the other's conflagration?

Mentally, I fought against his approaching lips. This was the guy who put maggots in my food. Why was he hovering like he was about to kiss me? Why did I *want* him to kiss me?

Ayaz paused an inch from me, the question written in his dark, ageless eyes.

A groan of assent escaped my throat. The fire drew me forward, pressing my lips to his. Heat flared through my face as our lips touched, as his fingers slid around the back of my neck, as his tongue roused something hot and needy and primal from the dark depths within me.

Ayaz kissed with a wild possessiveness, claiming me with his mouth. He kissed with his whole body, fitting himself against me in perfect union. He threw everything he had into that kiss, leaving me gasping, breathless, reminding me that underneath all his monarch posturing he and I were born of the same fire.

He was a scholarship student, too, and a minority at this school. Has he had his hair tarred and rotting meat shoved in his locker? Has he been led to a rickety boat and commanded to row away as fast as he could? Has he stood here once before, unsure of what he'd find on the other side of this rock?

He sure kissed like it, like he wanted to drive out my fear and my questions and all the unfairness of the world and replace it with this smoldering *want*. And with his fingers tangled in my hair and his lips made of fire and this ache pooling inside me, I would let him a hundred times over.

Ayaz drew away, his dark eyes sweeping over me. His rich scent clung to my lips, and the force that pulled us together was stronger than ever.

Quinn whistled. "That was hot."

I touched my finger to my lips, now scorched by his touch. *Yes, yes it was.*

"We're wasting time," Trey snapped.

"That was *not* a waste," Ayaz muttered. His hand lingered on my arm before falling away.

I swallowed hard, trying to bring my hammering heart back into line. "Clearly, all this stuff you told me about being dead is bullshit. You're not an eskimo—"

"Edimmu—" Ayaz corrected.

"—because no *way* do zombies kiss like that."

Ayaz grinned, holding my arm as we scrambled up the side of the cavern and squeezed through the hole Trey had made. On the other side was a sheer drop. Quinn went first, sliding on his ass down the smooth stone. He turned around and held his hands up toward me.

This whole cave trip felt like a pointless exercise to force me to trust the guys. I had to take Quinn's jacket or freeze. I had to allow them to lift me across the water and toss me between them down this drop, or I'd fall and break my neck. I was reserving judgment until we got wherever we were going, but there was going to have to be some *serious* fuckery at the other end of this tunnel to make me believe all of this wasn't some messed up attempt to get me to like them.

Part of me still wondered if I'd walked into another of their traps, but then I caught a glimpse of Trey's ice-blue eyes – wide and frightened, the edges ringed with silver fire. In the flickering lantern light, his hair shimmered with crimson highlights. He nudged me, but it was surprisingly gentle. "After you."

I squeezed my eyes shut as I slid forward, toppling off the edge of the shelf. A yelp escaped my throat as I fell, before Quinn's powerful hands gripped my sides and he lowered me down.

"Oof," he grunted as he lowered me to the ground. "You might want to lay off the bacon in the future, Hazy."

"You're such a cock," Trey said as he slid down beside us.

I remembered Quinn at that party a few weeks ago, watching me scarf down potato chips and remarking about how cool it was to see a girl eat food with gusto. I knew he wasn't being serious. Quinn Delacorte was never serious, not even when he was trying to convince me he was some kind of zombie revenant eskimo. My skin still burned where he had touched me. My whole body was both ice and fire – confused, just like me. *How in the frigid cold of this cave and the horror of what I'd already uncovered did these guys still make my blood run hot?*

We walked along a wide tunnel, the ground mostly even and the walls hewn smooth – *too* smooth, like shimmering glass. I caught glimpses of more veins in the walls, crossing each other in a lattice. Each step fell heavy as we walked into darkness – the kind of darkness that had form and mass, that pushed back against you as you stumbled into it, oppressive and tangible.

The tunnel widened, and we stood on the edge of a vast cavern – ten, twenty, fifty times the size of the last. Only instead of being a natural cavern formed by the movement of water, this had been wrested from nature and turned into the kind of cyclopean architectural statement someone like Dracula would appreciate. Everything was *too* smooth, *too* perfect; the angles seemed to bend and shift in the flickering light of a series of candles in niches spaced around the walls. The fires barely penetrated the vast space, but illuminated small sections of the shimmering stone walls and the eerie veins that arced and crossed to form a delicate and decidedly too-regular pattern through the dome.

In the center stood a wooden structure flanked by glowing torches and strung with a scaffold and ropes. It looked a little like a gallows. I could just make out the edges of a trapdoor in the floor of the platform. The lock clattered, as if something pushed up against it from beneath. A cloak of dread shrouded the space – a creeping sensation that crawled over my skin the longer I looked at that trapdoor.

"This is impossible," I breathed.

"If you're referring to the structural integrity of the cavern," Ayaz said. "I can assure you it's stood for at least five hundred years."

"Thanks for the architecture lecture, Mr. van der Rohe. I meant that I've dreamed about this place."

"We all have, at one time or another," Trey said. "That's why it always feels familiar."

I turned to him in confusion. "You mean... everyone in this school?"

"Everyone on the planet," Trey corrected. I didn't expect that. "This place is... it's sort of part of our collective subconscious."

I jabbed a finger at the structure. "If you thought this would give me answers, you were mistaken."

"Answers are coming." Quinn dragged me back into an alcove. "I can hear their footsteps right now."

"What footsteps—"

"Sssssh!"

Trey clamped a hand over my mouth. I sagged back against him, too exhausted and cold to fight. The four of us huddled together in a large niche, backs pressed against the shimmering stone. The wall pulsated against my skin, giving off a mild warmth that was both comforting and unsettling. From here, we could see clearly across the floor of the cavern, but it would be unlikely anyone else would see us in the shadows.

Unless they didn't see with human eyes.

My ears pricked at a faint sound – shoes thudding on stone, coming from another tunnel on the opposite side. There was a drumming sound, too – a percussion that seemed to form a perfect slow march, but as soon as I tried to catch the beat, it would slip away into something else.

A shadow flickered in front of the torches, then another. Dark shapes circled the room, chanting in low voices – words I did not understand. They stamped their feet on the ground in a furious beat that felt ancient and primal and also familiar – their voices rising and falling in a sublime and discordant harmony. Behind my back, the wall pulsed along with the beat.

Their song sent cold shivers through my already frozen veins.

One of the shadows stepped forward, climbing up onto the central dais, dragging a dark shape behind it like a lump of old meat. At first, I thought it was one of the things that had chased me in the gym, but under the torchlight I could see it was a human wearing a dark cloak.

The figure raised a hand and called forth two others, who climbed up on the platform beside it. Chains dragged across the wood as they unshackled something.

With a heave, they unbolted the trapdoor and lifted the lid.

Hatred poured out.

CHAPTER THREE

All my life I lived in a place where hatred was baked into bone. The color of your skin, the people you called friends, the life you were born into and couldn't escape – all these things painted a target on your back that attracted malevolence like flies to shit. Those on the outside hated because they were afraid that if they didn't separate themselves from us then they would become one of us. But that was nothing on the cruelties we could visit on each other in the name of wringing out the tiniest shred of power.

Hatred burrowed into my thoughts and lived close to my heart, so trust me when I say that what poured out of that trap-door was every ignorant abhorrence, every vicious deed, every revolting thought that had ever been visited upon a human. An avalanche of misery rolled across the cavern and crashed into me, tossing me outside of my body and sending me reeling from the dizzying spectacle of its spite.

The hatred crawled across my consciousness, forcing me to confront memories and possibilities that were more monstrous than the unknown. It grasped me close, feeding me with ineffable loneliness and the shuddering terror it couldn't help but invoke. And in that terror I *knew*.

I knew that everything the guys had hinted at was true.

They *were* all dead. Dead but walking. Kept alive somehow by this *thing* that Parris had called from the deep, this thing that fed on their hatred, and grew fat and rich off their evil deeds and dark thoughts, biding its time until it was strong enough to... to...

To escape.

A scream rose in my throat, pushing against my teeth, fighting for freedom. A warm hand circled my waist, dragging me back from the creature's grasp. "I know it's horrible," Quinn whispered, his breath hot against my earlobe. "You can't scream. If you scream, they'll find us. Screaming's pointless, anyway."

I opened my mouth, but no sound passed through my lips. How could I even scream? This was fucking *beyond* screaming. My mind was being torn to pieces by a battering of perverse imagery that assailed me through the very air I breathed. Unimaginable tortures and abuses played out inside my skull.

Through the haze of vile visions, I managed to stare out into the cavern. I noticed in a detached way that the cloaked figures had stepped back from the platform, leaving the slumped object on its edge, right beside the open trapdoor. Open now, the trap-door revealed a dark void – a well of darkness that had form, that flowed and moved and shifted as the malevolence grew inside it.

"Behold, our Great Old God, the one who came to our young world from the sky, on a trail of devoured stars," the first cloaked figure cried, raising its hands toward the platform. "Your dreams have reached us once again, revealing your desires. We, your loyal servants, have returned to you, bearing this gift."

The figure swept a hand across its shadowed face, flinging back a dark hood to reveal pale skin that glowed in the torchlight, sliced with bow-shaped lips colored crimson. Her dark hair fell in waves of shadow down her back.

Headmistress West.

"We long again for you to rise up from your deathlike slumber, to leave your dark prison and dance among the stars, for you to ride upon your cloud ship and play with your sisters and brothers, as you did when the universe was new. We honor you and your limitless knowledge of the universe." She swept her cape around her body as she fell to her knees. As one, the other teachers in the room sank to the ground, pressing their foreheads into the stone floor.

The demon or god or fucking shadow whatever creature raged within its prison, satiated by their obeisances. Headmistress West raised her head, her voice booming through the domed space.

"Hazel Waite eludes us. But she can't have gone far. We will find her, and we will tear her open and discover her secrets. We will figure out why she hurts you."

Okay, what?

"Please accept this boy as a gift. His soul will repair the wounds she has inflicted."

Ms. West lunged forward and grabbed the lump. A knife flashed in her hand as she cut away the straps and bag that bound it. A body rolled out and slumped against the platform, its limbs flopping, its face lifeless. It was bound in rope, with a foul gag stuffed in his mouth. As the robed figures hauled it up onto the platform and flung the ropes around it like a harness, the torchlight shone on a pair of glassy eyes and caught the golden threads of hair I recognized so well.

Greg.

My throat closed. *They're going to lower Greg into that pit.* And I knew without knowing how I knew that it wouldn't kill him. Not completely. Death wasn't the thing to fear in this room. When Greg came out again, he'd be just like Loretta. All the Gregness about him would be gone.

No. They're not doing that to Greg. Not for my sake.

Trey's grip tightened around my shoulders. But he had nothing on me when someone I loved was in danger. I tore myself free from his grip and leapt to my feet.

I stepped into the cavern, my head high. "Hello, Headmistress. Hi, faculty members. Greetings, malignant demon of the void. I'm Hazel Waite. I heard you were looking for me."

CHAPTER FOUR

Headmistress West spun around, her face as cold and impassive as ever. The only indication of her surprise to see me was a slight upward movement of one eyebrow, which was quickly reined in again.

"Miss Waite." A slow, evil smile spread across her face. "We're so pleased to see you safe and well."

My legs trembled, but I didn't dare back down. If I gave an inch to that... whatever it was, then I'd be the next person down that hole.

"Wish I could say the same." I managed to keep my voice calm, even as my whole body convulsed. "You've been out looking for me. It's odd to have all this trouble for a scholarship student, especially when this school usually doesn't give a shit about us."

Behind me, I could hear the boys whispering, arguing about how to deal with this curveball I'd just thrown them. As if I needed their help.

I shuffled forward a step. The entity swelled – not with power this time, but with something that would have been fear if a creature that *ate stars for sustenance* could feel fear.

"You've been causing no end of trouble at this school." Ms. West's features remained locked in that smug half-smile.

I dared a smile back at her, intending to look a bit sinister. But with the entity's vile visions pouring into my head, I couldn't force my muscles to obey, and it came off as a wobbly grimace. "I aim to please. So... what exactly have I walked into here? It looks an awful lot like you're trying to sacrifice my friend Greg to some cave demon. Which is obviously an insane thing for the headmistress of such a fine institution to be doing. I thought I'd pop out and ask you to explain yourself."

Her creepy frozen smile didn't falter. "No, no, that's what we're doing. Every year, four students enter this school. They are carefully selected, for we have very strict criteria. They must be exceptional, for it is their minds that our god most desires. They must be orphans, without anyone who will look for them. And they must be able to be broken. Four enter the school, but none will ever leave."

"What happens to them?" I took another step. I had no idea what it was I was doing, except that I needed to reach Greg.

"A small sacrifice, but necessary. The alumni of Miskatonic Prep are the rulers of our country, of the free world. They need our god's power in order to do their work, and so we must all make sacrifices for the greater good of our nation." With a flick of her wrist, the headmistress indicated the trapdoor. "Our god needs sustenance, just like you and I. Only instead of food, He Who Once Devoured The Cosmos now requires human souls."

Jesus fucking Christ. As if people like Trey's dad didn't already have enough power, they are literally dragging up ancient demons because they're that afraid of the unwashed masses.

"Is that what happened to Loretta?" I whispered. "You brought her down here and lowered her into that... that..."

"We did her a kindness," West explained. "Loretta had nothing left to live for. She was at the bottom of the points table, which is how we choose our next sacrifice. She was groomed for the god's needs – ready to give up her life and slide into oblivion. Souls that are broken are the most delicious to our god, and so she was enjoyed by him. But we are not unkind. For her sacrifice, she was given a second life, a better life, free from her pain. You were a dangerous influence on her – she was starting to believe that she had a chance to be someone in the world, and of course we all know that's not true. Now she has friends and status and peace – the things she always desired but could never have outside these walls. We don't usually allow scholarship students back into the student body, but Courtney felt Loretta could better serve our deity by returning to the school and helping to break your spirit."

As if what I was hearing wasn't sinister enough, West peeled away another layer of the school's evil. Loretta was sacrificed to this... this deity, not just because she was a scholarship student, but because she fell to the bottom of the points table and the bullies of this school had tortured her so completely she no longer wanted to live. *That's why they choose us – because we're orphans. Because no one will help us.*

But someone helped me... Trey gave me his points so I wouldn't be at the bottom. It was supposed to be me.

Loretta died instead of me.

Because *of me.*

The injustice of it boiled in my blood, turning my veins into rivers of fire. "Where do I fit into this?" I demanded, taking another step forward.

Inside its prison, the deity reeled. A fresh wave of torturous images burned into my skull, as if it were lashing out in desperation. *You said I hurt it, but how? Why?*

Ms. West circled me, her heels clacking on the stone floor, studying me carefully. "You are fascinating. You don't fit, Hazel Waite. Our god doesn't know what to make of you."

"If he's a god, isn't he supposed to be all-knowing and all-seeing and all that jazz?"

"Oh yes, but when one's life stretches over eons, when one

sees the universe make and unmake itself in the blink of an eye, when the death of a galaxy is as insignificant as a speck of dust on your collar, then you may begin to understand why he cannot turn his eye toward you. That is why he needs us, to feed it and tend to its needs and to find a way to understand what you are and why you affect him so."

I rolled my eyes. For real, this was too much. "Fine, whatever. Just explain why I don't fit into your insane cultist plot."

"Our Great Old God grants us his power to make the world in his image, to place his disciples in the mightiest and most influential places where they will gather the most followers and prepare for the day when he will be free of this prison. And in return, he asks for yearly sacrifices to sustain this power. The more broken the spirit of a sacrifice, the more enjoyment our god relishes from the devouring of them, and the more loyal servants they make when they rise again. That is why we first send them to the school, where our student body will prepare them for sacrifice. But you... you have resisted all attempts to break you. Trey and Courtney were tasked with preparing you for sacrifice, but their efforts have yielded some... undesirable results."

Trey and Courtney... have been bullying me in order to make me fit to be sacrificed to their god? My stomach lurched, but I couldn't deal with that yet, not while I was facing down Ms. West and that horrific *thing* she wanted to feed Greg to. "So basically, I'm like Brussels sprouts and cod liver oil to your god?"

"For now," she said. "But we will figure out a way to break you. We always do. That is why you cannot be allowed to leave the school. I can't have students telling wild stories about Miskatonic Prep, not when we still have so much work to do."

I shuddered as a wave of hatred rolled over me, momentarily knocking me back with the force of the vile visions it flung in my direction. This time, instead of shuttering my mind against it, I leaned into the horror, searching for something I could use to escape this situation. And as I dug deeper, I felt the entity's grip on my skull loosen, felt its shadows recoil from my mind, and I grasped at a possible answer, a single tiny hope.

Something else is going on here. All this searching for me tonight wasn't just about keeping me at the school to save me for their god. It's about protecting it... from me.

"That's not the whole truth, is it?" I said. "Does everyone in this room know how important I am?"

Ms. West shrugged her shoulders. "You have a high opinion of yourself, Ms. Waite. You may be unusual, but you are just another insignificant sacrifice. You matter little in our great scheme."

I dug the shard of glass out of my bra and held it over my wrist. "Fine. In that case, I'll open my veins right here. Won't that please your god?"

The god reared back, its malignancy giving way to shuddering terror. It didn't seem very pleased.

Headmistress West stepped forward, holding out her hand. "You don't really want to die, Hazel."

"You're right about that. But I'll do it."

She took another step toward me. I jabbed the shard into my wrist. I was so cold I barely felt the pain of the glass cutting my skin. A few drops of blood splattered along my arm.

A sound like the universe tearing roared inside my head. The ground beneath my feet trembled as the entity fought against its bonds.

The headmistress dropped all pretenses of calm. She lunged at me, grabbing for the shard. Trey swooped in and flung himself between us, grabbing her and yanking her away from me.

"You don't know her like I do," he snarled as Ms. West struggled against his grip. "Hazel will do it."

"Interesting," I grinned. "When I hurt, your god hurts. I wonder what would happen to him if I did this." I dragged the glass over my skin, raising a line of blood. The ground rolled beneath me as the entity's pain battered its formless body, sending a fresh wave of horror into my mind. I gritted my teeth as I kept on cutting.

Bring it, you fucking cosmic monster. I've lived enough hatred in my life that I'm not afraid of yours.

"Stop her!" The headmistress fought against Trey as other hooded figures stepped forward, raising their hands to grab at me.

"You're not touching Hazel," Trey growled. Quinn and Ayaz stepped out from the shadows, flanking me on both sides.

A cold smile settled over the headmistress' face. She stopped struggling. "I see the junior Eldritch Club has a new pet."

I turned to Trey. "The Eldritch Club?"

Still keeping one arm tight around Ms. West's neck, he lifted the cuff of his sleeve, touching his fingers to the tattoo on his wrist. "It's a secret society that's been part of Miskatonic Prep for generations. Only the best students are accepted, and once you're a member, you belong for life. We are the god's chosen children, his priests and priestesses, his favorites."

"And all the monarchs are in this club?" I remembered Quinn's identical tattoo.

Trey nodded. "Our parents are the senior members. We control the school. We prepare the sacrifices."

"You break them." It was all starting to come together – every horrifying piece of the puzzle. Bit by bit, the monarchs tore down the scholarship students with bullying and torture, taking away their chances even to excel academically, until like Loretta they wanted to take their lives. That was monstrous. It was unthinkable. It...

If their job was to break me, then why are they trying to help me? Why give me Trey's points? Why try to put me into that boat?

Or are they really just trying to stop me from killing myself to save their precious god? I can't deal with this. I can't...

I can't think about it. I have to save Greg and Andre. That's it. That's all that matters.

"Take your hands off me, Trey," Ms. West commanded. "Or I shall have to report your insubordination to your father."

Don't do it, Trey.

Trey's lip quivered. He released her neck. She sagged to her knees, clutching her throat with long, trembling fingers. Trey stepped in front of me, facing off against the headmistress and the other teachers.

"Hazel is ours," he said.

"No one is yours." Ms. West held out her arms. Two figures cast aside their hoods and stepped forward to take her arms and haul her to her feet. Professor Atwood and Dr. Morgan regarded me with wary expressions. "We are all children of the Great Old God. You must be put in your place."

She flicked her wrist again. Two more robed figures stepped out of the circle and grabbed Greg, lifting him between them.

No!

"You don't control me." I shoved Trey out of the way and stared down Ms. West with what I hoped was a defiant smirk. "Your god doesn't control me. I've just proven that. You can throw Greg into that pit, but all that's going to do is make me *more* dangerous. Ask Trey and Quinn and Ayaz how hard I fight back. Alternatively, I'll make you an offer you can't refuse."

"Hazel, what are you doing?" Quinn's voice trembled.

Ms. West held up her hand. The two figures paused, Greg's limp body suspended from ropes between them. "We're listening."

"Here's my deal. At the end of the fourth quarter, I'll give myself to your demon god. Willingly. When the year is up, you can conduct whatever experiments you want on me to make me worthy, and it can suck my brain out through a straw in my nose if it wants. I don't care."

"*No,*" Trey growled. Ayaz moved in front of me, but I shoved him back.

"Let her speak, boys," Dr. Morgan said.

"You can't just give up like this!" Quinn cried. "That's not you. You don't know what will happen."

"It's my body to give up," I shot back. "Under my own terms."

Ms. West's lips curled back. "Your country will appreciate your sacrifice. It will be for the benefit of all. What are your terms?"

I sucked in a deep breath. *I hope like hell I'm doing the right thing.* "I'll do this only if you agree to let the other scholarship students go. Your god cannot touch Greg or Andre. They get to walk out of this school with their minds and lives intact. Would that please your, er... deity?"

"They will have to remain until the end of the year," Headmistress West said. "And they are not allowed to know the secret of this school. They cannot learn of Miskatonic Prep."

"I don't intend to tell them." I glanced down at Greg's lifeless body. "But I can't guarantee they won't find out on their own."

"We may have ways of altering their memory if it comes to that," Headmistress West said.

No, you fucking don't. I'm not letting you lay a finger on my friends.

"They won't find out," I promised. "My life for theirs, that's my terms. If you break or anyone else breaks our agreement, I *will* kill myself, and I'll do everything I can to torture your creature while I do it. Do we have a deal?"

From the depths, an odor like rotting flesh rose up, striking at my nostrils like a weapon. And I knew without knowing I had been given my answer.

"Our god is most pleased with your offer." Headmistress West held out her hand to me. I took it. Her talons scraped across my skin as we shook. Her hand was ice cold and waxy, like my mother's skin had felt when the firefighters dragged her from the blaze.

"You have all witnessed our agreement tonight," Ms. West addressed the room. "Return to the school. Hazel has agreed to be sacrificed at the end of the year. Our god will wait with eternal patience to be sated by her soul."

The teachers threw the trapdoor closed, wrapped the chains through the bolts, and locked it down tight. Instantly, the room felt a little brighter, a little less oppressive. Dr. Morgan dragged Greg's limp body down from the ropes and dropped him at my feet. He stepped back and flashed me a cold smile.

"He's yours," he said. "Although you may be too late. His mind is not as strong as yours – many turn insane in the very presence of our god, before they even meet him in his prison."

I rolled my eyes. "You're insane, all right."

Quinn swooped in and scooped up Greg, throwing him over his shoulder. Trey grabbed my hand and dragged me out the opposite tunnel. Headmistress West's tinkling laughter followed us.

Walls of shimmering stone pressed down on us, their angles always appearing slightly skewed. Quinn ran ahead, with Greg's body flopping against his back. Trey and Ayaz jogged on either side of me, keeping pace with my shorter, wobbling legs. Ayaz's hand rested on the small of my back, the gesture urging me onward even as my limbs screamed and my mind rebelled against all the horrors the entity had thrown at me.

The roof of the tunnel raised and the floor sloped into a set of wide steps. We clambered up them and through a small opening at the back of a supply closet. Dusty brooms and pails knocked against me as I fought my way outside, collapsing onto a cool marble floor. There were no lights on, and I could just make out an empty notice-board and a sign pointing to a locker room. A rancid smell filled the air, making me cough and choke.

Dimly, I realized that I recognized the hall and that smell. I'd been there only once before – on my way to the gymnasium.

Warm, strong hands grabbed me under the shoulders, lifting me, taking the burden of my weight. "Hazel, what have you done?" Trey hissed.

I glanced at his cruel mouth, then at Quinn's stricken face, then to Ayaz, whose expression held only darkness. Something in the Turk's eyes told me he had some inkling of what I was planning.

"What I've done is save two innocent lives," I said, wishing my voice sounded strong and not tiny and terrified. I broke down into a coughing fit as the vile stench piled into my mouth.

"You've also doomed yourself," Trey's voice cracked. "You felt his presence touch your mind, but that's nothing. *Nothing*. Do you have any inkling what it is like when the god embraces you? We tried so hard to save you, but you probably should have killed yourself. It would have been kinder."

"What I've done is brought some time." Determination set my jaw. "Now we've got until the end of the year to figure out how to banish that deity into the shadows and bring you all back from the dead, once and for all."

CHAPTER FIVE

"I don't care about school rules, I'm not trusting you alone in the dungeon tonight." Trey pushed open the door to his dorm room and ushered me inside. "We can't have you running off to make more fucking deals with malevolent deities."

Students weren't supposed to sleep in each other's rooms. It was an instant 50-point demerit if you were caught, although it didn't seem as if the teachers much cared what the monarchs did in their fancy suites that were more like apartments than dorm rooms. I desperately didn't want to lose any of the hard-won points I'd gained during the first quarter, but I was also tired and cold and frightened and *no fucking way* did I want to sleep alone in the basement with the rats and that fucking demon sleeping beneath the school.

I collapsed onto Trey's enormous sofa. Quinn staggered in after him and dropped Greg down beside me before sliding to the floor. Trey frowned. "You've smeared dirt all over the carpet. You're cleaning it up."

I bit back a retort. As soon as we'd dragged our weakened, filthy bodies up the flight of stairs leading from the gym, Trey had reverted to his usual dicksome self. I pointed to the trail of muddy prints he'd tracked across his own cream carpet. "You're rocking your own creature from the Black Lagoon look, so chill. We should get Andre up here, too."

"This isn't a fucking sleepover."

"Fine." I stood up. My legs wailed in protest. "Bye."

"Where are you going?" Ayaz moved to block the door.

"I'm not going to leave Andre alone in the basement. Not when that thing is..." I couldn't finish the sentence.

"All right!" Trey yelled. "Quinn, go get the other charity case, if it will shut her up."

Quinn got up, deliberately smearing his hand along the wall as he headed out the door. I slid back onto the sofa, nestling Greg's head on my legs and pressing my fingers to his wrist, feeling a steady pulse. I held my hand over his forehead. *He's freezing cold.*

I went into Trey's room and dragged his duvet out, placing it over Greg's body and curling up around him, trying to warm my own freezing limbs at the same time. I stroked Greg's face, hoping like hell he was unconscious the whole time, that he hadn't had to endure the things the creature had fed into my head, that he hadn't felt the god's malevolence coursing through his veins.

If the god was *that* powerful and *that* malevolent while it was still – according to Ms. West – trapped within the earth in a deathlike slumber, then what could it do if it was awake and free? I couldn't contemplate that now. I needed to stay sane.

"Where's Ayaz?" I asked, noticing he was no longer in the doorway.

"He has to get something," Trey muttered. He moved around the kitchen, slamming cupboards and banging crockery on the counter. Each clatter sent a shuddering headache through my temple.

I hurled my body up again and leaned over the counter. "What the fuck crawled up your ass and died?" I demanded. "Among other things, tonight I found out you're undead and you and your secret club have been torturing me so you can sacrifice me to a *demon*. When I wrap my head around it fully, I'm going to unleash a serious amount of pain on your ass, and you'll deserve every bit of it."

Trey slammed one of his uber-fancy ready-to-eat meals on the counter. He shoved a bowl across at me so hard I had to lunge at it to stop it from careening over the edge and smashing on the tiles.

"Dish yourself some of that," he barked. "You need strength."

"Don't order me around," I shot back. "I don't need food. I need answers and I'm still waiting. What's got your goat?"

Trey popped the top off a bottle of beer with such force it dented the ceiling. "You shouldn't have made that deal."

"What's it matter to you? You're already dead. You've got nothing to lose. It's me whose life is on the line here. Me and my friends."

"Exactly," Trey growled. He emptied half the container into the bowl and shoved it into the microwave, slamming the door so hard the machine slid a few inches across the counter.

"No. Not exactly. My life, my deal. I thought you'd be happy, since feeding me to this demon was exactly what you were trying to do in the first place. And why do you have all this food and drink, anyway? If you're dead, you don't need to eat."

Trey grunted in reply. The microwave beeped. He didn't even bother sliding on an oven mitt, just picked up the steaming bowl and slammed it on the counter. I touched the rim, then jerked my finger away. Piping hot. *How are his hands not in agony right now?*

Because he's dead, duh.

But that also didn't make any sense. Quinn was dead too, and he'd howled with pain when Trey threw the itching powder into his eyes. And Quinn's eye had swollen from where his dad had hit him. So why...

No, I can't think about all this now. I need to sleep. And eat. Spicy meat smells wafted from the bowl. *Damn, that looks good.*

"Fine, whatever." I picked up the spoon and used it to hook the edge of the bowl and bring it closer. "Don't answer me. But don't expect things to be the same anymore. You've made it clear that you hate me and Greg and Andre, but—"

"Is that what you think?" In a second, Trey swung around the island and leaned over the chair. His muscled legs pressed up against the inside of my thighs. A fire curled in my core. Those ice eyes stared me down, challenging me. The tension between us sung with a rumbling note, like the string over a violin pulled taut.

Fuck you, Trey Bloomberg. You don't intimidate me.

I planted my hand on his chest, shoving him away. Fire rushed up my arm, spreading across my chest, warming my whole core. Just touching Trey made heat burn in all the dark and dangerous places inside me.

Trey's eyes smoldered. He slid back between my legs, reaching up with a cruel finger to pull at my bottom lip. My breath hitched as my heart raced ahead. I no longer wanted to shove him away. My fingers curled into my palm, nails digging into my flesh. The scar on my wrist buzzed with fire.

Trey pressed his finger into my bottom lip. "I've been taught to hate everything you are and everything you stand for. But I can't get you out of my fucking head."

He closed the distance between us in a moment. Our mouths crashed together as a wave of heat engulfed my body.

Trey's kiss sizzled with all the same desperation of our last one – a restless need that he'd stamped down and buttoned up and hidden deep within his heart of stone. He wrapped his arm around my waist, pushing me hard against him. His body was the only thing preventing me from melting into a puddle on the floor.

The fire inside me roared to life. Trey's hardness ground against my inner thigh and a moan escaped my lips. *I shouldn't be kissing this guy. He tormented me. He wanted to sacrifice me to a demon.* And yet I couldn't tear my lips from his. I knew there was so much more going on inside Trey's head than what he was showing to Ms. West. With his lips and tongue he gave me the tiniest taste of it, and I was ready to fall into him and lose myself.

The door slammed. I jumped so high that the chair toppled backward. Trey leaned over to steady it, smashing his forehead against mine.

"Ow!"

"Fuck!" Trey growled.

"Did I interrupt something?" Ayaz dumped a battered box on the counter. "I found it. You're lucky – the ink is still in good condition."

Trey backed around the other side of the counter. Probably for the best. I think even if there was an entire football field between us, this tension would still sizzle, trying to draw us together.

Ayaz unpacked the contents of the box onto the counter, handing Trey a cable from a power unit to plug in. Surprised, I picked up the tattoo machine and a packet of needles still in their packets. Flashes of memories I didn't want to face tugged at my battered mind.

"Why do you have a tattoo machine?" I demanded.

Ayaz fiddled with the regulator. "How'd you know that's what it is?"

A memory bloomed inside my battered mind.

I raced up the stairs and flopped down on Dante's bed. 'My mom's working tonight. Can I sleep over?'

Dante buzzed with excitement. He kept tugging at the ring in his earlobe, fidgeting with the stacks of sketchbooks stacked beside his bed, darting back and forth across the tiny room. He didn't seem to hear me.

I waved a hand in front of his face. 'Are you listening to me, bro? Is your foster dad home again? We could go to the club instead, if you want.' Dante's current foster dad was an alcoholic. He was on the road a lot for his job, but when he came home a cloud descended on their place and dulled the brightness in Dante's eyes. On those nights, we would either climb into my tiny bed and listen to the water dripping through the leaking roof, or hang out backstage at Mom's club. The working girls fawned over Dante and begged him to draw their portraits, but I hated being there, having to see Mom go off with strange men only to come back reeking of drink and pot and cheap cologne.

'Nah. For once, it's good news. Look what I just got.' Dante pulled a box from under his bed. He lifted the lid to reveal a medieval torture device.

'What is it?' I glared at the vicious-looking needles, the power unit, the tiny box of tools, little colored vials like an ancient apothecary kit.

'It's a tattoo machine,' Dante grinned, dropping it into my hands as he swiped up a bag of fruit. 'Some guy was selling them behind the school for fifty bucks. I've been practicing on oranges all day. Check this out.' He held up an orange with a lopsided smiley face drawn in short, uncertain lines. 'How does it look?'

'It looks unhygienic.' I held the machine between two fingers and dropped it back in the box.

Dante puffed out his lower lip. 'You're no fun. Guess you won't let me ink you.'

'You'll be six feet underground before I let you anywhere near my virginal skin.' He grinned, and I grinned, and we both let the innuendo pass over us, unacknowledged and unfulfilled.

"My friend Dante had one." I squeezed my eyes shut, pushing the memory aside. I really didn't want to think about Dante. *Not now. Not tonight.* "I repeat, why do you have it *now?*"

Ayaz flipped down his cuff, showing me that runic tattoo on his wrist. "This is the Elder Sign – the symbol of the Eldritch Club. I have to place one on your wrist."

"That's not happening." I folded my arms across my chest.

"Hazel, I *have* to."

"Dude, I'm exhausted. I smell like a garbage truck. I just found out there's a demon living under the gymnasium and the entire student body is walking zombies. I don't need to *also* get a tattoo tonight, especially not from the guy who is sleeping with the high priestess of fuckery."

"It's a god, not a demon," Ayaz corrected, ignoring my

comment about Ms. West. "And this is for your protection. This sign marks you as one of the god's chosen few. If you have it, the other students aren't supposed to touch you."

"If it's for protection, then why did someone paint it on my locker?"

"Duh, to protect you." Quinn swaggered into the room with a shirtless and sleepy-looking Andre trailing behind him. "For the smart girl, you're slow tonight. We painted it there. The girls had something evil planned for you that day and we needed to stop them, so Trey painted it there to warn them to back off."

"More evil than tarring my hair?" I demanded.

"Yeah. We had to let them do that. It was either that or..." Quinn shook his head. "You don't want to know."

"But I'm already protected by my pact. Besides, that's the symbol of your secret club," I pointed out. "I'm betting only monarchs can wear that, and I'm not a monarch."

"You are now," Ayaz washed his hands under the sink. "We decided."

"Really? You just decided? I get that your word is law in this school, but I feel like Courtney and Tillie and the others will have something to say about me officially becoming part of the gang. Don't you have to have a secret meeting and sacrifice a goat and dance around in your underwear before you issue a decree like that?"

Ayaz grinned. "I wish. We should make this underwear dance mandatory. Especially now you're in the club."

I glared at him. He shrugged. "Sorry. Sometimes my inner Quinn comes out when it's least appropriate."

"I resent that," Quinn quipped, leaving Andre slumped at the table. He leaned over the counter and brushed a finger against my collarbone, smudging a line of mud across my chest. I slapped his hand away before he got too close to my breast. "I'm the height of propriety."

"Uh-huh." Wearing gloves, Ayaz filled the reservoir with black ink, unwrapped a liner needle from its case and slotted it into a disposable plastic tube, and then attached the tube to the armature bar. I'd seen Dante do this a hundred times, but it felt strange to see someone else do it, as though Ayaz had stolen something from my memories. "This is ready."

I balled my hand into a fist and slammed it into the counter. Pain spread across my knuckles. *I don't want this. My first tattoo was supposed to be from Dante. It was going to be one of his beautiful drawings, not some hideous stick symbol of an ancient god.*

But Dante was gone. All I had right now was this school and these guys. These three dead bullies who made my heart ache and my body flare with heat.

Why they wanted to protect me after they have done everything they could to destroy me... we hadn't fully established that bit yet. But I'd just made a deal with a malevolent god. I needed all the protection I could get.

I sighed. "Fine. But only if Greg and Andre get them, too."

Andre's eyes widened. Trey and Ayaz exchanged a glance – one of those unspoken conversations that often occurred between them. Ayaz must have won because Trey threw up his hands and stormed into his bedroom, slamming the door behind him.

Ayaz sighed. He flicked the switch on the power unit. A loud buzzing filled the room. A deep furrow appeared between Ayaz's eyes as he pulled my arm across the counter toward him and rolled up my sleeve.

"Don't you need a stencil?"

"This isn't a work of art," Ayaz pointed out, pressing the needle against my flesh.

There was a stray cat that hung out around the tattoo parlor where Dante interned. It would crawl into my lap while I sat in the corner and read, purring like mad. If I ever tried to touch it, it lashed out with sharp claws, tearing chunks out of my skin. The tattoo felt like that – a sharp, tearing sensation. As the needle broke my skin, something dark reared up inside my head, pressing hatred against my skull. The god, lashing out as it felt my pain.

Take that, you fucker.

When it was done, Ayaz wiped the blood away and taped a clear dressing over it. I stared at the design. I hated it.

"Do Greg next," I said, tapping the edge of the dressing, my fingers itching to touch it.

Ayaz shook his head. "He's asleep."

"I'll wake him up."

Ayaz glanced toward Trey's door. "I don't know... he did just had an encounter with the god. His mind might not be up to this."

"If I'm in the club, then so are Greg and Andre. Otherwise, I can't guarantee their protection. Ms. West may have agreed they can leave this school, but that doesn't mean Courtney and her cronies won't keep up their torture, will it?"

From the way Ayaz's lip curled, I knew I was right. I shoved the last mouthful of Trey's stew into my mouth and heaved my body off the chair. Just walking across the room made me wobble. I desperately needed sleep. But I had friends to look after first.

I slumped down beside Greg and poked him in the shoulder.

"Greg, Greg... wake up."

Nothing. Greg's glassy eyes stared, unblinking. He felt so cold, so clammy. I threaded my fingers in his, casting around for something that would draw him out of the darkness. "Greg, come on... Andrew Lloyd Webber is doing another reality TV show, and they're casting for young voices for the role of Raoul de Chagny."

Greg's eyes flew open. *Gotcha.* "Hazel... where am I?"

He's awake.

Overcome with relief, I wrapped my arms around him and squeezed. Greg's eyes widened as he took in the enormous room, the TV that took up an entire wall, the kitchen suite and the cathedral windows overlooking the quad. Behind him, Andre leaned against the door frame, looking completely unimpressed.

"Where... where am I?" Greg whispered again, rubbing his palm against his temple. "Why do I feel like I have a brick inside my head?"

"Do you remember anything?" I squeezed his hand.

"I was walking to the bathroom when... someone hit me from behind..." Greg winced as he touched the back of his head. "I must have passed out because I had these horrible nightmares, the most vivid nightmares about a cavern and a cult and an imprisoned demon that ate stars... but they can't be real..."

If only you knew the half of it, I thought but didn't say. I was forbidden from telling Greg anything about the creature. It was better he believed that was only a nightmare. "You're safe now. Do you feel okay? We were worried you might have hit your head so hard that you..."

...that you were turned mad by the very presence of that god.

"Apart from a killer headache, I'll be fine, I—I think. What's going on?" Greg pulled a strand of hair back from my face. "Wow, you look like shit. Your clothes are ripped and you've covered in mud."

"It's a long, long story," I whispered. "Let's just say that things have changed around here."

"I'll say. Where are we? Do you have a new wealthy benefactor you've been holding out on us?"

"Unlikely. We're in Trey's dorm room."

Greg scrambled up, his eyes wide. I grabbed his hand, squeezing tight. "It's okay. He's on our side. Sort of."

"What..." Greg spied Ayaz on the other side of the room, the machine buzzing as he formed the tattoo on Andre's skin.

"Motherfucker," he swore. "Look what those bastards are doing to Andre."

"It's for his own good." I showed him mine. "You're getting one next."

"You..." Greg's face screwed up in confusion.

I tightened my grip on his fingers. "Courtney and the other

monarchs nearly killed you tonight. They have this secret club with their parents, you see – the Eldritch Club. It's like one of those collegiate secret societies where rich bastards dance around in their underwear and make secret deals and outrageous bets. They have it in for you because you're my friend and I've pissed them off. So they knocked you out and left you in this ancient cave on the school grounds. They just *left you there*. You could have died from the cold or starvation if I hadn't found you."

I knew from experience that a lie that was as close to the truth was easier to maintain. I wished I felt guilty for lying to Greg, but I had no room left inside me for fresh guilt. I was already burning alive from the stuff.

Greg glanced at the dried dirt on his arm. "Is this why I smell like a slaughterhouse?"

I nodded. "Trey and Quinn and Ayaz found me and told me what happened. We located you and carried you back here. You're so cold. I think if you'd been out there much longer..."

My breath caught. I didn't want to think about what would have happened to Greg if I hadn't been there to deal for his life.

"I don't know that I am okay," Greg rubbed his head. "I feel all foggy, like something's been picking around inside my skull. I should see the nurse."

I pushed him back against the couch. "You can't."

"Why not?"

"How much do you trust me?"

Greg winced again as his head knocked against the sofa arm. "Considering you're one of my only friends in this place, a whole hell of a lot."

"Then trust me on this – you don't want the nurse. The faculty... they're not *in* this club, but they're controlled by it. They do its bidding. I don't know if that includes Old Waldron, but we can't take the chance. You know some weird ass shit is going down in this school, right? Like, Loretta coming back all strange and being moved upstairs?"

Greg nodded.

"Tonight, I found out what all that shit's about." I thought fast, trying to concoct a lie that was close to the truth without breaking my oath. "The rich bastards who run this school deliberately choose scholarship students who are orphans. It's a centuries-old tradition, where the alumni pretend they're doing this big favor, pulling all these smart kids out of the gutter and giving them a better chance at life, when really it's about finding four new victims for the Eldritch Club members to bully."

Greg's eyes widened.

"It's sick, right? Scholarship students have even died and... and..." I tried to say *and they're buried in the cemetery down the back of the school*, but my tongue wouldn't form the words. It froze in my mouth like a piece of dead meat.

It must be some part of my pact with the god, some spell preventing me from breaking our vow. I hope Ms. West has bound herself by the same strict criteria.

"And?" Greg pressed.

"...and other bad stuff," I finished off. "The senior members of the Eldritch Club – like Vincent Bloomberg – run the *world*, and they believe they can do anything they like to people like us and there are no consequences."

"This is some *Handmaid's Tale* level chaos," Greg said, rubbing his eyes.

"Tell me about it," I said darkly. I hated lying to Greg. *Hated it.* But the truth was so much worse than the lie I'd told him, and if I had the chance to save his life and give him a future, I would take it. "The guys have agreed to give us this El Dorado Sign—"

"—Elder Sign—" Ayaz corrected, not looking up from his work.

"—whatever. It's their symbol. It says we're under their protection and the other students can't touch us. Which is good, because apparently they were planning some next level shit for all of us this quarter."

"Do I have to get it tattooed?" Greg whined.

"You can get it removed when you're a rich Broadway director." I yanked his arm out straight. "Be a good boy and hold still for Ayaz."

Ayaz changed the needle and tube and came over. Greg kept his eyes closed the whole time. When Ayaz finished, Greg let out a long breath. His face was deathly pale as he settled back into the sofa.

"Don't scratch it." I slapped his hand away from his wrist. "You need to sleep."

"You really believe them?" Greg glanced over at Quinn and Ayaz. Quinn slouched in an overstuffed leather chair, rummaging through Trey's liquor cabinet. Ayaz packed up the tattoo machine, placing each instrument carefully back into the box. "They're the bullies."

I sighed. "It's complicated. I believe them. I've seen too much tonight with my own eyes *not* to believe them. But I don't *trust* them. I don't think I can ever trust them."

Andre climbed on the sofa and slumped next to Greg, digging around in his pocket for his pad and pen. Andre scribbled a note and passed it to me.

"They like you," it read.

I rubbed my lower lip. My skin still buzzed where all three guys had kissed me. I'd never even had a boyfriend before, and tonight I kissed *three* dead monarchs.

But why? Quinn I understood – sex was his protective shield. He flirted and fucked because it was better than facing his bitter reality. But Ayaz ran so hot and cold, his mind and heart so closed off, that I couldn't even believe his kiss was real.

And Trey... Trey hated me from the moment I arrived at Derleth Academy. He may have been made into this monster, but he embraced his role as the King of Kings. The kiss in the locker room I could understand... he'd just faced down his father and so desperately wanted comfort, but he was too proud and too mean to ask. It was a moment of weakness and I was the closest victim.

But tonight? What was *that* about?

They like fucking with me, I wrote, handing the note back. Andre gave me a sly smile as he tucked the pad away.

The clock on the oven read 3:14AM. I could barely keep my eyes open. Quinn went into Trey's room and a moment later returned, dragging a very naked Trey by the ear.

"Ow. What gives?" Trey complained.

"Hazy gets the bed. We all agreed. Look at her, dude. She needs sleep."

"It's my bed," Trey roared. "She's got her own, downstairs, with the rats."

"And she's not going anywhere near it tonight, not before we've dealt with the student body. The two charity cases can sleep on the sofa. You and I are staying awake," Quinn said.

"It's fine," I said, my eyes fluttering shut. "I'm not a damsel in distress. I'll just stay here with Greg and Andre. Trey doesn't need to give up his bed—"

Ayaz already had his arms around me, lifting me off the ground. I was too weak to argue. He dumped me unceremoniously on the bed. The door pulled shut behind me, leaving me all alone in Trey's bedroom.

Trey's bedroom.

I slid off the bed, exhausted but eager to peek into this private side of Trey and maybe understand him better. But there wasn't really much to see. An enormous bed mussed up from where he'd been lying only moments ago. A stack of books on the nightstand. A poster of the lacrosse team and some awards and trophies stacked in a glass cabinet along one wall.

I paused in front of the trophies, reading a few of the titles. Player of the Year. Class President. Captain of the Debate Team. All carrying the crest of Miskatonic Prep. All from twenty years ago. Beside them, a row of ribbons with Derleth's crest, naming him Valedictorian for every subsequent year. Trey had been king of this school in every way, holding on to his crown with an iron fist for the last two decades.

Does he ever get tired of it? Does he ever wonder what's the point?

Curious now, I flicked through the stack of books. *Wuthering Heights*, a history textbook, some horror novel called *At The Mountains of Madness*. In the top drawer of the bedside cabinet I found a mess of condoms, chocolate wrappers, and a college prospectus with dog-eared corners.

I picked up the prospectus and opened it across my knees.

All the faces had been scribbled out in angry red pen. Words scrawled across the page in violent script.

NO FUTURE. NO HOPE. NO TOMORROW.

I ran my hand over the page, feeling the bumps in the paper where he'd pressed the pen so hard he'd scored right through. On that single page, I saw more of the real Trey Bloomberg than I'd seen all quarter.

Imagine being stuck in senior year for two decades.

Trey Bloomberg was rich, beautiful, clever, well-connected. He had everything going for him.

Everything except for a future.

The prospectus weighed heavy in my hands. I replaced it and shoved the drawer shut, wishing I hadn't snooped. I rubbed my hands together. Bits of dried mud flaked off and fell on the pristine cream carpet. My knee and wrist throbbed with pain. Even though I was struggling to keep my eyes open, I needed to clean up before I crawled between the sheets.

I let myself into Trey's ensuite – all white marble and black chrome – and turned on the shower. Multiple heads pummeled my body with hot water while I lathered up with Trey's expensive shampoos, dragging my fingers through my ruined hair, washing away the mud and cold of the caves. But not even fancy-ass bath products could slough away the crawling chaos of the horrors the deity had visited upon my mind.

After I'd showered and dried myself with three of the fluffiest towels ever unleashed upon the world, I lay down in the bed, setting the shard of glass on the corner of the bedside table. I pulled the covers up to my head. Trey's scent wafted up from the sheets — spring herbs, wild-blossoms, fragrant cypress wood — light and airy and calm.

I closed my eyes, hoping the blissful oblivion of sleep in a non rat-infested room would soon overtake me. Instead, the deity sought me on the edges of my dreams, calling me back to the cavern. Every time I felt myself slipping under, its visions crept through my skull, and my eyes flew open again.

It was as if that thing was made of hatred, as if its very constituent parts were the prejudice and rage and thirst for power it had extracted from those it consumed. I wondered what it would extract from me, what power it would draw from my own innermost thoughts.

Or would the things I'd done be too dark even for it to stomach?

CHAPTER SIX

"Rise and shine, Hazy."

I opened one eye. A disembodied head bobbed on the opposite wall, sandy hair sticking out in all directions and wearing Quinn's signature smirk. Pain and fire tore through my skull.

The deity beheaded Quinn! It's possessed his skull and sent it to torment me.

I scrambled up the bed, grabbing for my shard. My feet tangled in the sheets as I tried to escape.

"Don't come any closer or I'll fuck you up!" I yelled, holding the shard over my wrist, just over the Elder Sign tattoo.

"Hazy, Hazy... it's just me." The severed head pushed the door wider, revealing his whole body. His very taut, *very* naked and tatted body.

My mouth fell open, and my tongue dried on my throat. My arm trembled as I struggled to hold it out. *This isn't how this dream usually goes...*

"Shit, I'm sorry. I didn't mean to scare you." Quinn flopped down on the bed, his muscled ass pointing to the sky as he took the shard from my hand and set it back on the bedside table. He clasped my hand in his. He felt warm, alive. But I knew that was a lie.

I sighed and rubbed my eyes. "I'm not sure I've slept at all. I've been having these horrible nightmares..."

"I know. You were screaming in your sleep," Quinn whispered. "Trey said not to disturb you, that at least you were sleeping. But I couldn't take it anymore. I came to see if you were okay."

The dreams flooded back to me – mere snatches of my nightmares that each held unimaginable terror. A black, slimy mass covered in eyes and mouths, a towering giant woman with branches made of flesh protruding from her body, a subterranean city made of shimmering stone and built atop the body of a slumbering god, a eyeless tortoise with a triangular head and two whip-like tails that lumbered across the earth devouring everything in its path, Quinn with his limbs torn off by monstrous tentacles, Ayaz absorbed into a towering pillar of amorphous alien flesh, Trey and Greg and Andre turned to flesh-eating zombies by a red vapor, Dante's fingers trailing over a naked breast, my mother's face in the window as the fire tore through the building. Flames consuming the cosmos.

Even in sleep, I couldn't escape the horror of this school and its secret.

"I'm not okay," I whispered. My nails dug into his arm. *Quinn's here. He feels so alive.*

"Me neither."

Quinn's lips sought mine, hot and needy. This wasn't anything like Quinn's other kisses; this one was full of secret parts of himself he hid from the world. This was the Quinn buried down deep, the scared boy who just wanted to be held.

The dead boy who wanted to live.

We faced down our fears in each other's arms. Quinn tried to force out the darkness in me, and I tried to swallow his pain.

Quinn's hand brushed across my breasts, his touch light,

searching, but tinged with need. His finger brushed my nipple, which hardened under his touch.

In the wall behind my head, I heard the faintest *scritch-scritch*. A warning.

I froze.

"Hazy?" Quinn's voice was husky, breathless. He froze too, his muscles tensed.

I scrambled out from under him. "Get out of this bed."

"As you wish." Quinn wrapped his arm around my waist and threw me over his shoulder, sheets and all. "We're out of bed."

"Quinn, you bastard, let me down." I grabbed hold of the doorframe. He sighed dramatically, set me down, and adjusted the sheet in my hands so that his fingers brushed just above my breast, sending a flush of heat through my body...

I shoved him out the door and slammed it behind me. My heart hammered in my chest. *Fuck, that was close.*

I'd never heard the rats on these upper stories before, but it was just as well I did. Those tiny claws scratching against the wall had stopped me before I did something really stupid with Quinn.

I scrambled around the bed, searching for the clothes I'd tossed aside last night. *What's the time? I'll have to race downstairs to get some fresh clothes. I hope I'll make it to breakfast before the dining hall closes... hang on, why can't I find any of my clothes? This better not be another of Quinn's jokes...*

...or a new torture...

I imagined walking into the living room wearing just the sheet, Trey tearing it from my body while Quinn snapped a hundred photographs, which they plastered all over school with a horse's face Photoshopped over my head. It'd be a good Photoshop job, too – Ayaz had a rare artistic talent.

I never should have trusted them. My knees trembled. I slumped down in a chair in the corner, knocking over a stack of fresh clothing. *My clothing.* Someone had collected a fresh set of jeans, Dante's old basketball tank, and fresh socks and underwear from

my room. I ran my hand over the edge of my black bra, feeling a
rush of heat at the idea that one of them had touched it.

What is wrong with me?

I pulled on the clothes and ran Trey's hairbrush through my
hair, trying to clear all the confused thoughts from my head. I
wanted to trust the guys, because fuck knows I needed allies at
this school if I was going to defeat a cosmic god. I wanted their
kisses, their touch... earlier, in bed, I didn't want Quinn to stop.
But after everything they'd done to me last quarter, being close to
them made me feel untethered, like I couldn't even trust myself.

And that wasn't even taking into account I'd seen their graves
last night, that they were walking ghosts or zombies or edimmu,
and that there were *three* of them. Even if I wanted them – which
I didn't, it wasn't *possible* – I couldn't have them all. I had to
choose, and how could I choose the best of three shitty options
when they were all locked into a competition with me as the
prize?

Why did it have to be *them?* Why couldn't I have feelings for
Greg... well, not Greg, since he was gay, but Andre? Someone else?
Anyone else? Why did I always fall for the worst possible guys?

I am so screwed up.

I walked into the living room to find the weirdest sight – Greg
and Andre sitting on Trey's enormous couch, elbowing each other
with glee as they played some dungeon-crawling game on Trey's
Playstation. Ayaz pottered around the kitchen with an apron
looped over his broad shoulders, cracking eggs into bowls, while
Trey leaned against the wall, drinking orange juice like he was a
judge at some orange-juice drinking competition as he surveyed
the room with cool detachment.

"This is awesome," Greg held up his controller and grinned at
Trey. "I can't believe you still have this game. It's like twenty years
old."

Trey grunted.

Andre's eyes followed me as I headed to the kitchen. I could practically hear the cogs in his head turning. Greg may have believed my story about the monarchs, but I wasn't sure Andre did.

In the kitchen, I peered over Ayaz's shoulder as he stirred eggs in a pan. He was shirtless under the apron, his skin glowing under the lights. *Wow, he's cut.* My throat dried up and the tips of my fingers sizzled. I had to clamp my hands behind my back so I didn't reach up and touch him.

He might've kissed you in that cave to satisfy some sort of honor, but he's sleeping with the headmistress. That is a) gross and b) untrustworthy. Even if he is cooking breakfast for you—

An amazing smell hit my nostrils – eggs, peppers, tomatoes, a hint of chili. "What's that?" I asked.

"It's called *menemen*," he said, adding a handful of chopped herbs to the pan. "My mother used to make this every weekend for brunch, with homemade bread, of course."

"It smells amazing." I held up a plate so he could scoop out a generous helping. On the table was a stack of warm bread, some chopped vegetables, and a container of thick, creamy yogurt.

"You made all this?"

"Yes." Ayaz didn't look up from the pan. "Not all of it today. I made this batch of yogurt a few days ago."

"You know this school has a dining hall that serves three meals a day precisely so you rich kids can get used to being waited on hand and foot?" I lowered my voice. "You also know you're supposed to be dead, right? Why do you need to eat?"

"We don't need to," Ayaz said. "I just like it."

"Can you taste the food?"

"Kind of." He ran his finger along the rim of the pan and licked it. Heat pooled between my legs as I thought about those lips around a part of me. Ayaz picked up a plate and started dishing up some of the eggs. "I get the aroma and the faintest ghost of the taste on my tongue, but I never have the sensation of being full. I—"

Ayaz snapped his mouth shut. He shoved the plate into my hands and turned back to the stove. Over his shoulder, I noticed Andre leaning over the counter, watching us with a thoughtful expression.

"Ayaz made breakfast," I held out a plate to him. "You want some?"

Andre took the plate, but he kept staring at me, his eyes searching my face. How much did he hear?

It doesn't matter if he heard, he's not going to guess the truth.

Ayaz shoved a second plate into my hands without looking at me. Andre's eyebrow lifted.

"Ayaz was just telling me about his food allergies," I said, spooning a generous dollop of yogurt on top of my breakfast.

Andre just kept staring at me.

"Is he dumb?" Trey came up behind us, grabbing the plate out of Andre's hands. "He never talks."

I spun around to face Trey. "Don't talk about Andre like he's not here. He's *mute*."

"Same thing." Trey shoved a forkful of eggs into his mouth and sauntered off.

I turned back to Andre, fuming on his behalf. He shrugged his shoulders and accepted another plate from Ayaz. Trey's comment rolled off him because he'd heard it so many times throughout his whole life, and that was *wrong*.

One way or another, I'm going to make these guys see Greg and Andre as people in their own right, I vowed. As if I didn't already have enough impossible tasks to achieve this year.

Quinn walked out of Trey's bathroom, a towel wrapped around his torso. I noticed Greg's eyes following him across the room. Quinn leaned across the counter, plucking a cherry tomato out of a bowl and pushing it between his lips. I bent my head to my breakfast, trying not to think about Quinn's lips on mine only a few minutes ago. *There's far too much naked testosterone in this kitchen.* "So, what are our plans for the day?"

Today was Saturday, the first official day of the end-of-quarter break. We had a week off school before second quarter started. Somehow I didn't think I'd be getting much of a vacation.

"If we're throwing ideas around, I'd love to stay here and keep playing this game," Greg piped up.

"Sounds like a plan. I'll play with you." Quinn flopped down on the sofa and grabbed the second controller.

"Hazel and I need to do some studying," Ayaz said, throwing extra chili on his breakfast. "We've got that *very important project* we need to start on." He meant, of course, finding a way to defeat the god.

"Your history project?" Greg asked. "I thought you were already halfway done with that."

"No, this is something else," I said quickly. "And we should probably get started, so—"

"No, you don't," Trey said. "I need to study with Hazel."

The two of them stared each other down. Finally, Ayaz stepped back. "Fine. But I get her when you're done."

"If there's anything left of me by then," I muttered. The absolute last thing I wanted to do was spend a single second longer with Trey Bloomberg. He confused and enraged me way too much as it was. "What do we have to work on, anyway? We're only in two classes together and we don't have any assignments—"

"You asked for my help for physics," Trey nodded at me. "Well, I'm offering my assistance, but that offer is only good for today. Get your stuff. I want to get to the library before someone takes my table."

As if anyone would *dare* to sit at the monarchs' favorite table – the one under the giant cathedral window overlooking the athletic fields. I searched Trey's face for some inkling of what this was about – I was kicking his ass in physics class, and he knew it, so this wasn't about studying – but he was impossible to read. "Let me finish my breakfast first," I shoveled another forkful in my mouth. "We'll have to go to my room for my books."

"No need." Trey practically shoved me out the door. Heads turned in the dormitory hall as we made our way down the marble staircase and across the atrium. Whispers followed me as I trailed behind Trey. I caught snatches of the familiar 'gutter whore,' but no one was brave enough to yell anything around Trey.

In the library, every table was empty except for the one under the window. A group of freshman had spread out their books and were laughing and swapping snacks they'd nicked from the dining hall. Trey glared at them and nodded toward the doors. "Go."

The entire table scrambled to collect their books and bags. They fled for the exit with such haste that one of them left behind their slice of brownie.

Trey picked up the slice and took a bite, somehow avoiding getting any crumbs on his pristine clothing. We sat down on opposite sides of his table. He pulled his physics book out of his bag and flipped it open.

"Are we really going to sit here and study?" I demanded. "Because this is ridiculous."

Trey slid the brownie across the table to me. "Take it. Unlike Ayaz, I've no interest in food."

I shoved it aside. "Why are we here? I should be with Ayaz, trying to figure out how to get your life back."

Trey steepled his fingers. "I'm trying to prepare you," he said.

"For what?"

"For being a monarch. You're wearing the Elder Sign now. That means you're under my protection, but only as far as everyone agrees that it does. I'm the King of this school, and what I say is law. But hatred for you runs deep... deep enough that my word might not be enough, not unless they *believe* that you're one of us. And that starts by being seen with me."

"That's stupid. And not necessary. I made a pact—"

"The only agreement you've made is that you and the other two charity cases make it to the end of the year alive. Anything else is fair game. For someone so clever, you're shit at making deals. Technically, they wouldn't be in violation of the agreement if they cut off all your limbs. Don't think the headmistress won't consider it. She's quite creative."

"I don't doubt it," I said, folding my arms across my chest. A cold fear shuddered down my spine. "Is she going to cut off my limbs?"

"She might," Trey shrugged. "If she thought it would give her an answer. I don't think she'll touch you until she understands why your pain hurts the god, but she's not the one you have to worry about now."

"You mean Courtney? You said she was going to do something to me last night. That's why Ayaz came to my room?"

Trey's jaw tightened. "Courtney has a new boyfriend."

"What's that got to do with—"

"His name is John Hyde-Jones."

"I know him." John was a hulking guy with a thick neck in my Ancient History class. He sat in the back with the monarchs, making lewd remarks about the Greco-Roman mosaics in his textbook and slapping every girl's ass who walked by his desk. He had an intellect to rival a gardening hose, but his father was a senator and he exuded an aura of danger. I always gave him a wide berth.

John + Courtney = a match made in hell.

"Courtney gave John your room key. He and a couple of his buddies were going to wait until you were asleep and—" Trey shook his head. His eyes flashed with danger, but this time I didn't think it was directed at me.

I didn't need him to fill in the words. A cold fist curled around my heart. I stared down at the desk, unfolding my arms and letting my hands flop against the wood. My fingers curled over to touch the scar on my wrist, peeling off the dressing on my new tattoo – the ink that was supposed to protect me but might've put me in the firing line.

Neither of us spoke for what felt like forever. Trey's unspoken words hung in the air between us.

No one would have heard me scream. No one would have helped me.

I forced my mind back from the precipice – I was already dealing with too much horror, I didn't need to imagine what would have happened if Ayaz hadn't come for me first.

Finally, I raised my head and met Trey's icicle eyes with my defiant ones. *You may have tried to break me, Courtney Haynes, but I have more allies than you know.* "They hate me that much?"

"You've been systematically tearing this school and all its institutions apart ever since you arrived. Of course they hate you. They're not used to a gutter whore having a voice. They want to silence you, Hazel." Trey flipped a page in his textbook. "That's why you shouldn't go back to your room until we can get the lock changed."

"But the teachers… were they in on this, too?"

Trey shook his head. "When the guys found your room empty, Courtney alerted the headmistress. Ms. West thought you were making a run for it, so she had everyone out looking for you. It would be much harder to find you if you left the boundaries of the school, since none of us can cross the sigils on the barrier. It's like butting up against a brick wall. But a scholarship student could, and an escaped student would threaten the entire system – that's why they only choose orphans, so no one will come looking for them and they have nowhere to run to. If you'd got in that boat, you'd be safe in Arkham by now, telling your story to a police officer who thinks you're high."

"And Greg and Andre would be doomed."

Trey shrugged. "We're all doomed."

My fingers slid from the burn across to the tattoo, shooting a jolt of pain down my arm that also caused a fire to flicker in my head as the god felt it, too. *Interesting that I now seem to be able to sense the god's pain as well as my own.* "Tell me about the fire," I whispered.

"Quid pro quo, Hazy," Trey flashed me a smile that was

completely devoid of mirth. "I show you mine if you show me yours."

"What do you mean?"

"I want to know about the fire that killed your mother."

No.

"You already know everything," I hissed. "You read about it in my file."

"Not everything. I don't know how you got that scar you keep touching."

I squeezed my eyes shut as heat flared in my hands. The scar glowed so hot I tore my finger away. When I opened my eyes again, the corner of Trey's textbook had caught on fire. He yelped in surprise and smothered the flame with his sleeve.

I shoved out my chair and stood up, my whole body shaking. "This study session is over."

CHAPTER SEVEN

"I'm ready," I said to Ayaz, rolling up my sleeves. "Show me the book."

It was Sunday, the day of rest. Only I would never rest again. Yesterday, after I left Trey in the library, he remained there for the rest of the day. I went back to his room and played Playstation with Greg and Andre and Quinn in an effort to avoid having to talk about Trey's book's spontaneous combustion. Ayaz baked *lahmacun* (flatbread spread with minced beef, salad, and lemon juice) and set out homemade *baba ganoush* and *tzatziki* that tasted divine.

It felt weird to act like a proper teenager for once, hanging out and eating snacks and trash-talking each other, even if it was on a sofa which probably cost more than my mother ever earned in a year while eating food from a country I'd never be able to visit.

Today, the charade was over, for me at least. Greg and Andre were playing air hockey in Quinn's room – they must've made an impression on him, since he'd allowed them free rein in his man cave for the week. Trey and Quinn left for 'break' – in order to keep up appearances for the scholarship students that everything was fine and dandy, most of the Miskatonic Prep students needed to pretend to be off on ski vacations or in Paris with their families. In reality, they were shepherded into a series of luxury cabins deeper in the woods, where a week-long party raged.

At least that got them both out of my presence for a week. I didn't know how much longer I could deal with Trey's penetrating gaze and Quinn's easy smile and the tension that stretched between us.

This year, Ayaz had opted to stay behind, which was why I now sat across from him on his Scandinavian sofa, about to get a crash course in Parris' occult practices.

"Are you sure you're okay with this? That book can be pretty dark."

"I've already looked at it, remember?" I tapped my knees. "Bring it. I'm not afraid of paper cuts."

Ayaz frowned. "Are you going to take this seriously?"

"As serious as this coffee," I said, lifting the tiny cup of Turkish coffee to my lips.

"I don't have to help you with this, you know. I could be enjoying a party in the woods with undead girls who fuck like they have no future instead of sitting here trying to help you on your futile quest for freedom."

"This is your freedom, too," I pointed out.

Ayaz rolled his eyes. "I've been through all this before. This deity has controlled the most powerful people in the world for the last five hundred years. But sure, we're going to figure out how to defeat it and bring a bunch of Edimmu back to life in just a few months."

"Of course we won't with that attitude." I pounded my fist on the table. "Bring on the book."

Ayaz went to the bathroom, returning a few moments later with the book. I noticed he'd removed all the scholarship students files he'd kept hidden inside it. "It's the one hiding place the maintenance staff won't look," he said. "None of them want to touch anything in a guy's bathroom. We have to clean them ourselves. The faculty thinks it teaches us personal responsibility."

"Oh, sure. Because cleaning a bathroom is totally one of life's most horrific hardships. What's this binding?" I ran my fingers over the rough cover. "It feels like leather, but, like, not the stuff used to make jackets—"

"It is leather, made from skin," Ayaz said. "Human skin."

I jerked my hand back. "Is there anything at this school that isn't horrifying and gross? Any idea whose skin it is?"

"Parris, of course. He had his disciples make the binding from his skin after he died. Apparently, it imbues the spells inside with additional potency." Ayaz opened the cover and flipped through the pages.

"How did you come into possession of Parris' diary, anyway?"

"It's called a *grimoire*. It's less of a diary and more of a... spell-book, for want of a better term. It contains magic rites and sigils Parris worked on, as well as notes about some of the rituals his group performed – those are in a diary format. I got it from Trey's dad."

"Why would Trey's dad give this to you?"

"That's a long story." Ayaz opened a drawer and pulled out a stack of paper and pens. "In my home country, parents with enough money often pay to send their children to receive their schooling in the West – usually in the United Kingdom but some-times in America, Australia, or New Zealand. My father is a low-level diplomat. We are Muslim and of Arab descent – a minority in Turkey – and there had been some political turmoil they didn't want me mixed up in. My family had some business dealings with the Bloombergs, and they wanted to solidify their ties with the US. Vincent wanted a way into the oil and shipping wealth of our country during a time the US was staging attacks on Turkey in the First Gulf War. To improve his reputation he offered to have me stay with his family and to sponsor my admission into Miskatonic." A darkness passed over Ayaz's face. "My parents were only too happy to leave me in his care."

"Your parents just let you live with a stranger who'd publicly admitted prejudice against your faith?"

"It's not at all uncommon." Ayaz brushed it aside, but the darkness in his eyes told me he wasn't as cool with it as he pretended to be. "If they refused to do business with Islamophobes, they'd never do business at all. Besides, I'm not a Muslim any longer. There's nothing like being raised from the dead into a living nightmare to make you lose your faith in Allah. My parents trusted Vincent because he was rich and powerful, and he could give me a better life."

"Was this before or after the fire?"

"Before. I lived with the Bloombergs since I was ten years old. Vincent took me under his wing. It started out as political posturing for him – a way for him to stand up to people on the left who opposed him and say, 'Oh, I'm not a racist or an Islamophobe. I'm a good person. Look, I'm lifting this poor Middle Eastern kid up from the gutter.' When really, I was a wealthy kid maneuvered into a strange country to further two families' political aims. But after a while, I fancied Vincent really did like my company. Not as much as Wilhem – that boy could do no wrong in his eyes. But he saw something in me he didn't see in Trey. Or maybe, he saw too much of himself in Trey, and he didn't like his reflection. I took an interest in the occult and the Eldritch Club, and so Vincent gave me this book my first year at Miskatonic Prep. I never understood its significance until after the fire."

"If Trey's so desperate to please his father, then why doesn't he hate you?"

"Who's to say he doesn't?" Ayaz shrugged. "Trey's always been good to me, but for all I know it's a calculation – a chess move in the game he plays against his father."

Ayaz's eyes fluttered closed, his impossibly-long lashes tangling together as his mind traveled to some other place and time. I caught a whiff of him – that honey and roses scent of forbidden pleasure – and my lips burned with memories of our kiss. The kiss he'd taken because he'd felt left out. Because somewhere inside he was still that ten-year-old boy in a big, strange house, wondering why he'd been abandoned by the people who were supposed to love him.

But I couldn't square away that glimpse of him with the guy I'd caught fucking Ms. West in an empty classroom. Ayaz was an enigma to me. More than anything I wanted to open him up and lay him bare.

"Or maybe because of his loneliness, he needed a friend more than he needed someone else to loathe?" I ventured.

Ayaz snorted. "No. He saw that his father liked me, and he thought if he befriended me then whatever magic I exerted over Vincent would rub off on him, too. Enough questions." Ayaz's eyes sprung open. Whatever memories that had assailed him were firmly shut away in a box again. He flattened out the book. "We need to get to work."

"What are we looking for?"

"We have two separate problems – getting rid of the god and bringing the edimmu back to life. The first has to be our priority, so anything that could give us a clue on how to destroy the god, or how to banish it back to its own dimension. Failing that, if we could figure out how Parris summoned and trapped it in the first place. Most magic is a kind of karmic balancing act, so performing the same spell backward is often enough to undo its effects."

"So all this stuff, spells and rituals and summoning, it's all real?"

"You've had your brush with the Great Old God. What do you think?" Ayaz fingered the edge of the book. I nodded. When he put it like that, I couldn't deny what I'd felt that night, what I still felt every time I closed my eyes. "As far as I can tell, there's no exact spell in here that correlates to, 'here's how to summon a

Great Old God,' but Parris has written about his research. It would help if you learned Medieval Latin."

"Oh sure, I've already got a full academic load, a leading role in the school production, and a Great Old God on my case, but whatever. I'll learn Medieval Latin."

"It's fine." Ayaz tossed another book across the table to me. "This is an occult book from the library. It's written by E. Eldridge, one of Parris' students, and it's been translated into English."

"How do you know Medieval Latin?"

"I've been at this school twenty years," he said. "Trey spends his time trying to stay at the top in some vain hope he'll win his father's approval. Quinn's fucked his way through the entire student body several times over. I learn things."

"What things have you learned, apart from Medieval Latin?"

"Theoretical physics. A few other dead languages. Advanced alchemy."

"You're taking that stupid alchemy class?"

"Not stupid." Ayaz pointed to a squiggly shape on the page in front of me. "I can tell you what that means."

"Okay, Nostradamus, what is it? It looks like someone testing their pen to see if it's out of ink."

"It's a sigil. I told you how in magic these are considered to be pictorial signatures – like how a demon might write its own name. They can also be the map of a ritual or directions to a place of power. Or they can trap power. Parris wrote sigils like these all over the walls in the caves and cairns on the boundaries of the school. They are what keep us edimmu trapped inside. They form an invisible barrier we can't cross. You'll see them everywhere once you know what you're looking for."

"There was one carved into that rock you and Trey moved," I recalled.

"Exactly. That sigil is part of the god's prison." Ayaz traced a sigil on the page of his book. "See this? It's the sigil of the demon

Bael. This is Halphas, and here's Asmodeus. By drawing these sigils, not only can the magician summon a demon, he or she can also control it. But Parris wasn't interested in demons. He wanted more power than a demon could offer him. I think what happened is that he found the sigil that drew this god out of another dimension, only he had no control over it. He couldn't put the god back in the box."

"So he trapped it here?"

"Exactly. The void beneath the gymnasium is the god's prison. And I think everything the god does – all the power he feeds the members of the Eldritch Club, all the sacrifices he demands – is an attempt to weaken Parris' protections. If that god escapes—" Ayaz shuddered.

"But that's not going to happen, right? That god has been trapped down there at least five centuries. Surely it would have escaped by now if it could."

"Except that twenty years ago it started a fire that killed 245 souls," Ayaz said. "And then it resurrected those same people to live in a time-locked prison in order to feed it more power. I can't help but think it's gearing up to make a move. Remember, the god doesn't measure time the way we do. For it, twenty years isn't even the blink of an eye."

"When you put it like that..." I turned the page in my book, staring down at more images of sigils and other occult symbols. "You'd think Parris would have just left a note explaining what he did, to make it easy for his disciples to figure out what he couldn't."

"It's not that easy. He couldn't write down the sigil. Even that might have given the creature too much power. And remember, Parris wasn't prone to altruism. He was more concerned with obtaining as much power as possible from the trapped god than with sending it back. But somewhere in this book, he's given us clues, I'm sure of it."

"Uh-huh." I turned another page. "And in the twenty years

since you've been searching for this sigil, what have you uncovered so far?"

Ayaz shook his head. "Absolutely nothing."

I glared at him.

"What? I had to teach myself Medieval Latin. Besides, I never thought I had a deadline before."

"Right." I cracked the spine on the book as I flipped back to the beginning. "We're better get studying, then."

CHAPTER EIGHT

My back pressed against cool, pulsing stone, frozen in place as I watched Dante tattooing tentacles over my mother's naked breasts. As he finished each one they came to life and slithered over her skin, wrapping around her limbs and squeezing tight while she writhed in ecstasy. I cried out and he turned around to look at me. His eyes reflected orange flames and his mouth was a black hole hanging open, disgorging masticated stars.

My alarm rang, startling me out of another horrific nightmare. I slammed my hand into the annoying buzz, swatting Loretta's ancient clock off the chair beside my bed. It crashed against the wall and clattered to the floor, the glass face shattering and mechanical innards bouncing across the stones. The rats in the walls skittered away from the noise.

Oh yay. The first day of the second quarter is already off to a great start.

I was back in my own dorm room, down in the dungeon with the damp and the rats. Quinn and Ayaz had "borrowed" (read, stolen) some tools from the maintenance shed and installed two new locks and a deadbolt on my door. The locks they'd cut off a couple of disused classrooms. It made me feel a little safer – it was probably enough to stop John Hyde-Jones, but not enough to hold back the god's hate-filled visions from my dreams.

I sat up in bed, wiping sweat from my forehead with the corner of my sheet. Hanging from the doorknob of my wooden closet was my Derleth uniform – knee-length red-and-black tartan skirt, white shirt, black blazer edged with red piping, and the black-and-red striped tie. My palms itched as I slid out of bed and stood in front of it, running a finger over the embroidered star on the school crest.

How can I put this on and pretend everything's normal when there's a demon beneath the school and a clock ticking down to my death?

Scritch-scritch. The rat claws churned, as if sending me a reply.

I pressed my finger into the scar on my wrist. My mother's voice rang in my ears, clear and golden. *You can do anything, my love.*

Like she'd know. She'd never been to a boarding school of the dead.

After everything I saw last week, it seemed impossible I was about to go back to classes and pretend everything was fine. But if it would protect Greg and Andre, then it was worth it.

Besides, I had a few plans of my own. If Courtney Haynes thought she was going to continue to torment me and my friends, she had another thing coming.

While spending the week with Ayaz, the knowledge of just what the Miskatonic Prep students had done to the sacrifices gnawed away at me. The monarchs of this school had tormented four students a year, every year for twenty years, until the students wanted to die. Until they were so broken they wanted to be sacrificed to the god. And while it seemed like Trey and Ayaz and Quinn at least had some kind of conscience about it, Courtney and her ilk took *pleasure* in their task.

I may be trying to give them their lives back, but that didn't mean they didn't deserve to pay for their crimes. I couldn't just let Courtney and Tillie and the others walk out into the world as they were – they would continue the fine traditions they'd started at Derleth Academy, blazing a path of torture across the world without remorse. I needed to make them face the monsters they'd become.

It was time they experienced a little torture themselves, courtesy of Hazel Waite, the gutter whore turned newest Eldritch Club recruit.

Revenge ideas stirred in my head, sending excited jolts through my body. I didn't know when or how yet, but I knew I'd make every last student of Miskatonic Prep pay for what they'd done, starting with Courtney and the other monarchs. I just didn't know how the three Kings fit into my plans. They had been horrible to me and to my friends. But when I thought of Quinn's scream when Trey threw that itching powder into his eyes, or Ayaz's hand brushing mine when he handed me a coffee and my veins caught alight, or my lips burning with the ghosts of their kisses, *How do I choose between what they were – my bullies –* and what they are to me now?

I guess it depends what they do next, whether they prove to me – to us – that we can trust them.

I pulled on the uniform, struggling to get the tie straight. I always used to copy Loretta while she did hers, but she wasn't here anymore. I twisted it into a mockery of a knot, grabbed my battered bookbag, and pulled the door open.

Here goes nothing.

Greg and Andre met me in the hallway. Andre had his sleeves rolled up, showing off his Eldritch Club tattoo. Greg's eyes were ringed with red – I imagined that like me he was still fending off the Great Old God in his dreams.

He greeted me with one of his customary warm hugs. "We ready for this?"

"We're gonna knock 'em dead," I said without a hint of irony, flashing him my own not-quite-healed tattoo. "Things are going to be different this quarter."

The three of us linked arms and took the stairs together.

Unlike the sweeping marble staircases throughout the rest of the buildings, our staircase was narrow and metal, so it was a bit cramped, especially when Andre tried to squeeze his enormous shoulders around the corner.

We emerged on the dorm floor. Students fluttered between their rooms, tossing books at each other, laughing and talking, and acting like totally normal teens who weren't at all under the power of a malevolent cosmic entity. Girls compared lipstick colors as they strutted down the hall, tartan skirts rolled up as high as they dared.

All these students are dead.

They looked so normal, but it was all a show, a farce designed specifically to break us. I shivered. Greg squeezed my hand. He thought I was afraid because of Courtney.

If only you knew, Greg. I'd give anything to go back to my worst nightmare being Courtney fucking Haynes.

Ayaz came down the staircase at the end of the hall. A couple of girls who were walking past stopped in their tracks, their jaw practically hitting the floor at the sight of the monarch in his crisp white shirt and black dress slacks. It was kind of gross, but also... I got it. Ayaz was hot as hell, with his dark hair and smoldering eyes and those cheekbones that could cut glass...

I may have been doing a bit of drooling myself.

Try to remember, he's sleeping with the headmistress. Or, as she should be known, the Deadmistress.

I snorted at my own silent joke.

The girls chased Ayaz down the hall, giggling as they caught up with him and started to grill him on his class schedule. He met my eyes over their heads, and the corners of his mouth tugged up, just a little. He pushed his way through the gaggle of girls and came right up to me. His hand flew to my cheek, stroking my skin. I heard one of the girls gasp.

It was one thing to cook me breakfast and help me banish a

god behind closed doors, but for him to acknowledge me in public... *things are definitely changing around here.*

Ayaz grabbed my hand. "Come on."

"But Ayaz," one of the girls stepped forward. "Wouldn't you rather—"

"No."

Greg and Andre trailed after us as Ayaz dragged me into the senior common room – a space I'd never been allowed to enter before, except for my first day when I been snooping. Then, the common room had been deserted. Now, it was *packed* with students. Even though class was starting in less than twenty minutes and the dining hall was still open, what looked like the entire senior class was stuffed in like sardines, leaning against the walls, sitting on the floor, and perched on the edge of tables.

Trey sat on the kitchen island, swinging his legs casually, like he was waiting for a doctor's appointment or for his private jet to be prepped. Behind him, Quinn whistled to himself as he made himself a coffee in the fancy espresso machine. Ayaz joined them, swiping a hand through his dark hair. The three of them standing there, so cool and casual, commanded the space. This was their domain. They belonged here.

And we didn't. No wonder I felt like I was naked, and Andre was staring at his shoes. Greg smiled, but I could still see the haunted look in his eyes. The god was haunting him, too.

Toward the front of the crowd, Courtney folded her arms and glared at me. "What's this about, Trey? Why is the gutter whore in our space?"

"This is just an informal gathering to let you all know that from this moment on, the scholarship students are off-limits," Trey said. "We've had our fun with them last quarter, but that stops, now."

A collective rumble rippled through the room. "This is fucking bullshit," John Hyde-Jones growled from the back of the room. "Those plebs deserve to be *crushed*."

Every word from his lips made my stomach twist as I thought about what he'd planned to do to me.

Courtney snorted. "You may be King of this school, Trey, but you don't make those rules. Our traditions have been passed down for generations. The strong prey on the weak. It's the way of the world, and none of us should fight it."

"Oh, yeah?" Trey lifted my wrist and yanked up my sleeve, exposing the Elder Sign tattoo.

Silence dropped like a bomb, obliterating every whisper of dissent.

Courtney's eyes flashed with rage. She stood up and stalked over to me. I glared right back at her, stepping forward so we were nose-to-nose. She grabbed my wrist and raked her nails over the tattoo, as if trying to scratch it off.

A jolt of pain lanced through my wrist. Inside my head, the god cried into his void. If Courtney felt its pain too, she didn't show it. Her nails dug into my skin.

"It's not a scratch-and-sniff," I snapped, yanking my arm from her grasp. She grabbed Greg's arm and flipped it over to see his tattoo, and then her eyes fell on Andre's and she shrieked.

"You gave them the sign. You can't do that!" Courtney faced off against Trey. "You don't have the authority to—"

"*I* am in charge of the Eldritch Club at this school," Trey said, his demeanor cool, calm. He looked completely bored with everything Courtney had to say. "Not you, Courtney. You want to talk about rules? You want to talk about who belongs? I don't need to remind you that before you started fucking Quinn, you and your filthy new money were never part of the inner circle."

"And now we're not fucking anymore," Quinn said gaily, lifting his coffee like it was a toast. "Perhaps you won't be in much longer."

"When I tell your father about this, he's going to kill you," Courtney spluttered.

"My father left me in charge of the club," Trey growled. "He wouldn't be pleased to know the new money slut is making trouble."

Tillie stood up, tossing her silky hair over her shoulder. It must be some witchcraft that kept it so straight and long and shiny. "If you won't hear it from new money, then hear it from old. She isn't one of us, Trey. None of them are. You're making a mockery of everything the club stands for. For everything this *school* stands for."

A few murmurs of assent rose from the crowd.

Ayaz stepped forward. "It's ridiculous we're still measuring our worth by our parents' wealth. They're not the ones here, we are. Maybe it's time we—"

"Save the pretty speeches, Ataturk. No one cares what you think anymore. It looks like Trey has got another pet, which means that you're about to lose your throne," Courtney sneered at Trey. "Have you thrown Ayaz out of bed to make way for the gutter whore? Or do both of you stick your dicks in her at the same time?"

Ayaz growled low in his throat, like an animal. Trey threw his arm out just as Ayaz threw his body forward. "Don't. She's not worth it."

"Yes, listen to your master, you Turkish dog," Courtney chirped. "Although how much longer will he be the master, I wonder? He's been so corrupted by the gutter trash that he's allowed three *scholarship students* to wear our most sacred symbol even though they haven't been initiated."

Initiated?

Another grumble of assent rose through the students, louder this time.

Of course. What top-secret elite society was complete without a pointless, humiliating initiation ritual? I glanced over at Greg. He'd shrunk back behind Andre and was self-consciously tugging down the cuff of his shirt. *If it protects Greg and Andre...*

I shrugged. "Fine. Whatever. If it'll make you happy, I'll go through your initiation."

"Hazel, shut up," Trey growled.

"We'll do it too," Greg said, his voice wavering a bit. His eyes met mine and in them I recognized my own defiance. He didn't know what was at stake, but he was willing to trust me and to fight for himself. Andre nodded, crossing his enormous arms across his chest and glaring at Courtney, daring her to take him on.

"No," Trey said.

I glared at him. "I didn't come to this school asking for special treatment. None of us did. You think we're not worthy to get in unless we complete some initiation. Fine – then prove it."

Courtney's smile was pure evil. "You heard her, ladies and gentlemen. Shall we set the initiation for the first party of the quarter? That should give us time to ensure it's done *properly*."

The warning bell rang. No one moved.

Trey nodded at Courtney, but his eyes locked on mine. As usual, those icy-pools gave nothing away. "Set the initiation."

Ayaz's eyes blazed as he met the gaze of every student in the room. His challenge made several step back with unease. "You all know the rules," he growled. "I'll snap the fingers of anyone who breaks them."

The students filed out of the common room. Greg gave me one of his wavering smiles. "Hazel, what did we just agree to?"

I shrugged. "Probably a world of pain. But if we get through it, they'll leave us alone for the rest of the year."

"That'd be nice." Greg and Andre exchanged a glance. "I hope you've got a plan."

Before I could answer, Quinn wrapped his arm around me. "You're one crazy wench, did anyone ever tell you that?"

Trey kicked the island. I yelped as the wooden cabinet splintered, the door drooping on its hinges. Inside, crystal glasses clattered.

"Fuck," Trey gasped, pulling back his leg to kick the next door. His hands balled into fists at his sides, and his shoulders shook with uncontrollable rage. "Fuck!"

I stepped in front of him, throwing my hands up before he tore the room to shreds. I had no doubt that he would do it. My mind flashed back to the day he dumped the itching powder over Quinn's face, how his anger consumed him, eating him up until he saw nothing but a black tunnel with no way out.

I knew a little about what that felt like.

"Trey, calm down. What's the big deal? We'll do the stupid initiation ceremony if that will make it safer for us. What does it involve, dancing over hot coals while reciting arcane Latin poetry?"

Trey flung himself away from me, too angry he couldn't even answer. Quinn answered for him. "You're taking that ancient history elective, right? You know the story of King Minos' labyrinth and the minotaur? It's like that."

"Explain."

"They drop you into one of the caves surrounding the school. You have to find your way back to campus. If you make it within a three-hour window, you're in the club."

"That's it? We go on an obstacle course and we get to be in the secret club?"

"It's not as easy as you think. There are miles of caves through these cliffs. It's easy to get lost or completely turned around. As your sponsors, we're not allowed to know where you're dropped in advance. Courtney and Tillie will do their best to make sure you fail. And if you make a wrong turn... let's just say there are things down there you don't want to encounter in the dark."

CHAPTER NINE

The date Courtney set for our initiation into the Eldritch Club was Halloween night, because of course it was. Apparently, the rich bitches needed a week to decide on just how they were going to torture us in the labyrinth of caves.

Oh, goody.

Meanwhile, the student body at large was occupied with the upcoming Halloween dance. It was one of the big events on the Derleth/Miskatonic social calendar. When the entire student body sans three students were soulless revenants and couldn't step foot outside the boundaries of the school, they tended to go all out for a party. At our table in the dining hall, conversation centered around costume designs. Trey, Ayaz, and Quinn continued to command the monarch's table, together with their loyal posse – Barclay, Arthur, Kenneth, Rupert, Paul, Mary, and Nancy. Greg, Andre, and I sat on the end, trying to ignore the dagger eyes other students threw our way. No one dared to insult us openly while the Kings were around, but they definitely weren't happy about our new station.

On the opposite side of the hall, facing off with us like an opposing army, Courtney held court at what had once been the table reserved for scholarship students. She now commanded an army of her own, led by her boyfriend John and his equally thick-necked, creepy-smiled friends. I watched Loretta as she laughed with her new circle. When she used to sit with us all she'd do was shift food around her plate.

She was more alive as a revenant than she'd ever been.

That broke my heart a little. But I couldn't focus on her. Loretta was already lost to me. I had to concentrate on keeping Greg and Andre alive. I was especially worried about Greg, who'd confessed he was barely sleeping since we'd rescued him from the caves.

I expected class to be awkward, what with all the teachers knowing about my pact, but things were so completely... *normal*. It was weird how everyone slipped into this routine – the teachers taught, the students passed notes and plotted Halloween hook-ups, like they hadn't just been trying to rape me or sacrifice Greg to an ancient and malevolent god.

After twenty years of this farce, everyone knew their role.

The only thing that wasn't normal was the way Trey, Quinn, and Ayaz closed in around me. Trey walked me between classes, glaring at anyone that so much as looked at me. Quinn acted like we were practically an item, always throwing his arms around me or lifting me over the threshold of a classroom. Ayaz brought me thoughtful gifts – a drawing he'd made of me, a bacon sandwich when I had to miss breakfast because of an early rehearsal.

"Andre's right – the Kings are all hot for you," Greg announced as we flung tulle and velvet at each other. We were raiding the costume and props room for outfits for the Halloween party. Quinn had just told me that the party was an alumni-sponsored event, which meant senior members of the Eldritch Club would be showing up.

I had to look like Hazel Waite, monarch of the school and

Eldritch Club member. Difficult, considering the only clothing I had with me was my Derleth uniform, my black dress, and a few threadbare t-shirts. Luckily, Dr. Halsey allowed us free rein on the drama departments costumes and props, as long as we didn't ruin anything.

I snorted at Greg. "It's a game to them. They're just trying to keep Courtney and her cronies away from us. Which is nice, but it's not the same as being into me."

Greg rolled his eyes. "Sure. You keep telling yourself that."

"Even *if* it was true, which it isn't, I'm not going to date any of them, not after the things they did to me. To all of us. And I don't want to hear another word about it. Where is Andre, anyway? I thought he'd want some say over his own costume."

"I don't know. He keeps disappearing on me as soon as class is over." Greg rubbed his red-ringed eyes. "I assumed he was at choir practice but apparently that's only on Thursdays."

"Maybe he's found himself a girl. Or a guy." I pulled out a white Venetian mask and held it up to my face.

"I hope so, but I haven't seen him with anyone, and of course he won't say... ooooh, I like that." Greg fished out a beautiful blush pink gown and held it under my chin. "These would look amazing together."

"Yeah, they would. On someone else." I tossed them back into the pile. Very cute, very *not* me. "You have a real eye for this. You're such a gay cliche."

Greg grinned. "I know. It's on purpose."

"Huh?"

"That gay guy – the camp, fashion-loving, show tune-singing, fabulous-talking guy – he's a character. Most people can't help but love him. If I'm him, then it's easier being gay. Does that make sense?"

"Not really. Are you saying you just pretend to like musicals?"

"No, no. I love musicals. And acting. And playing a part. But I only got into theatre because I thought that's what gay people were supposed to be into." Greg placed a crown over his head. It fell down over one ear. "I grew up in this tiny rural town in Nebraska. All I knew about being gay was what I learned in church – that it was a sin and that sinners went to hell. But I didn't know that being gay was what I was. I just knew that no one liked me and I felt things that weren't the same things other people felt. I knew I didn't belong. I came out to my parents accidentally when I was twelve. My sister had a boyfriend and I had a huge crush on him. I announced that I wanted a boyfriend, too. It was like they didn't hear me. They just pretended I never said anything."

"That must've hurt," I said.

"Yeah." He held up a pig costume and wrinkled his nose. "Insert many years of teen angst, until I started talking to other queer people on the internet and seeing gay men in TV shows – they dressed a certain way and acted a certain way and people liked them. No one had ever liked me. So I tried to be like them. And it worked – with my mom, at least. She started taking me shopping, giving me money to buy hair products, driving me to rehearsals at the local musical theater. It was like she felt safe with this version of me because she'd seen it on TV."

"What about your dad?" I remembered what Greg had said about his dad taking him shooting.

"We never went shooting together after I came out," Greg's shoulders sagged. "I get it – Dad felt uncomfortable around me, like I'd somehow spoiled the father/son bond we had by liking men. But I also didn't push it – I was trying to find myself in the world of queerness and there didn't seem to be any room for shooting deer or skinning rabbits unless you were talking about the hottest fur trends at New York Fashion Week. For all I know, Dad might've had the hard word from Mom about not letting a minor shoot a gun. But the result was – no shooting, and we grew apart because I thought he didn't accept who I was. I'll never find out the truth, now. They were good people. They tried hard to accept me for who I am, but I think I was just too much of a disappointment."

"I can't ever imagine you being a disappointment," I said. Greg's story was so sad. In speaking his truth, he'd lost who he really was. He felt like he didn't fit anywhere. I could understand that. "How did they die?"

"They were driving my sister to the mountains for a week of hunting and fishing and camping. I can't remember why I didn't go with them. Maybe we'd had an argument and they forced me to stay home, maybe I offered to stay so it wouldn't be awkward for them. All I remember about that day is getting the call from the state police. It was a drunk driver who ran them off the road. Mom and my sister died in the crash. Dad died in the hospital, minutes before I got there. It was as if he couldn't even be bothered to wait for me."

"I'm sure that's not true."

"I was supposed to inherit the farm, but it turned out my mom had all these gambling debts so their assets were seized. My conservative Christian relatives refused to care for me because of the gay thing, so I went into the system and... this is *perfection*."

Greg held up a black velvet dress with a white lace collar, the kind of dress Wednesday Addams would wear if she was trying to seduce a billionaire. The skirt was *mega* short.

"No." I folded my arms. "Not happening."

Greg's eyes gleamed. He set a pilgrim's hat on his head. "We'll go as the Witches of Salem. Shunned and persecuted because they were different, because they didn't fit in. It's perfect."

"You're not giving up on this, are you?"

"Not on your life."

I snatched the dress from his hands. "Fine. But only if I get to turn Courtney into a toad."

The warning bell rang. Greg shoved the pilgrim hat under his arm. "We've got physics. You need to swing by your locker first?"

"Go on without me." I slid my hand in my pocket, feeling around for the small tube I'd taken from the art department and hidden there. A Halloween party with elaborate costumes was the perfect time to start my revenge plans. "I have something I need to do first."

CHAPTER TEN

"I never thought I'd be invited to a monarch party." Greg's voice wobbled as he rubbed product on his hands and slid them through his hair. "If only I wasn't too terrified to enjoy it."

"At least the one good thing about these costumes you chose is that I can wear comfortable shoes," I muttered, tugging on my battered boots. I was wearing a pair of school uniform stockings that I'd ruined earlier in the year with an enormous run beneath the short black velvet dress with its white lace cuffs and collar. Greg and Andre looked straight out of Providence in their black shirts and wide pilgrim hats, even though Greg seemed a little listless and not his usual flamboyant self. He'd gotten creative with our costumes though, making us individual nooses to slip around our necks. We used theatre makeup to make our eyes wide and dramatic. It was pretty cool. I just wished we weren't wasting these costumes for the Miskatonic Prep crowd, but for an actual fun party with actual cool people.

Although I couldn't help but wonder what Trey, Quinn, and Ayaz would think when they saw my outfit. A sliver of heat sliced through my chest at the thought.

I straightened up and struck a pose. Greg grinned at me and made a clicking motion with his hand. "Honey, you look *fierce*."

Inside the walls, the rats scritch-scritched their assent.

Andre handed me a note. "Greg knows what he's talking about," it read. I laughed and hugged him. My arm brushed against the survival pack he had strapped underneath his shoulder. The other good feature of these outfits was that they allowed us to conceal all sorts of things that might help us survive the initiation.

"Are you guys sure you want to do this?" I asked. "I'm not backing out, but you don't have to get dragged along—"

"And miss the chance to join a secret club and stick it to Courtney?" Greg grinned, but his smile wobbled at the corners. "Not on your life. The Eldritch Club doesn't know what it's got itself in for."

Please let everything go okay tonight. I hadn't been told what would happen to us if we failed, but judging from what Courtney had planned for me so far this year, it would be brutal.

There was a knock on Greg's door. I flung it open to find the corridor full of monarchs, dressed in white sheets edged with purple. Trey had a bloodstain in the middle of his, and Quinn carried a comically large knife. Julius Caesar, killed by his loyal friends Brutus and Cassius.

"You're supposed to wear tunics underneath those," I said. Although I had to admit, I liked the amount of naked, tattooed (in Ayaz and Quinn's case) and muscled shoulders and pecs on display.

"It's a Halloween party, not a parade of historical accuracy," Trey snapped.

"You look hot, Hazy." Quinn swept me into his arms. He tried to kiss me, but I turned my head away so his lips brushed my cheek instead. I needed to be careful tonight. This was their territory, not mine. Even after everything they'd done to help me this quarter, I still wasn't convinced they weren't about to turn on me again. Their cruel smiles still haunted my memories.

I was starting to worry that after discovering their secret and the god beneath the school, I'd leaned into the Kings more than I should, accepting their help and their attention while I dealt with all the shit. I was starting to let my guard down, to give in to the fire inside me that told me to trust them.

But that wasn't right. It wasn't me. I'd thought about leaving them out of my revenge plans, but I realized that was impossible. They had to *pay* for what they did, otherwise things would always be this way between us – I'd always be walking on eggshells, waiting for them to betray me. So even though it felt wrong, they were back on the revenge list – just as soon as Greg, Andre and I were part of their secret club.

Trey grabbed Quinn's arm and yanked him off me. "Tonight isn't about looking good. It's about survival. You sure you're ready for this?"

I nodded, lifting the hem of my skirt just high enough – okay, *way* too high – to reveal the supplies strapped to my thigh. A candle and lighter, a short length of rope, a compass, some first aid stuff. My shard of glass rubbed against the inside of my wrist.

"Ayaz has grilled so much information about path-finding and surviving in caves into my head I think I've forgotten everything else I've ever learned."

"Geek." Quinn jabbed Ayaz in the arm.

"Then let's go." Trey held open the door. Greg, Andre and I marched out to join them. At the top of the staircase, we met the other monarchs, all dressed in similar romanesque costumes. Nancy whistled as her eyes swept over my outfit. She was dressed as Medusa in a floaty empire dress that hugged her in all the right places, her wavy red hair piled high on her head and entwined with realistic plastic snakes.

"Girl, you look wild. We are going to own the dance floor tonight." Nancy gave my noose a tug. "Love this touch. Historically accurate, you know. Most people think the Salem witches were burned at the stake, but they were all hanged except for Giles Corey, who was pressed to death beneath heavy stones."

"Delightful." I straightened my noose. "You don't think it's going to cause trouble with the alumni, given the history of the school?"

Nancy laughed as she passed me her lipstick. "Hell yeah I do. And I love it. It's about time someone shook things up around here. This place has been the same for *decades*."

Oh, Nance. She didn't know that I knew just how accurate that was.

"We ready?" Trey glanced around the group. He was met with shouts and cheers. Ayaz and Quinn linked arms with me. Greg and Andre took their places on the ends. The monarchs of Derleth Academy, united.

We marched through the dining hall doors as one. Strings of fairy lights hung from the rafters, making the whole room glow with twinkling light. Rock music that was twenty years out-of-date pumped from an expensive audio-visual setup on the raised platform where the teachers normally ate. Now that I knew the school's secret, so many of its weird quirks made sense. Of course their music taste was stuck in the past; they hadn't listened to new tunes since the fire.

Heads turned as we stalked across the room – students, teachers, and alumni followed our movements with awe, with trepidation, with barely-concealed rage. Faces of alumni flashed around me, and now that I knew the secret of this school I couldn't help but wonder how they all remained so young, so vibrant. Their children had been teenagers twenty years ago, but nearly everyone in this room still looked barely middle-age.

Of course, the god is giving them youth as well as power.

I noticed Vincent Bloomberg standing with the Deadmistress at the front of the room. His wine glass froze at his lips. I noticed a pair of fake horns sticking out of his dark hair.

The devil. Of course.

Heat flared through my chest, a fire stoked by rage and fed with fear of tonight's ordeal. The two of them presided like a royal couple over a room of dead teenagers frozen in time, all so they could wield a power from beyond our universe. How could Vincent Bloomberg leave the campus at the end of the day, knowing his son was trapped here for eternity? How did he sleep at night?

Like a baby on fucking four-hundred-count Egyptian cotton sheets, I bet.

The students were going to get theirs for what they'd done, and Courtney would be a quivering amorphous mess by the time I finished with her. But I reminded myself to save the majority of my hate for the orchestrators of this horror – not the Great Old God itself but the humans who were willing to do anything for its power. The parents like Vincent who hadn't fought for their children's lives but had instead robbed them of a future in order to feed their own vanity and lust.

You think you're the devil, Vincent Bloomberg? I'm about to get Dante's Inferno on your ass.

Quinn swiped drinks off the table and handed them around our group. As we toasted each other, my shoulders tensed from the burden of so many eyes on me. I raised the drink to my lips, then caught Courtney – wearing a slutty cat costume complete with glittery ears and cat-face pasties over her otherwise bare breasts – staring me down from over the rim of the cup. I set mine down without taking a sip. It would be just like her to try and poison me tonight.

Trey took my hand. "We're having the first dance," he said, loud enough for everyone to hear.

All around us, conversations stopped. Trey's jaw set. He took my hand, escorting me to the center of the room. People stepped aside to make room for us, until there was a wide circle around us. The music swelled – some gothic rock band sang with dark, crunchy guitars and a violin keening for forgotten souls.

Trey's fingers laced in mine. His other hand gripped my hip with fierce possession. I had no idea how to dance like this – you'd get beaten at a Badlands party for waltzing or whatever the fuck this was – but he led me in a circle like a pro, his body sweeping me across the floor like I was a Disney princess and he was the Prince Charming.

Prince of Darkness more like, with the fairy lights catching crimson strands in his hair and his fresh cypress and wildflower scent pulling me under his spell.

I knew this couldn't be real. The way Trey looked at me, his eyes burning into mine. The tug of his haughty lips, the way his body molded into mine. This was all a production for the man in the devil horns – a song-and-dance routine for an audience of one. As Trey swung me around the room, Vincent Bloomberg's eyes burned into the back of my skull.

I didn't want to be a pawn in Trey's teenage rebellion. Even if we did have this crazy, messed-up chemistry. But the violin swelled and a mournful voice cried of lost love, and Trey held me on my feet and I almost, for a moment, *believed*.

"Who's this band?" I asked, trying to break the spell and bring me back to center. My voice came out breathless.

"They're called Blood Lust," Trey replied.

"They're good." I never paid much attention to music, but tonight the pounding bass and that damn violin were waking dark and hidden parts of me.

"Mmmmhm." Trey leaned in close, his cheek resting against mine. My heart pattered in my chest. "Every girl in this room wants to be you right now. What do you think of that?"

"I think they're all fucking idiots," I replied. Trey chuckled, his laugh reverberating down my spine. "Why bother with this farce? Why do you all put on this show for your parents – is it so they feel better about trapping you in this nightmare?"

"These parties are all we have to look forward to." His breath caressed my earlobe. "Apart from torturing scholarship students."

"If you're trying to make me feel pity for you, you've failed miserably. If you'd exerted half as much effort trying to undo this curse or whatever it is as you've spent tormenting people, you'd be free by now."

Trey's fingers tightened in mine. "Don't you think we tried? They have all the power – I'm nothing but a soulless void walking the earth, trapped out of time. If we don't obey them, they undo the magic that binds us here, casting our spirits adrift. That's worse than what I am now – at least here, I have some control, some agency."

"Your father wouldn't do that to you."

"You think so?" Trey smirked, but there was no humor in his eyes. "We've saved who we could, but we can't openly defy them. We're powerless against them."

We saved who we could. Did that mean they had helped others before me? I held on to that nugget, not wanting to ask more right now, to find out it was untrue. "Poor little rich boy. So you discovered what it feels like to be powerless. I'm weeping for you."

"I don't need your pity. You can't run away this time," he whispered, his voice edged with danger. "Tell me about the fire."

My back stiffened. "Not happening."

"I don't—"

"Surprise." Quinn's head popped up between us. Trey frowned and dropped my hands, slinking away. Quinn grabbed me and spun me in a wide circle until the room lurched and the faces and lights blurred together. Other bodies moved in around us. Nancy grabbed Trey and swung him around. The music changed to something modern and upbeat, and Quinn started grinding up against me. I tried to let loose and enjoy this farce of a teenage party put on by people who'd trapped their own children as revenants. I was a pretty good actor, and it helped to have Quinn's hands sliding over my hips.

The rest of the party was pretty lame. Tables of fancy food I didn't dare eat, a playlist of out-of-date music, and boring conversations I'd never be allowed to take part in. Most of the kids filtered out around nine, leaving the faculty and alumni behind to discuss their secrets.

Students mingled in the quad, whispering about tonight's afterparty and pulling hip flasks filled with booze from the folds of their costumes. I couldn't see Courtney, Tillie, John, or any of their other friends anywhere. They must have already made their way down to our meeting place. We waited for our whole group to gather.

"Where's Quinn?" Trey demanded.

"The party can start now. I have arrived." Quinn jogged up and struck a pose, his toga flapping around his bare legs. "I was just saying goodbye to my mom."

I glanced up at the dining hall entrance, and noticed Quinn's parents standing together under the arch. Damon Delacorte held court amongst a group of alumni, telling some elaborate story with lots of gestures and facial expressions. Quinn's mother clutched her husband's arm, tossing her head back and laughing at one of his wild tales. They looked like the perfect couple, if you didn't notice the dead look in the woman's eyes or the faint shadows of bruising on her neck and wrists.

I wonder how she feels about what goes on at the school. Clearly, Quinn was her beloved son. How much of a say did she get over what happened after the fire? Did she like these alumni outings because she could see Quinn again, or was it a painful reminder of what she'd allowed to happen to him in exchange for her perfect life?

I wanted to ask Quinn about it, but he was skipping ahead of the group across the lacrosse field in a jolly mood, quoting lines from Shakespeare's *Julius Caesar* and pretending to stab Trey from behind the rose bushes. We hit the trees and followed Quinn's bobbing lantern to the narrow steps leading around the back of the grotto and down into the ancient ruins.

"I know you're going to make it tonight, Hazel." Nancy grinned as she gathered her gauzy dress in her hands and she descended the steps. Paul followed behind her. One by one, the monarchs disappeared down the side of the cliff while the roar of the ocean raged inside my head. Greg and Andre pulled up the rear until Ayaz and I were the only ones left.

Ayaz cleared his throat. "Remember that the vertical lines on a sigil point to—"

I closed my hand around his shoulder. "You've told Greg, Andre and I everything we need. It's up to us, now."

"I hope you know what you're doing," Ayaz muttered as he followed me down.

"Me too," I muttered as I clutched the edge of the cliff, grateful for my sturdy boots. "Me too."

At the bottom, the three Kings flanked me and we walked across the overgrown garden toward the rotunda. My mind cast back to the last time I'd been here, when the guys tried to convince me to get on a rickety boat and sail away from Derleth forever.

Which is exactly why you can't trust them, because they're selfish. If the Kings knew me at all, they'd never have asked me to leave Greg and Andre behind.

I told myself that, and I knew it to be true, and yet the idea of including them in my punishment still made my stomach churn with dread.

A group of students gathered between the crumbling columns of the rotunda. I'd expected to see the afterparty in full swing, but the place was mostly deserted. Members of the maintenance staff flitted silently up and down the stone path leading to the woods, carrying trays of food and a sound system. Even for their illicit parties, monarchs didn't lift a finger themselves.

We marched up to the rotunda, facing off against the monarchs that made up the Eldritch Club, who fanned out in a circle around a crackling fire. Courtney stood in the center of the circle, her green eyes shimmering in the pale moonlight. She wore a sexy cat costume that accentuated her feline features and predatory stance.

"These three outsiders have dared to lay claim to our club's protection," Courtney lifted a stick out of the fire, and I could see the tip was wrapped with a gas-soaked cloth, making a torch. The fire danced over her face, giving her the appearance of a pagan queen. "We all know they are not worthy. Tonight, we shall be proven right."

"I'm not making you captain of my cheer team," I sneered.

I ducked as the tip of the torch sailed through the air, where a moment ago my head had been. "Don't you dare address me," Courtney snapped. "You're not my equal. You're a gutter whore, and after tonight you're going to be a *dead* gutter whore."

Just like you, I wanted to retort. But Greg moved closer to me, his fingers reaching for mine. I squeezed him back and held my tongue. My agreement wouldn't allow me to speak and reveal the secret of this school, even if I'd wanted to.

"You know the rules, Courtney," Quinn stepped forward. "You can't interfere once they're inside the caves."

"Of course." Courtney flipped her hair over her shoulder and grinned at Quinn. "I wouldn't dream of breaking our *precious* traditions. Not that you've done us the same honor, allowing that piece of trash to wear our symbol."

"She'll earn her place," Trey said, his voice full of scorn.

"We'll see about that." Courtney held out a blindfold. "Turn around," she commanded.

I snorted. "So you can blindfold me and walk me off a cliff? No thanks."

"She can't do that," Trey said. "It's against the rules."

"And Courtney always plays by the rules, does she?" I folded my arms. "I'm going into this with my eyes wide open."

"Fine." Courtney trilled, a triumphant grin spreading across her face. "If she refuses the blindfold, she forfeits the initiation. Derek, cut that tattoo out of her arm."

"With pleasure." Derek, a friend of John's and a hulking lump of a guy who looked like he should have bolts sticking out the sides of his neck, lurched toward me. A silver blade flickered in the air as he raised a beefy arm.

Jesus fuck! They weren't kidding.

Shifting my right foot back, I slid the glass shard out of my sleeve and pressed it between my knuckles. If Derek thought he was getting anywhere near me with that knife, he had another thing coming.

Ayaz stepped in front of me, glaring at Derek. "Put that down, man. She'll wear the blindfold."

"No, I won't."

Ayaz squeezed my arm. "We all did, Hazel. It'll be safe. I'll be beside you the whole way there. I won't let anything bad happen to you."

I wanted to yank my arm back. *You've already let bad things happen to me.* But I didn't have a choice. Greg and Andre were already wearing theirs, and students snaked up the narrow stone path, leading them into the forest. I pulled the black scarf over my head and let Courtney tighten it. She pulled the knot so hard I swear it pushed my eyeballs back into my head.

In the darkness, my other senses pricked, parsing every scuff of a shoe, every murmur, every crash of the waves against the rocks for danger. Ayaz rested my hand on his elbow, covering my fingers with the warmth of his palm. "I'm here, Hazel."

Once again, as much as I fucking hated to trust anyone, I found myself leaning against Ayaz, allowing myself to take cues from the movement of his body to feel my way over the uneven ground. His fingers on mine felt warm and solid, guiding me true.

Part of me almost *wanted* him to betray me, so I wouldn't feel so conflicted about what I had to do. The other part of me – the part that was all fire and madness – didn't want him to ever unlace his fingers from mine.

Hands shoved me forward. "After you." Courtney's mocking voice cried in my ear.

Ayaz gripped me as I struggled up the steps. My fingers scrabbled for the edges of the steps, feeling my way up the path. Behind me, someone kicked my calves as I struggled. "Walk faster," John Hyde-Jones growled. My body stiffened as I caught the menace in his words.

Finally, I felt the ground even out, the rock beneath my feet give way to dirt and twisted tree roots. The air warmed as the trees sheltered us from the worst of the wild ocean wind. I hated how much I leaned on Ayaz as my feet slipped over the uneven ground, but I didn't pull away.

We walked for miles. I called out to Greg and Andre, but club members shushed me. Apparently, we weren't allowed to communicate. My feet ached from tripping on roots and scuffing on rocks, my shoulders strained from the tension of not being able to see. Every step I took I expected to topple over a ravine or walk onto the tip of a sharpened sword.

We stopped twice, briefly, while the students recited an incantation in a creepy guttural language and banged a drum in that uncanny rhythm that was impossible to follow. Ayaz whispered to me that Greg and Andre had both been dropped at their positions. Mine would be the last, the furthest from the school.

How sporting.

I counted my steps as we walked, attempting to make a rough guess at how far we'd come. We must've been right at the very edge of the school grounds, close to the sigils that kept the students trapped inside, when Courtney called out for us to stop. Fingernails scraped my face as the blindfold was torn away. "You're up, gutter whore," Courtney hissed.

Bright torchlight blinded me. Ghoulish faces pressed in all around, spinning me in a circle as they chanted their curses. Ayaz's hand was torn from mine and I lost all the guys in the frenzy. Tree limbs, faces, rocky crags... they all sped past so fast I couldn't focus on a landmark. The infernal drum beat in my ears, further disorienting my senses.

White hot pain seared my leg. I screamed, my body collapsing in on itself as the pain built like a cresting wave, blinding me until all I saw was the inside of my skull. The world faded into a single point, and I could no longer hear or register anything except the pain.

Adrift in an ocean of agony, I thrashed like a stranded beast, desperate to free myself of its grip. But there was no escape – only a cold resolve that once my body stopped being on fire I would burn every one of those motherfuckers down.

Inside my head, the god screamed, its shriek the sound of the universe tearing asunder. The ground beneath my feet rumbled in protest, but I was so disoriented I had no way of knowing if it really was shaking or if it was a product of my pain-filled mind.

Dimly, I understood what had happened. Courtney burned the back of my calf with her torch. *The bitch*.

"Go back where you came from, *gutter whore*." Thick, lumpy hands groped my breasts, then shoved me. I toppled backward. The white lights blinked out as I was swallowed by stygian gloom. I flung out my hands to break my fall, but all I grasped was foul air.

The darkness swallowed my scream as the pain engulfed my body, and I was lost to the void.

CHAPTER ELEVEN

I fell forever, until it felt as though I were no longer falling at all but suspended in the darkness, a puppet waiting for her strings to be jerked by a cruel master.

But, eventually, gravity won. I landed hard on my back. Pain sliced down my spine, momentarily competing with the needles stabbing into my leg. I gasped for air in my crushed lungs. The god screamed inside my head and flung an assault of waking nightmares into my mind.

I don't know how long I lay there, wallowing in the agony of the fall and the foul images the god visited on me, before my mind was able to cut through the pain and remind me there was a ticking clock on my own personal sword of Damocles.

I reached down between my legs and felt around for the survival kit I stashed on my thigh. I let out a breath I didn't realize I was holding as my fingers closed around the candle in its tiny holder and the lighter. It took me four tries with my trembling hands to get the candle to light. When the flame flared up, it did little to penetrate the gloom of my prison. Far above my head, I could just make out a pinprick of light from the moon. The hole they'd thrown me into was so high that the moonlight didn't even penetrate into the cave. No way would I be able to climb back out that way.

I set the candle down on the rock beside me and focused on standing up. Every movement caused fresh pain to shoot up my leg. I touched my hands to the red mark on my calf and nearly threw up. My stockings had melted against my skin. *Yup, definitely a burn.*

I turned over and slowly, slowly, pulled myself to my feet. The pain seared up my spine and exploded in my head, fighting with the god's visions for top billing. My eyes watered, and I had to stop to take several shaky breaths. Based on my estimation of the distance, it would take me well over an hour to get back to the school from my current location, provided I could even make it out of the cave. But that was with two functioning legs, which I definitely did not possess. Walking on the burn was going to take much longer, if I could even do it.

Courtney had broken the rules, but she'd also all but ensured I'd fail the initiation.

No.

The tears burned my cheeks. I wiped them away. *Courtney doesn't get to win that easily. I will make it back to the school on time, even if I lose my leg in the process.*

I'm going to be god-food at the end of this year, anyway. This isn't about me – it's about protecting Greg and Andre.

In the darkness, my fingers sought another burn – the scar from a fire that had hurt me much deeper than Courtney ever could.

I can do this.

First, I thought over what little I knew about first aid. The fact that the burn hurt was a good sign – it likely meant it wasn't as serious as it could have been. I took off my shoes and peeled the stockings off in a wave of pain so intense I had to roll over and throw up. That done, I slid down to the pool of water and plunged my leg under the surface, hoping like hell there wasn't anything living in there.

While my leg soaked, I tried to force out the god's pain screaming between my ears. I pulled out the small first aid kit Ayaz had insisted I bring. I took one of the clear dressings and peeled off the backing. I pulled my leg out, patted the area dry with my balled-up stockings, then applied the dressing and shoved my boot back on. It still smarted like hell but that was all I could do until I got back to school.

If I get back to school.

Gritting my teeth and holding the candle in my hand, I made my way slowly around the cavern. With every step, my leg screamed. By the time I finished a circuit, my face was slick with sweat and tears, but at least I knew what I was dealing with.

The rocks formed a series of steps leading down toward a tunnel on the other side of a small pool of black water. Toward the top of the steps on the opposite side of the cavern were two further caves, both leading off in different directions. Out of the corner of my eye I caught the sickly phosphorescence of those otherworldly veins – not as many as in the caves nearer the school, but they were definitely present. I held the light up to the walls, searching for a sigil. Ayaz had taught me that Parris had drawn sigils in many of the caves to seal his rituals and as maps of the property and the cave networks. All I faced was bare rock.

If I could find one of his sigils, I could tell which path to take. Instead, I had to pull out some old-fashioned MacGyver shit.

As we'd walked to my current location, I'd noted the terrain had sloped downward. My guess was that we'd headed west down the peninsula, in the direction of Arkham. I pulled a compass out of my bra and held it against my chest, trying to line up the arrow. It spun wildly, refusing to settle on one direction.

Great. Just great. Something in the cave – some magnetic rock, most likely – was fucking with the needle. I needed another way to choose which direction to take.

Trying to ignore the god's protests and the glint of the veins, I hobbled down to the edge of the pool again and held up the candle, as near the entrance to the tunnel as I could reach. The light didn't even flicker. Instead, the darkness seemed to swallow it. An oppressive presence slid from the entrance. Good. I didn't want to go that way.

I clambered up to the next entrance and did the same thing. The flame bent over. I'd found a breeze. Ayaz had told me any breeze was likely coming from the surface. I leaned inside the cave and swung my candle around. The cave seemed to head in a general upwards direction. I slapped my palm against the damp wall, leaving a deep impression of my hand in the mud and silt that I could use to find my way back if required. I hoped it wasn't required.

I stepped into the cave and scrambled between the rocks as fast as I could move with the candle in one hand and my leg howling with pain. Every few feet I slapped my hand into the wall.

After an indeterminate amount of scrambling, the cave ended in another, smaller cavern. The sides were steep rock, curving outward. The breeze came from another hole in the roof. I might have been able to climb up there with two good legs, but in my current state it was impossible. Courtney was counting on that.

I groaned in frustration, kicking a small stone down into a small puddle, splashing cold water over my already freezing legs. But there was nothing I could do. I backtracked to the first cavern and tried my candle on the third tunnel. The flame bent again, although not as far as it had before. It was my only choice, so I gritted my teeth against the pain and forced myself onward.

By now I was so cold that except for the faint pulse of pain from the burn I could barely feel my legs. My teeth clattered together; my mind swam with nausea and a sickening sense that something was behind me. As the sensation crawled up my spine,

I spun around, casting my light around the tunnel, but I could see nothing.

The sensation of being watched continued as I struggled up an incline, dragging my injured leg over craggy rocks. My heart pounded in my ears, and underneath it, a terrifying wet sound, like someone trying to breathe with water in their lungs. At first, I thought I was imagining it, but the wheezing gargle grew louder until I could no longer ignore it. I sped up, my leg screaming as I put too much weight on it in my mad scramble to escape. But the wet breathing kept following me, closer and closer...

The tunnel opened out, the ground evening out into a slick, smooth surface with a water trench hollowed out along the center. I swept my candle around the space. On the far wall, I noticed a pattern of dark lines inside a circle on the wall, too regular and even to be natural.

A sigil!

I lurched myself up the slope. My boots slipped on the slick surface. Behind me, a dark presence loomed from the shadows. *It's right there. It's almost got me.*

I cried out as I slid backward. My nails scraped the rocky wall. I rested far too much weight on my burned leg and propelled myself up, screaming as I scrambled a few feet before my foot slid out from beneath me again and I landed flat on my face.

Inside my head, the god screamed.

My candle flew from my hand. It flickered once against the rock before going out, leaving me alone in the cloying darkness with *something* breathing wet, fetid air against the back of my neck.

.

CHAPTER TWELVE

Panic rose in my chest. I churned my legs and arms, no longer certain what I was doing, only that I had to get away.

Something slimy slid over my ankle. I jerked my leg back, pitching myself forward. My cheek grazed cold, sharp rock, and pain seared my skull. I gripped the wall with one hand and wrenched my body forward, just as the creature reached out another slimy hand to touch my foot.

Get away from me!

Heat flared in my hands, burning down my arms like lava flowing through my veins. In the darkness, a shape seemed to glow from the other end of the tunnel – a burning ring of fire.

The sigil.

I only registered its shape for the briefest of moments. The heat in my hands exploded, rolling along my skin like a wave. I slipped on the rocks, my arms useless as the fire danced along my skin, burning up bone and flesh and sinew. I was my mother, then Dante, burning in a pyre of my own making, while the god raged inside my head.

Light flared through the tunnel, blinding me. The familiar roar and crackle of flames tore at my eardrums. Something screamed – it took me a moment to realize it was me. Fire consumed my body. I was a ball of radiant flame, burning bright and long and hot, so hot.

The heat rolled off me, crawling over the walls and floor of the tunnel, seeking out its prey. I rolled on my back, throwing my hands up to protect my face, trying to see through the fierce light. Through the roar of the flames and the screech of the god's screams, I made out the faintest howl as the creature slunk back into the darkness, its wet body sliding back down the tunnel to escape the heat.

And another sound. Footsteps squelching. Someone beating at my body with something soft. A harsh female voice calling through the flames.

"Stop, stop, you'll kill us both." A shadow dropped down over me, waving its hands in my face.

"Stop what?" I yelled.

"Stop the fire!"

I didn't know what she was talking about, but she sounded afraid. Heat burned across my cheeks. I raised my hands to my cheeks. *Please, don't let anyone else die in a fire. Not again.*

A coolness rolled down my arms. The cold settled over my stomach, creeping to my legs and my face. The light faded, and I could begin to make out the shape of a woman, a few years older than me, with long dark hair and eyes like black diamonds, covering my body with a large jacket.

I sat up, my eyes adjusting to the dimmer light cast from small pockets of flame dancing across the rocks, sending off showers of sparks that sizzled when they hit the damp surfaces.

Where did the fire come from? How can there even be a fire in a cave? There's nothing to burn.

Except me. I could burn. I was burning. So why do I feel fine?

The woman rolled away from me. She wore skintight black leggings with hiking boots. One of her legs was on fire, the flames licking the edge of her wool socks. She shrieked as she thrust her leg into the stream of brackish water running along the middle of the tunnel. Her face twisted in relief as the flames sizzled out. She withdrew her dripping leg and peeled back the fabric. Unlike my calf, hers was unharmed.

"Praise Allah for small miracles," she muttered under her breath as she crawled back over to me. She looked familiar, but I was positive I'd never seen her before in my life. "Are you injured? Can you stand by yourself?"

"Who are you?" I demanded, ignoring her question. "Are you a teacher at the school?"

She snorted. "That's unlikely."

"Then what are you doing here? Why'd you set the cave on fire?"

She rolled her eyes. "You hit your head when you went down or something? That's just what I need – if you've got amnesia than Allah is truly cruel. Look, I didn't set the cave on fire, *you* did."

"I didn't make the fire!" My palms blazed with heat. Every part of my glowed with residual warmth. I shuddered at the sensation I'd felt only a few times before in my life. *It can't be true. Not again. Please.* "That creature attacked me. The fire must've—"

"Nope," she shoved a hand under my shoulder and tried to yank me upright. All she managed to do was scrape my burned leg over the rock. I yelled, and she dropped me. "It was you. Now get up."

"I can't just *make* fire..." I gasped as a fresh wave of pain ravaged my body.

"Fine. Believe it was me if that'll make you move faster. You've got to get up. We're leaving. That creature has a family who'll be none-too-happy when they see what you've done to it."

"How do I know you're not a friend of Courtney's, leading me into a trap?"

The woman rolled her eyes toward the stalactites, losing patience. "Because I just put out the fire that was about to burn you up? If all I get for my trouble is the third degree, I'll just leave you here and you can try your luck with the creature's mother."

"No." I used the craggy wall to pull myself to my feet. I'd like to think I knew a gift horse when I saw one. "I'm up. I'm coming with you."

"You've burned your leg," she said, pointing.

"Thanks," I said sarcastically. "I hadn't noticed. And I didn't burn it, Courtney did."

"She a blonde bitch with green eyes?"

I nodded.

The woman pointed back down the way I'd come. "I saw her here last night. She must've set a trap for you. There's a sigil low on the walls over there. As soon as you walked into this tunnel the creature was summoned to come and feed. Good thing you had your firepower, or I might not have got to you in time."

I opened my mouth to tell her again that I didn't start that fire, but then I remembered that I was in the middle of a cave and this strange woman had just saved my life and ruined her leggings in the process. I probably owed her a passing attempt at an explanation.

I rubbed my palms together, trying to staunch the heat flaring across my skin. "Yeah. I don't know how I did that. It just happens sometimes, usually when I'm afraid or really fucking angry. It's only happened a few times in my life."

I was being more honest with this stranger than I'd ever been with myself. Nearly being eaten by a slithering shadow had that affect on me.

"Well, good thing you made it happen today." She nodded toward the sigil. When I didn't move to follow her, she tilted her head to the side, studying me with those piercing – and eerily familiar – dark eyes. "If it helps any, my brother would tell you to trust me."

"Your brother?"

"Yeah. I've seen him with you. He's one of your boyfriends,

although why he'd let them dump you this far from the school, I don't know. Maybe you pissed him off with your sunny personality?"

Ayaz. I realized where I recognized her – she had the same intense eyes and dark hair as Ayaz, only her hair hung in matted clumps around her face from the mud on the cave surface. She shone a flashlight toward the end of the tunnel and slid an arm under my shoulder again, providing me with additional support as I hobbled along the wall, trying not to lose my footing on the slope.

"He never told me he had a sister at this school," I said. "Only a younger sister..."

My voice trailed off as I started to put the pieces together. A name floated on the tip of my tongue.

"You're Zehra?"

"That's me." Her smile was brilliant – a flash of white teeth and full lips. I imagined that was what Ayaz's smile looked like if he ever bothered to use it.

"Why are you here, in a cave? Are you dead like your brother?"

"I'm very much alive, and I aim to keep it that way. Which is why I need you to talk less and move more." The beam of her flashlight shone on the sigil I'd seen. "Did you see that glowing just before your fire started?"

"I think so." My temples throbbed. "I'm not sure what I saw, to be honest. One moment something slithered over my foot and the next my body and the whole cave was on fire."

"Interesting. You know how to read sigils?"

I nodded. "Your brother taught me."

"Good." She traced a line that ran toward the center of the sigil. "Then you'll see how to get back to the school from here. The easiest way is to follow the ridge until you reach the road, then walk through the front gates. You're going to have to hurry, though."

"Gee, thanks," I said sarcastically as my burn screamed. "I didn't already know that."

"That girl – Courtney – she intended that creature to kill you. The Eldritch Club doesn't expect you to return."

"Then they're going to get a big shock," I grunted as I pulled myself around a large boulder. Across the top of the cave, a faint slash of light and a whoosh of fresh air signaled an exit. "But why are you helping me?"

Zehra beamed that brilliant smile of hers again. "Because you're Hazel – you stole my brother's heart and you have fire in your veins. You're the first one who's made me believe I might be able to get my brother back. Watch your step here."

"Thanks." She fell in behind me as I scrambled up the last steep slope. Fresh moonlight kissed my skin. I turned around to offer a hand to Zehra, but she'd disappeared.

"Where'd you go?" I called out, but the only answer was the hoot of a lonesome owl. "Zehra?"

I had so many questions, but she didn't want to stick around to answer them, and I had somewhere important to be.

Or did I?

I turned my gaze downhill, where faint pinpricks of light peeked through the trees – the town of Arkham at the base of the peninsula, lit up like a Christmas tree. None of the edimmu could cross the borders of the school, but *I* could. All I had to do was run down that hill to the safety of those lights, hotwire a car, and drive as fast and as hard as I could in the opposite direction.

I let the idea sit with me for a few moments, the tantalizing taste of freedom pooling on my tongue. Then, with a sigh, I turned away from Arkham.

I scrambled over the scattered rocks, sucking in gulps of fresh, chilled air. I pulled my tired body from the muck, dusted as much of the grit and mud off my body as I could, and took off in a hobbling run down the ridgeline.

With every step, pain jolted up my leg, sending waves of

nausea through me, mingled with garbled visions from the injured god. In the same way that Greg now had horrible dreams because he'd been in the god's presence, I and it were now somehow connected. I could tell when it was hurting by the way it lashed out at my mind, which could be something I could use to my advantage.

But right now, I needed to focus. I forced myself to ignore the pain and the god and keep going. After a while, the pain became background noise to the wild thoughts and theories swirling in my head. *Why was Ayaz's sister waiting for me in that cave? If she isn't a student at the school, then what's she doing here? What was that creature Courtney sent after me? Could I somehow get her in trouble for breaking the rules of the initiation?*

How did I make that fire?

I had no answers to any of it.

My chest was heaving by the time I reached the road. Sweat poured down my back, soaking through my ruined dress, but I didn't slow down. I had no way of knowing how much time I had left. My ankles rolled as I pounded along the gravel road toward the school.

The tall iron gates came into view – the same ones I'd passed through on my first day in this hellhole. When I reached them, they were locked. *No, no.* I ran at them, slammed my body into the metal. They didn't budge. My lungs screamed. My body begged to lie down in the trees and forget about the whole thing. I lifted the chain and found that the lock hadn't been bolted. I unlooped the chain, shoved the gate open, and ran through, tearing along the drive toward the athletic fields, where the initiation ceremony was to end.

Lights flickered in the lacrosse field. A circle of students carried torches, counting down in loud voices. "...nineteen, eighteen, seventeen..."

I poured on speed. My body had gone numb from the waist down.

"...fifteen, fourteen, thirteen..."

I tore across the field, barreling through their ranks and collapsing in a heap on the pitch. Tillie scrunched up her nose. "She looks like a swamp creature."

I grinned up at Courtney, waving a hand. "Hi!"

The look of rage on Courtney's face as it dawned on her I had escaped her monstrous trap and was now part of her secret club made every agonizing moment worth it.

"Fuck, Hazy." Quinn sank to his knees, cradling me in his arms. "You made it."

"I knew you could do it," Ayaz said. Behind his shoulder, Trey's ice eyes swept over my body, but he didn't say anything.

"No thanks to Courtney," I growled, rolling my leg over to show off the burn on my calf.

"That was an accident. I can't help it if you were thrashing around like a dead fish," Courtney snapped.

"Hazel, you made it!" Greg crawled toward me. He fell into my arms, the two of us rolling on the turf, smearing mud all over each other.

"Of course I did. And you? They didn't make you saw your own arm off to get a key?"

"Nope." Greg shuddered. "It was scary enough down there as it was. I kept thinking I heard things..."

"You're fine, that's what matters. Where's Andre?" I searched the field for him.

Greg shook his head. His face darkened. "I haven't seen him. I don't think he made it."

CHAPTER THIRTEEN

No. It can't be.

Andre was bigger and stronger and smarter than the two of us combined. He was much closer to the school than I had been. How could he not be here?

What have they done to him?

"Andre?" I sat up, shoving Quinn's arm off my chest. The burn blazed with pain, but I ignored it as I staggered to my feet and shoved aside one of Courtney's minions. "Andre!"

"Hey!" The minion – I remembered her name was Amber – yelled. John stepped toward me, his hands balled into fists. Beside me, Greg stiffened.

A hand slid around my face, clamping over my eyes. I screamed and kicked out, trying to knee the bastard in the balls as I shook my glass shard out of my sleeve. *No fucking way am I going back in a hole.*

"Hazel, stop," Greg yelled.

The hand left my mouth and my captor spun me around. I found myself face-to-face with Andre. A wild grin spread over his face.

I grabbed his collar and shook him. "You bastard! I might've cut you."

Andre's mouth opened in a silent laugh. Greg fell into my arms. The three of us clung to each other, our bodies covered in the marks of our ordeal. Their strength gave me hope.

Behind Andre's head, a dark face watched us, the mouth set in a firm line. *Loretta.* I started at the sight of her – what initiation had she endured in order to become part of this secret club? Had Courtney left her in a cave in the dead of night, without a single friend to give her strength? How much of who she was had been obliterated when the god took her life?

Loretta caught my eye and stepped back behind Tillie, turning her face away as if she couldn't bear to look at us.

Is she upset that she no longer identifies as one of us, or is she angry that we survived and infiltrated her new circle?

All thoughts of Loretta flew from my mind as the circle of students closed in around us. Trey and Courtney glared at each other. John cracked his knuckles. A palpable tension crackled in the air.

I stepped back, sliding away from Greg and Andre. If this got ugly, they'd be safer the further they were from me. I palmed my shard and rolled up my sleeve.

"I'm one of you now." I flashed my wrist at Courtney. The Elder Sign shimmered in the moonlight. "We all are."

"You'll never be one of us," Courtney glared. "You've ruined *everything.* The Club is supposed to be for only for the elite, the children of this country's leaders. Now it means nothing. We won't stand for it."

"Oh, poor princess," I cooed. "Have the big bad weirdos come to crash your little club?"

"Look at them," Courtney smirked. "A fag, a dunce, and a whore strutting around like they're the shit. No way are they the equals of anyone in this circle. So why are they being allowed to act as though they have power here? Why haven't they been put back where they belong? It seems our noble leader—" she glared at Trey, who stared back with a detached arrogance that made it clear just why he was the leader "—has fallen from grace. One taste of a gutter whore's pussy and he's willing to throw away everything we've worked to create here."

"Maybe this stuffy school needs a bit of shaking up," I said sweetly. "This is your last warning. We beat your initiation. We've earned immunity. Turn your hatred to the people who actually deserve it – your parents."

Courtney tossed her hair over her shoulder. "*No one* deserves punishment more than a whore who won't learn her place." She tugged at one of her cat ears, as if she intended to throw it at me. Her eyes widened as the ear refused to come off in her hand.

"What's wrong, Courts?" Tillie stared at her friend.

"My ears won't come off." Courtney tugged at both ears, her eyes widening. "Ow. It hurts!"

"Let me try." Tillie grabbed one of the sparkly ears and pulled. Courtney's shriek could have broken glass.

"You're scalping me, you bitch!"

Tillie forced Courtney's head down, parting her hair and peering at the ears. "It looks like they're glued on."

"But that doesn't make any sense. I just used that spirit gum from the drama department, the same stuff we always use. It can't —" Courtney paused as she caught sight of the smirk spreading across my face.

"What did you do?" she screeched.

"Nothing," I smiled sweetly. "I was just thinking how tragic it would be if someone accidentally swapped the spirit gum with superglue."

"Superglue?" Tillie grabbed one of her devil horns and tugged. The horn stayed exactly where it was. She screamed. All around me, Courtney's friends yanked and pulled at their slutty costumes, but everywhere they'd used gum to stick down a seam or hold on a prosthetic was now glued firmly to their skin.

"But... I put that on my pasties..." Courtney tried to dig her fingernails under the glittery red cups that covered her nipples, but they wouldn't budge.

"Did you have something to do with this, Hazy?" Quinn gasped, his whole body shaking with laughter. Behind him, Ayaz and Trey exchanged a glance, but neither of them laughed. My body rumbled with glee, the laughter bubbling up inside me and spilling over with joyful hysterics. Beside me, Greg chuckled and Andre clutched his stomach and did his silent laugh.

"Happy Halloween," I grinned at Courtney. I linked arms with Greg and Andre, and we headed off in the direction of the school. "We'll see you bitches at the after party."

CHAPTER FOURTEEN

The Halloween party was scheduled to rage all night. While part of me was desperate to return to school to shower, dress my wounds, crawl into bed, and think about everything I'd seen and heard tonight, I knew that leaving now would only be a sign of weakness. Courtney and her posse slunk back to the school in an attempt to find some way to remove their various appendages, which meant we could make a show of power to the rest of the school if we got there first.

Trey must have had the same idea, because he stalked off toward the forest without waiting for anyone else. The rest of us hurried after him. Nancy and Paul pressured Greg for details about his ordeal, and he launched into a dramatic retelling of how he escaped the cave, complete with a song he made up on the spot. Andre even passed a couple of notes to the others. I realized that neither Nancy, Paul, or any of the other monarchs and monarch-adjacents in our group had made any derogatory comments about his muteness or Greg's flamboyance. They were all right.

Were they still on my revenge list? Did tolerance make up for their past transgressions? Probably not. I hadn't realized when I started thinking about it that this punishment thing was hard. I couldn't get past the fact that I wanted to hurt people I was sort of, sometimes, occasionally, maybe starting to like.

I've got to find a way to get over that, and soon.

As we neared the steps down to the pleasure garden, Quinn yanked me off the path.

"Argh, what are you doing?" I rubbed my shoulder.

"I bought something for you," Quinn riffled around in the folds of his toga. He shoved a bottle of gin into my arms. "I knew you'd get all dirty in the caves so... hold that for a moment while I find... wait, I think I've got it."

I tried to peer into his toga. He pulled out another bottle and dumped it in my arms. "What do you have in there, an entire bar?"

"While I'm excited that you want to see what's under my toga, that will just have to wait until I've found... ah hah!" From the depths of his outfit, Quinn whisked out a hanger, upon which hung a red dress my mom wouldn't have worn to work on account it was too slutty.

I snickered. "Are you sure you're the spaghetti straps kind of guy?"

"It's not for me, Hazy. It's for you."

"I'm not wearing that."

"Yes, you are. You want to show Courtney who rules this school? You gotta look the part. Besides," Quinn cracked his trademark grin. "You wear this dress, and you'll be midnight shot with fire – you make this poor dead boy's every dream come true."

"This may come as a surprise to you, but I don't live to fulfill your spank fantasies." I fingered the hem of the dress.

"Aw, come on, Hazy. You know you're all covered in mud."

He had a point. I snatched the dress out of his hands, fingering the sparkling embroidery along the sweetheart neckline. "Where did you get this from?"

"I got my mom to bring it for me. She gave it to me at the party tonight. She thinks it's a gift for Courtney."

I remembered seeing Quinn's mother as we left the alumni party. "Are you allowed to have your parents bring you expensive gifts?"

"Not really. The faculty and the Eldritch Club frown on it. They think it's unhealthy if we get too much stimulus from the outside world." Quinn gestured to the dress. "Some of us have parents who are more understanding than others."

I filled in the blanks of what Quinn didn't say. The senior Eldritch Club members wanted to keep the student body focused inward on tormenting the newcomers so they wouldn't join together to rise up against the Eldritch Club. It was so glaringly *obvious* I couldn't believe clever people like Quinn and Trey and Ayaz (okay, mostly Trey and Ayaz) didn't see right through it. "Why don't you just stand up to them? There are over two hundred students at this school, and only what, five-dozen active senior club members? Why don't you all just tell them, 'no, actually, we don't want to sacrifice orphans any longer'?"

"You think it's that easy?" Quinn's smile had frozen.

"To do the right thing? Yeah, it's that easy."

"Like fuck it is. Power isn't just about outnumbering someone," Quinn said. "If it were, ninety-nine percent of the world's wealth wouldn't be in the possession of the top one percent."

"What do they have on you that stops you from just eating their brains? They can't threaten your life if you're already dead."

"You mean besides the fact that we're not brain-eating zombies?" Quinn stuck out his arms and mimicked a shuffling walk. "The Eldritch Club are so desperate to hold on to their power they'll sacrifice their own children to an interdimensional cosmic entity. You think death is the worst they can do to us? There's a reason every Miskatonic student falls into line, even if their parents weren't members of the club. Rebellion is pointless –

the only thing we can do is drink and fuck and try to enjoy eternity."

"If that's true, then why did you try to save me?"

Quinn shrugged. "We've done horrible, unforgivable things. Don't make us into heroes, Hazy."

I snorted. "Yeah, no danger of that."

Laughter and music wafted up from over the ridge. "Put your party dress on," Quinn said, his voice sad. "A night of Bacchanalian hedonism is just what you need."

"As if I'll be able to relax with the whole school breathing down my neck and Courtney on the warpath. I'm holding you personally responsible for anything that happens at this party. If I end up in a Carrie situation, then I'm pushing *you* over a cliff. We'll find out if dead monarchs can fly."

"I swear." Quinn made the sign of the cross.

"Your word doesn't mean shit. The last party I came to with you, you lured me into the grotto so your friends could steal my clothes. Turn away." I gestured for him to turn around.

Quinn's eyes swept over my body one final time, but he obeyed, turning until he was completely facing away from me. He put his hands behind his head.

My eyes on Quinn's back, I peeled off my ruined Halloween outfit, scrunching up the dress and using it to wipe as much of the mud as I could off my arms and legs. An icy breeze blew from the ocean, raising goosebumps over my bare skin and caressing my nipples into hard points.

"I didn't lure you into the grotto," Quinn said.

"Bullshit. No peeking," I snapped as his head jerked to the side. He promptly jerked it back.

"It's the truth, Hazy. I asked you to swim because you're fucking hot and I wanted to go swimming with you. Trey told me to invite you to the party—"

"And you're Trey's bum boy." I pulled the dress over my head, shaking my hips to pull it down. It fit perfectly, damn him.

I think you're fucking hot and I wanted to swim with you. Quinn's words sent a wave of heat flaring along my spine.

"—but I was going to ask you anyway." Quinn leaned back, the muscles along his forearms bulging. I was such a sucker for thick forearms. When Dante played basketball, my eyes stayed fixed on the corded muscles that flexed as he moved. I shook my head as my fingers sought the burn on my wrist. As if on cue, the matching burn on my leg flared with fire. *I don't have Dante anymore, and Quinn... he's...*

"But not because you have some deep connection to me. You don't even know me. You just like pissing people off." I sighed, sticking out my hip. "You can look now."

Quinn's eyes widened when he saw me. He licked his lower lip, and a fresh wave of heat sizzled up my back. "Damn, Hazy. You're going to break hearts tonight."

"Good." I took his arm. "Let's go."

We descended the steps together. I tried to ignore the flaring pain of the burn on my leg. Pain was good – it meant I was still alive. At the bottom, Andre and Greg were standing with Nancy and Paul and the other monarchs. They clapped as Quinn and I stepped into the pleasure garden.

"A round of drinks for the triumphant spelunkers!" Quinn cried, pulling the bottles and a cocktail shaker from out of his toga. "I've been honing my cocktails. Who wants to try a 'Quinn Fizz'?"

The group moved over to the bar area, where the school's silent staff were still setting out glasses and filling punch bowls. They scattered when Quinn took over. More students crowded around to watch him fling bottles in the air and juggle spoons like he was in some fancy nightclub. Greg had disappeared but I noticed Andre at the other end of the bar, making a series of hand gestures to one of the maintenance staff, a girl with frizzy brown hair. *What's going on there? Why isn't he using his pad?* I tried to push my way toward Andre, but Ayaz stepped in front of me.

"Do you want to dance or something?" Ayaz asked.

My heart thudded in my chest for reasons that almost definitely had to do with the honey and rose scent that filled the air around him. "I didn't know you were the dancing type."

"I'm full of surprises." Ayaz held out his hand. I stared at it for a moment, then took it.

A group of kids jumped around to the band, who were playing the same outdated 90s playlist they'd cranked out last time. I scanned the crowd for Courtney or Tillie or any of their friends, but they were nowhere to be seen.

"If you're looking for Courtney, you won't see her tonight," Ayaz said in his silky voice. "Word is it she's just pulled a huge chunk of hair out trying to get the ears off. I bet you're secretly disappointed."

Pulling her hair out? That gives me an idea...

"Good guess. I'm absolutely bereft without her." Ayaz and I walked into the middle of the dance floor. People shuffled away from us as we turned in slow circles around each other, like two animals locked in a battle of wits. Tension crackled between us as our bodies drew closer – predator closing in on prey. The throbbing pain of the burn – still covered in the dressing but visible to everyone in the short dress – only made it worse. Not even the lurching visions of the god could quench the flames dancing inside me. My heart beat in time with the frantic drums, and a rush of liquid magma surged through my veins.

Right now, *I* was the predator, claws out, ready to pounce.

The song worked itself up with a furious, frenzied pitch. Bass pounded in my ears. Ayaz's skin brushed mine as we leapt and sparred and spun around each other. Every touch singed my skin with unspoken promises. Something nagged at me, some urgent thing I needed to tell him, but the thought was lost in the corners of his black diamond eyes...

Oh, shit, that's right.

"I met someone in the tunnels," I pressed my lips to Ayaz's

ear, talking as loud as I dared so he could hear me over the music. "She helped me escape the trap Courtney set for me."

"Trap?" Ayaz's eyes darkened.

"Yeah. There was a creature that slithered out of the water and came after me. Apparently, it had been called up by Courtney specifically to go after me. But this girl jumped in and saved my ass." I decided not to tell him about the fire just now. "And the funny thing is, she looked like you."

Ayaz froze.

Someone bumped into me from behind. I stumbled forward, my chest pressing against his. Through the thin fabric, I could feel every curve of his muscles and the heat that rolled off his skin.

"She had your eyes, Ayaz," I said, staring into those dark orbs – a shroud that hid the man beneath. "And this amazing long hair, like a waterfall of darkness. Your sister is one badass demon slayer."

His fingers dug into my arm, hard enough that I cried out. "Did Quinn put you up to this?" he whispered, his voice tight.

"Quinn can't make me do anything," I shot back. "I *saw* her, Ayaz. Who is she? She's your younger sister, right? Because if your sister was young and you've been an Edimmu for twenty years, then she'd be about the right age..."

"She's my sister," he whispered. "That's Zehra. But I can't believe..."

"What?" I shook his arm. "We said no more secrets, remember? Tell me."

Ayaz's face darkened. "Not here," he whispered, tugging my hand toward the grotto. "Fancy a swim?"

Last time we'd been in this pool together, Ayaz had leaned in close and warned me that Trey was planning to hurt me. He'd also been sandwiched between two very attractive girls and had seemed intent on giving them a good time. My body tingled with the memory of his hands cupping a breast, touching a cheek, caressing beneath the water...

His hands on me in the cave, his tongue teasing out the flame inside me.

My head was all messed up. I was thinking about punishing this guy at the same time I had fantasies of his hands all over me. I couldn't separate the two things in my mind – *I want Ayaz. I want Ayaz to pay.* At the same time, I was having equally evil thoughts about his two friends.

I'm completely insane.

It was also freezing cold tonight, with a hint of drizzle in the air. I could only see a handful of other couples in the grotto, and if we moved further back into the cave, where the water was rushing out of the thermal spring, there would be no chance of anyone overhearing what we said.

And besides, maybe Quinn was right – a little hedonism never hurt anyone.

I swallowed hard. "Sure."

Ayaz pressed his hand to the small of my back, releasing a pool of heat as we headed off the dance floor. I walked ahead of Ayaz over to the stepped wall where the students dropped their clothes. I cast my eyes around for any sign of Courtney or Tillie, but didn't see them anywhere. I gritted my teeth and started to peel off the dress.

I've only had this thing on for twenty minutes.

I'd chosen my black bra set tonight – the same one I'd worn at the last party. It must've been my lucky underwear. Ayaz definitely thought so, the way his eyes traveled up my body as I stepped into the water. He stripped off, and it was my turn to gape. His toned chest was decorated in a smattering of ink in bright tattoos – beautiful images I recognized from Pre-Raphaelite paintings. His body tapered from broad shoulders into a narrow waist and a fucking adorable ass with tattoos of shimmering mermaids splashing around the cheeks. As he lowered himself into the water I got an eyeful of... everything. There was a *lot* of everything.

I swallowed. *You're here to tell him about Zehra. That's all.*

This is such a bad idea. You have a burn on your calf. Why are you getting into hot water? Because of a guy?

Hell, yes.

"Those girls you were with last time..." I started as he clambered across the uneven rocks.

He shrugged.

"They didn't seem to mind sharing you."

"If girls want to have me, they have to share," Ayaz said. His hand tightened on the small of my back. "Until now."

Is he talking about me? He can't be. Or is that a veiled reference to him kissing me because his friends did? "I thought you said Quinn was the one who slept with anything that moved?"

Ayaz shrugged again. "I said I like to learn. You don't always do learning in books."

Even through the waterproof dressing, the hot water on my burned leg smarted. But that hurt the god, so I didn't care. Besides, it had nothing on the sharp pain jabbing at the base of my spine. It felt annoyingly similar to the way I used to feel when I saw Dante with another girl. I paused on the rocky ledge, leaning over to look over at the students grinding against each other. Greg had jumped in with the band and was doing an excellent job on vocals. Andre stood beside Trey at the bar, both of them with a drink in their hands, staring into space without speaking. I grinned to myself. *A match made in heaven.*

Ayaz pulled me deeper into the grotto. Water bubbled from the spring in the wall and streamed down into the pool. Steam curled off the surface, filling my already-foggy head with hedonistic thoughts. Those dark, spontaneously-combusting caves and burning sigils seemed a long way off, especially with Ayaz's arm around my shoulder, his naked chest rubbing against my shoulder.

Ayaz spun me around to face him, placing his hands on my shoulders and pressing me against the grotto wall. "Kiss me," he whispered.

"Huh?"

"You heard me," he growled. Flecks of gold flared at the corners of his eyes.

He was making it my choice, my move. If I kissed him now, it would be because *I* wanted it.

Did I want it?

I didn't know. I wanted the Kings to show remorse for what they'd done to me and for how they'd driven Loretta to seek an end to her life. Sometimes I thought they got there, but then I learned about some new horror and I felt they could never be sorry enough. I wanted to have never come here. I wanted to burn this fucking school down and salt the earth beneath it.

But at the same time, the moon was high and Ayaz was beautiful. Tonight was Halloween, a night for ghosts to walk the earth and for witches to have their way... tonight I was the baddest motherfucking witch of them all, and I was naked in a hot spring with the ghost of a boy that in another world, another time, I could have fallen in love with.

Tonight, I embraced the darkness and the fire. I pressed my lips to his.

A soft growl rumbled in his chest as his tongue plunged into my mouth. The world faded away, everything outside me and Ayaz and our burning, singing flesh ceasing to exist. His eyes fluttered shut, those long lashes tangled together as he sank deeper into the kiss. The burn on my calf flared with heat but it was nothing on the heat burning between my legs.

This kiss was *everything*. It was the whole fucking universe.

It was also nothing. It meant nothing. It was a distraction, an act for anyone who might be watching us.

So what was that other kiss? What did it mean?

"Zehra is my sister," Ayaz whispered against my lips. His tongue ran along my teeth. "She was just a baby when I left. I used to video chat with her constantly when I lived with Vincent. Like, every day. She was so much fun, even as a little kid. Twelve years ago, my parents sent her here to enroll in Derleth. Either they lied about her family to get her in, or the scholarship committee got so greedy for an ideal applicant that they didn't check into her background too closely. They didn't know she'd had a brother who died at Miskatonic Prep. Zehra arrived here on the first day of the quarter. Trey had me break into her room to steal something precious from her. They always bring something precious with them. She had a photograph of my parents in her suitcase. That's when I knew it was her."

"Did she recognize you?" I asked, my tongue sliding against his teeth.

"I tried to stay away from her, but she ferreted me out. She was always a bright kid. Much brighter than me. I was supposed to be dead and here I was, walking the halls, no older than the day I died."

"But wouldn't—" Ayaz's lips forced mine open, his tongue driving out my words. I gasped against him, kneading the flesh of his back as he drew out the fire inside me. *God, his touch is magic.*

If kissing a ghost is this hot, I should do it more often.

"She was angry with me at first – that I had let them all believe I was dead. But then bit by bit she put the pieces together, like you have, and then she wouldn't leave me alone. I couldn't just let her stay here and become a sacrifice. She deserved more. I'd been left on my own in this country with nothing but my parents expectations, and look how that worked out for me."

Bitterness leaked into his voice. I linked my fingers behind his neck, pulling his head against mine, trying to drink in that bitterness, to draw it out of him. "At least here, you don't have to pretend you wanted to be a doctor."

Ayaz laughed against my lips. The sound was lyrical – music humming through my veins. "In a strange way, being stuck here, I have more freedom than I've ever had. I can read books. I can draw."

"You sound as though you're trying to convince yourself."

"Yeah." There was that bitter laugh again, all the music stripped away. "I am."

"So what happened to Zehra?"

"Trey, Quinn, and I... we tried to sneak her out of the school. We took her down to that dingy and shoved her out to sea. 'I'll go for help,' she said. 'I will come back with a legion to set you free.' She would have done that, too. Zehra could get anyone to do anything she wanted, just by smiling at them. But she never got the chance. The next day, Quinn found the boat splintered to pieces on the rocks. I thought... I thought there was no way she could survive."

"And you never heard from her again?"

Ayaz shook his head. "That's how I knew she was dead. She would have found a way to get a message to me. Quinn says he saw her once, hiding behind a tree, watching our lacrosse game. But when he looked again, she was gone. We looked all over the woods, calling her name, but she never showed herself."

"Quinn thought she left those articles for me to find," I remembered.

"But she couldn't..." Ayaz murmured, his eyelids fluttering. He was a million miles away. "...all these years I thought she was gone... I thought I was the one who killed her, who sent her off in that boat... you swear you saw her?"

"Flesh and blood and all. She held my hand."

Ayaz sagged against me. This King of the school trembled, wearing his vulnerability on his skin. Suddenly there was no space between us, no room to breathe.

Ayaz backed away. "I have to... I need to..."

I nodded. "I know."

Ayaz fled the grotto, launching his body over the edge with a wave of water that splashed across the dance floor. I watched him go, jogging into the darkness without stopping to collect his clothes.

As I climbed out of the pool, Trey's eyes swept over me, blue ice that cooled the heat in my skin. I bent down to pick up my clothes. By the time I pulled my dress over my head, Trey had disappeared.

Like a ghost.

Something Quinn had said came back to me. *You think death is the worst they can do to us?* I thought of the hatred that had poured out of the god's void. The three Kings acted as though they were above it all – Quinn wallowing in hedonism, Ayaz striving for knowledge, Trey's regal remoteness and desire for ultimate control. I thought they were untouchable, but now I knew better.

They might be dead, but their hearts still beat. They still felt, still *loved* – a love twisted by the desire for what they had once had and could never have again. And I could see now how someone evil could take that love and twist it into something rotten, something that could be used to keep those boys in line.

Love kept them bound to Miskatonic Prep. Love forced them to torture the outsiders until they didn't know any other way.

Love makes you vulnerable. I knew that all too well. It painted a target on your back and ripped all the humanity out of you until there was nothing but a broken shell.

I sucked in a breath. My finger pressed into the scar on my wrist. I hadn't allowed myself to feel anything since the fire. I'd come to Derleth Academy a broken shell. Now, my three tormentors were threatening to open me up again. They were burning me inside and out.

Somehow, I was burning them right back. And in that fire were all the feelings we thought we'd destroyed. All the hope and love and longing that made us weak.

The question was, would the resulting inferno destroy us all?

CHAPTER FIFTEEN

Courtney and her friends never showed up at the Halloween afterparty. I heard they spent most of the night trying to detach their various appendages from their bodies. Old Waldron's infirmary appeared to be stocked from the 1800s and didn't have anything that could dissolve the mess. Superglue was a bitch to get out, especially when you stuck it in your hair.

Or on your nipples. *Poor Courtney.*

Greg and I got 20 points each deducted by Dr. Halsey for ruining the costumes we borrowed. The night had been more than worth it – we got into the Eldritch Club, Courtney superglued her nipples, I met Ayaz's sister, and every time I thought about the grotto a deep, hot ache flared inside me.

Over the weekend, my burn blistered. I cleaned it out and changed the dressings, relishing the god's anguish as I rubbed it with antiseptic. It still emitted a dull ache when I walked on it, but nothing I couldn't handle.

In class on Monday, both Courtney and Tillie showed up wearing hats pulled low, covering their hair. When Mr. Dexter scolded them for breaking the uniform code, Courtney refused to remove hers and accepted a 5-point demerit. Tillie, however, couldn't face losing the points. She scrunched up her nose and flung her hat at the teacher.

"*There.* Are you happy?" She slouched in her seat.

I had to cover my mouth to stop a laugh escaping. The other students weren't so polite. Titters erupted around the room as everyone took in Tillie's nightmarish 'do. The hair on the top of her head stuck up in clumps from where she'd had to cut the ears out. Her entire scalp was red and peeling from whatever chemicals they'd used to try and remove the glue. Even Mr. Dexter's eyes widened, but he composed himself quickly.

"Thank you, Ms. Fairchild." He glared around the room. "I expect you all to maintain decorum until the bell, or I'll deduct points from the whole class."

While Mr. Dexter read out the day's announcements, I watched Tillie and Courtney from the back of the room. Tillie's shoulders sagged as she stared at her desk. She kept raking her nails through her hair, scratching at her irritated scalp. Courtney lifted the edge of her beanie and scratched at her scalp. She kept shifting in her chair, rubbing her palms over the front of her shirt. *I bet those nipples are sore,* I thought smugly.

A draft caught the back of my neck, reminding me that last quarter they'd snuck into my room and smeared black tar all over my hair. I'd had to cut off the dreadlocks I'd been sporting since freshman year, yet another link to my old life and my heritage destroyed by this school. Courtney and the other Queens deserved everything they got.

The bell rang. I leapt to my feet, eager to beat Courtney out the door. "Nice hat," I said sweetly as I walked past her desk. "It suits you."

"You're dead, bitch," she hissed, but there was no bite to her threat.

"Not as dead as you are," I smiled back at her. Courtney's lip curled back, but she didn't get out of her chair. Quinn threw an arm around me, guiding me toward the door.

I cast a final look back at Courtney as we headed down the hall. She remained rooted in place, staring straight ahead with a deer-in-headlights expression, like she couldn't believe what had happened to her.

You may be undead, but you're still vulnerable. I'd found the chink in Courtney's armor. She believed that she had power at this school. But I'd just shown her how fickle her power was, and how little it really mattered. She could be toppled just as easily as the kids she tortured, and once I took away her power, she would have nothing left.

I wasn't even nearly done with her yet.

Greg wasn't as enthusiastic as I expected when I revealed my revenge plan during our private rehearsal that evening. "I just don't think it's worth going after them like that."

"After they tormented Loretta? She wanted to kill herself."

"Yes, but she didn't. And they're her friends now," Greg pointed out. "What if this made things worse for her again? The superglue was funny, but you know Courtney won't allow it to stand without retaliation."

"I don't think they really are her friends." I slumped over the piano, my chin in my hands. "And as for Courtney retaliating, I plan on making it so that's the last thing she wants to do."

Greg frowned. "You're not going to hurt her, are you?"

"No..." A slow grin spread across my face. "Maybe a little bit."

"I don't like this, Hazel. Aren't we just stooping to their level?"

"People like Courtney think they can get away with treating others like shit. They didn't earn their privilege – it was handed to them, and they have the nerve to think we're less than because we had to work for everything we have. The only way they will learn is if we turn that around on them, show them what happens when they become powerless. I promise I'll do all the actual revenging.

I just need you to make the formulations, and then I'll have to figure out how to swap out—"

"If you're intent on doing this, Andre might be able to help with that," Greg said. "He's got a friend on the maintenance staff."

"He does?" I remembered I'd seen Andre gesturing to the brown-haired woman who worked in maintenance. Was that her? "Do you mean a lady friend? Is that why we hardly ever see him outside of class?"

"I think it might be," Greg grinned. "He won't talk about it, but I keep seeing him hanging out near the laundry chute, and he's got a big dopey smile on his face all the time. Bet if it helps you he'll finally spill the beans. I'll talk to him about it tonight."

"You mean you're gonna help me?"

Greg swiped a hand through his blond hair. "I wish you'd just leave them alone. Things are good now. But I'm also not gonna let you do this by yourself."

I hugged him. "You're the best."

"I know, I know." Greg kissed the top of my head. "This is it, right? After we do this, you'll call it even on the Queens?"

"Hell no. What we're plotting right now is just the warm-up. I need something bigger, something that doesn't just target Courtney but shows everyone at this school they can't treat people like trash and get away with it. I just don't know what it is yet."

"Just don't go getting yourself in deeper trouble. It may seem like we've got the protection of the three Kings right now, but that could change in a heartbeat."

"I know. Don't worry, we don't need them," I said with more conviction than I felt. "I don't need anyone."

When I said I didn't need anyone, it wasn't entirely true. I needed Ayaz to keep translating Parris' book because I couldn't read Medieval Latin. I needed Trey's protection. I needed Quinn's smile to make the long days go faster. And as much as I hated to admit it, I was starting to look forward to seeing the Kings, sitting next to them in class, feeling the jolts of fire when our arms brushed in the hall.

But just when I thought I might be falling for one of them, or all of them, just when I started to unclench my fists and let my guard down around them a tiny bit, I'd remember one of the horrible things they'd done to me, or get a flash of Ayaz fucking Ms. West, or recall the crossed-out photographs of previous scholarship students who they'd tormented.

I knew they should be included in my revenge plans, but what I didn't know was if, when the time came, I'd be able to go through with it if it meant hurting them. Greg's moralizing had started to rub off on me.

But I didn't have to worry about that now. I was still focused on the Queens. I worked with Greg over the next week on perfecting three 'concoctions.' I loved that word because it made us sound like mad scientists cooking up something. In a way, we were – a plot to destroy Courtney.

For his mid-year chemistry project, Greg had decided to formulate a small makeup range – he'd already been experimenting with different recipes at his old school, but the faculty there had put a stop to his experiment. "They claimed it was because my work was potentially dangerous," he told me. "But that's not true. Some kids were making organic weed killers, which are way more toxic. The school didn't want a boy making lipsticks."

But at Derleth, no one cared what Greg did because they saw him as expendable. It was like we were cattle on a ranch. As long as the cows ate their grass and popped out babies, the farmer didn't give much thought to their intellectual stimulation. At least it meant that no one asked questions when Greg wanted to spend extra time after class in the chemistry lab.

While Greg toiled with the chemicals, I snuck out of bed to rummage through the recycling. The maintenance staff cleared them first thing in the morning, and I needed to sneak my treasures back to my room without being seen. After a week, I had all the bottles and jars I needed. The Miskatonic Queens went through a *lot* of beauty products.

I had everything I needed for phase two of Hazel's revenge. All that was left to do was to countdown to D-Day.

CHAPTER SIXTEEN

"I can't believe you've scheduled extra tutoring with Dr. Morgan during the movie night," Quinn pouted over breakfast. "I was looking forward to snuggling with my girlfriend."

The Eldritch Club was hosting a movie night tonight in the dining hall. Students could bring blankets and pillows from their dorm rooms, and instead of our usual fancy three-course dinner, the catering would be pizza and popcorn and fries. It sounded like fun. Too bad I was going to miss the first half. But I had a very good reason.

"Yeah, well," I shrugged, popping a piece of bacon into my mouth. "It's a pity both me and your girlfriend will be missing it, because I was really hoping to meet her."

"Haha," Quinn stuck out his lower lip. He still labored under the belief that if he called me his girlfriend enough times, it would be true. Although every time he said it, Ayaz's back stiffened, which I... liked more than I wanted to admit. "Seriously, though, why are you worrying so much about your grades? You're hanging out in the middle of the rankings. That's better than most scholarship students could ever dream of. You should be kicking back like me." He leaned back and tried to put his arm around my shoulders. I shrugged him off.

"What you call 'kicking back,' I call 'being a lazy slug,'" I said. "Right now, I'm kicking Trey's ass. I don't want a bad grade on my Egyptian Pharaoh essay to ruin that."

At the other end of the table, Trey snorted into his eggs. It was true that I'd pulled 35 points ahead of him, but only because he'd given me 500 of his own points to save me from being sacrificed. We both knew it, but that didn't mean I wasn't going to rub his dicksome nose in it.

"I'll help you study. Here, look at this." Quinn grabbed my plate and sculpted my pile of crispy bacon into a pyramid.

"Didn't your mother ever teach you not to play with your food?" I growled, whipping a piece of bacon from his hand before he could add it to the stack.

"My mother taught me all sorts of things." Quinn waggled his eyes.

"You're disgusting."

Greg tipped the salt shaker on its side and placed it at the entrance of the tomb. "Here's the mummy off to its final resting place."

"Don't you start." Greg and Quinn cracked up laughing. They'd been getting along really well together lately, especially since we hardly ever saw Andre. Pity Quinn didn't have eyes for Greg – they'd make a cute couple and it would get him off my case about the girlfriend thing.

I'd never been anyone's girlfriend before, and I wasn't going to start with Quinn Delacorte. Although it was tempting. I still got a jolt of fire down my spine every time he touched me, and I *needed* more of his kisses in my life. But I knew he only wanted to go out with me because it would stir up trouble, and... my lips still burned from Ayaz's touch in the grotto. And Trey... the way he looked at me sometimes, like he was trying to see into my soul...

I needed to sort out my own feelings before I agreed to be

anyone's girlfriend. Especially since I was clearly crazy in the head for falling for not one but all three of my bullies. There were more important things to focus on right now, like my imminent sacrifice to the Great Old God beneath the gym.

Ayaz and I had been translating spells and reading occult books every spare minute, but we were no closer to figuring out what the god was and how to send it back into its void. Every day without answers was a day closer to the end of the year, when the god would come to collect. I'd made it my mission to break the hold the god had on this school and find a way to give the whole student body their lives back.

But today, today wasn't about saving the undead. It was about making them pay.

As I wrestled what remained of my breakfast off Quinn and Greg, a faint noise reached my ears. At first I thought it was the toaster on the buffet acting up, but then I realized that it was coming from the wall behind us. The unmistakable scritch-scritch of rat claws.

That's the second time I've heard them outside of the dungeon and the gym. I glanced around, but no one else seemed to have noticed. The din of the dining hall nearly completely obscured the noise unless you knew what you were listening to. I shrugged and went back to my food. Rats in the walls were just part of life here. Who cared it they were migrating around the school? Maybe it would do these spoiled rich kids good to encounter some rodents.

I forgot all about the scritching as we left the dining hall and headed toward the lockers. Andre dashed past me in a hurry to get to the breakfast buffet before it closed. His body brushed against mine and something cold dropped into my blazer pocket. A key.

The master key for the student dorms.

He came through for me. I knew he would.

The school day dragged on. I watched the clock like a hawk, counting down the minutes until the final bell. Even then, I had to wait. Rehearsals started immediately after the final bell. Today we were in the main auditorium, blocking some of the musical numbers. For the first time since learning our parts and lines, Trey and I would be together on stage.

The production was an original written by Dr. Halsey with the help of several drama students, including Courtney. It was obvious from the first reading that my part had been written with Courtney in mind. It was a rags-to-riches story with a love triangle, which seemed ludicrous in this school where everyone believed you were who you were born as. I played a waitress with ambitions to be a fashion designer, and I was been fought over by two guys – a rich all-American hero type, played by Greg, and a dangerous biker from 'the hood,' played by Trey.

Despite all the problematic aspects of the script, the songs were great and I loved dueting with Trey. As soon as he stepped on stage, his whole body changed. All his sharp edges ironed out, and the muscles in his face unclenched. Just for those few moments under the lights, he got to become someone else.

And that someone just happened to be locked in a passionate dance with my character.

We spun around the stage, the song rising in intensity as he lunged at me and I leapt out of the way, and then I chased him down and he'd hide. It was a dance of seduction, where our hearts and minds clashed against each other as our characters battled their own demons. Behind us, a row of backup dancers led by Courtney mimicked some of our movements to heighten the tension.

As I lunged at Trey during the first verse, his eyes widened and I really believed – just for a second – that he would rock forward and grab me. But he executed the steps flawlessly, spinning away and singing his lines about how he wasn't good enough, how he'd ruin me. And then it was his turn to come after me.

He leapt across the stage, landing on his knees and sliding toward me. Under the stage lights, his dark hair looked like dusk, bursting with flecks of starlight. Those blue eyes turned up to me, broad arms held wide, and his voice broke as he sang his last, mournful line.

My breath hitched.

My heart pattered.

Heat pooled in my core.

This isn't real. He's acting.

But it didn't feel like an act. It felt like Trey Bloomberg's mask was starting to crumble.

I don't know how I managed to get my next line out, but I sang it in a daze, my eyes locked on his, a million unspoken things passing between us. Trey grabbed me by the hips and lifted me over his head for our finale, tossing me into the air like a leaf on the breeze. His hands on me lit a blaze that burned long after he'd set me down and the wave of applause from our fellow cast members washed over us.

"Congratulations, you two," Dr. Halsey beamed. "That was perfect."

The only people who didn't look happy as we climbed off stage were Courtney and Tillie. I could feel their scowls on the back of my neck as I settled into the front row of seats to watch the next scene.

"Wow, Hazy." Greg leaned over to give me a fist bump. "You nailed it. You and Trey were *smoking*."

"He really can sing," I admitted, picking up my script to follow along.

Greg waved a hand. "Sure, he's technically proficient, but I was referring to the fact you two burned up the stage. Your chemistry together is *el fuego*. It'll melt the panties and jocks off everyone in the audience. I'm surprised the curtains didn't catch on fire."

"Gush much?" I lifted my head long enough to see Trey settling into a seat on the other side of the auditorium next to Ayaz. He caught my eye with his intense expression, and a fresh wave of heat rolled up my neck. "If you like him so much, you should ask him out."

"I don't think he's got eyes for anyone else," Greg winked. "I can see why you won't agree to go out with Quinn. Why choose one when you've got all three wrapped around your pinkie finger?"

The next scene started, so I wasn't able to tell Greg that real life didn't work like that. No one got to have three boyfriends, especially not someone like me. None of those guys would settle for being one of the many, and I wasn't sure if I wanted any of them after the things they'd done.

Instead, I spent the rest of rehearsal dreaming about all three of them kissing me, touching me. Lips and hands fought for dominance as they lay me down in Ayaz's big bed and...

Dr. Halsey announced that rehearsal was over, jolting me out of my fantasy. I rubbed my warm cheeks as I went down to my room and changed into jeans, Dante's basketball tank, and my leather jacket. *Stop thinking about them. You've got revenge to enjoy.*

I laced up my boots, slid the glass shard and the skeleton key into my pocket, and picked up my bag of tricks.

It's showtime.

I locked my door behind me and sat down on the metal stairs, just out of view of anyone in the dormitory above. Doors slammed, students laughed and joked with each other, and foot-steps clattered back and forth over the marble floor. "You coming, Courts?" I heard Tillie yell.

A door slammed. "Right here. I couldn't get my hair extensions to behave."

"Lucky you had your mom send you those last year. You look *fierce.*" That was Amber. "I'm going to have to keep wearing this hat until it grows out."

"The gutter bitch is going to pay," Tillie swore. "I can't believe the way the boys are fawning over her, like her gaping pussy is fucking magical or something. Come on. If we get there early, we can grab the best seats."

Their heels clapped against the marble floor, growing fainter as they headed over to the dining hall. A few minutes later, the corridor was mostly silent. Anyone who was anyone at this school would be at the movie night.

I bolted out of my hiding place. Upstairs, I walked quickly through the empty dormitory, scanning the corridor for stragglers. I knew I looked hella guilty, but there was no one here to see me. I made my way to Courtney's door and slid the key into the lock. I let out the breath I didn't realize I'd been holding as the lock clicked and the door swung open.

I slipped inside and shut the door behind me. Courtney had left all the lights on – rich girls never had to worry about how to pay the power bill – and the place blazed like a Fourth of July show. Her room was everything I'd imagined – an enormous four-poster bed hung with gauzy drapes, a closet that was larger than my entire Philly apartment, a kitchenette filled with wine bottles and mason jars filled with weird health foods. Everything in shades of white and lilac – it could have been a magazine photo shoot if not for the tornado of makeup and clothing and candy wrappers strewn across the room.

I resisted the urge to riffle through Courtney's things and headed straight for the bathroom. A line of bath products lined her shower caddy. All the students used the same fancy bath products – I guessed the school ordered them in bulk or something. That made my job easier. I swiped Courtney's shampoo, conditioner, and body wash into my tote and replaced them with three I'd brought along, making sure to tip a little from each down the sink so she didn't notice a change.

As I shut Courtney's door behind me, my gaze fell to her notice-board. Each room in the dormitory had a notice-board beside it so students could pin photos and knick-knacks and notes to each other. Courtney's was mostly covered with old valentines and pictures of her mother's collections cut from fashion magazines. My finger traced the edge of a note in Quinn's handwriting, feeling a blush creep over my cheeks as I read the contents.

My stomach did an awful clenching thing that had nothing to do with jealousy. Nothing whatsoever. *Never forget that Quinn slept with Courtney.*

Behind the note was a photograph. I recognized a young Courtney, probably about twelve years old, grinning madly at the camera as she showed off a shimmering gown in a lilac color that perfectly accentuated her feline features. I couldn't even imagine Courtney smiling like that now.

I flipped the picture over. A handwritten note on the back read, "My beautiful Courts. You're going to be a star one day, just like your mother. Love, Dad."

Hmmmmm. I wondered if I was holding in my hands the key to undoing Courtney. This picture was her weakness. I just didn't know why. Before I could change my mind, I unpegged it and shoved it into my tote.

Tillie's room next. Her room was pink – pink walls, pink sofa, pink bed, even some kind of weird pink stone for the kitchen countertop. I replaced her toiletries and got out as quick as I could, before the pink seeped into my pores.

Amber was last. Her room was mostly navy blue, and smaller than the others. I swapped out her toiletries as well, and quickly locked her door. *That hadn't taken long at all.* If I hurried, I might not even miss the opening credits.

I paused in front of the last door – Loretta's room. I never intended to make her part of this prank – she didn't deserve any punishment. But maybe there was something I could do *for* her, if I could just *understand.*

She had been through whatever horrors the god inflicted when it took her soul. I knew she wouldn't talk to me about it, but she used to keep that diary. Perhaps she wrote something down.

I stared at the key in my hand, then at the door. The notice-board beside Loretta's door was empty, apart from a nondescript wooden cross hanging from a single nail.

My heart hammered in my chest. I shoved the key into Loretta's door and pushed it open. The room was dark. Of course, Loretta had grown up poor like me. She'd never leave lights on.

I stepped inside and clicked on the light, illuminating a beautiful room decorated in a soft cream with cream and lilac furnishings. It looked like a junior version of Courtney's room, which was both comforting (that Loretta wasn't chained to a wall) and disturbing.

Courtney was clearly supporting Loretta to live here as a Queen. But why? She wouldn't be doing it out of the goodness of her heart. So what was Loretta's end of the bargain?

I shuffled through her bookbag and the stack of things on the desk, hunting for the battered journal Loretta carried everywhere. She used to hide it in the gap between our desk and the wall. It might've rankled another roommate, but we both knew that when you were poor you hid your precious things. *She's probably still hiding it. Old habits die hard. Maybe under the mattress or—*

"Hello, Hazel."

I whirled around, banging my head on the overhead shelves. Loretta sat in the middle of the bed, the blanket pulled up to her chin so she looked like a ghost rising out of the mattress. She fixed me with a vacant gaze that sent a chill down my spine. *I swear she wasn't there a moment ago.*

"Loretta, hi." I rubbed the top of my head. "You scared me."

Above Loretta's head, a rat *scritch-scritched* behind the wall.

"Why are you scared?" Loretta asked in a flat, uninterested voice. "*You're* the one sneaking around *my* room."

"Yes. So, about that... I was..." I searched around for a suitable story, but Loretta's blank stare unnerved me. I shrugged. "Yeah, I got nothing."

Loretta didn't reply. She kept staring at me with dead eyes.

Dead eyes...

"So..." I said, shoving my hands into my pockets and taking a step toward the bed. "We haven't really talked since this quarter started. How do you like your new room?"

"It's fine."

"I saw that you aced the English test the other day. Congrats! I messed up all the Shakespeare questions. I can never make sense of his thees and thous."

Loretta's blank expression was starting to creep me out.

I sighed. "You know you could hang out with us if you wanted to, right? We miss you, especially Greg."

Loretta's eyebrow twitched. *That got a reaction. Interesting.* I pressed on. "I can't pretend to understand everything that's going on with you right now, but I want you to know that I'm here if you ever need a friend."

"We're not friends," she said in her flat voice.

"Yes, fine, we're not friends," I snapped. "But I still won't let the Queens get away with what they did to you."

"They gave me all this." Loretta gestured to the room.

"Yeah, but they took so much more from you."

"If you say so. A word of advice," Loretta's eyes narrowed. "Don't mess with Courtney."

I smiled innocently. "Who, me?"

"You had your fun with the superglue, but don't try anything else. It won't end well for you."

"Thanks for the creepy warning," I shrugged. "But I can handle Courtney."

"No, you can't. Don't make the mistake of thinking you're invincible just because you came from the *hood*. They've got power over you that you can't even..." She shook her head. "Forget it. Just get out and leave me alone. Go join your *boyfriends*."

She spat out the word with such venom, a surge of anger rose inside me. *Fine, I won't try to help you.* I turned away from the bed and stalked toward the door. Rats scritched overhead. My hand closed around the handle and a rush of regret hit me. I was the queen of lashing out at people when I was scared. I should have learned to recognize it in others.

"I know what happened to you," I said, still facing the door. "I know about the deity beneath the school, and what it demands of its loyal servants. But it's not invincible. Something about me hurts it. I've felt it cry out in pain, and it's a terrible thing to behold. That means there's still hope. We're hunting for a way to fix things, to give you and everyone else back what was stolen. Loretta, I'll b—" I turned around.

A scream caught in my throat.

Loretta had vanished. The bedsheets were pulled tight and straight, as if she'd never been there at all.

CHAPTER SEVENTEEN

"Took you long enough," Quinn complained as I grabbed the edge of his blanket and slid down beside him. He had a great spot in the middle of the screen, near the back of the room. Greg and Ayaz sat in front of him, sharing a pizza with Nancy, Paul, and some of the other monarchs. Greg was laughing and chatting with Paul. It made me so happy. "You just missed the best fight scene."

The movie was *Gladiator*, which was such a weird choice – about a slave who defied his station to become a champion. Also, it had been made before I was born, and it showed in the special effects and actors. Sometimes, I couldn't believe it took meeting a Great Old God in a subterranean cavern to make me realize this school was stuck in a time warp.

All around us, kids crunched popcorn, unscrewed the caps on hidden hip flasks, and talked in low voices. There were quite a few kissing sounds and rustling of blankets. Dr. Dexter slumped in a chair in the corner, ostensibly here to supervise us. His head nodded against his chest, and occasionally he let out a loud snore.

As I leaned across Quinn to grab a handful of popcorn, he held the bucket just out of reach, his face an inch from mine. "It'll cost you a kiss," he grinned.

Feeling emboldened from my successful revenge mission, I leaned forward and pecked him on the lips.

"I know you can do better than that." Quinn's hand snaked around the back of my head, his fingers pushing through my short hair as he locked his lips with mine, teasing my mouth open with his tongue.

My body responded immediately, tightened with this hot, warm feeling that happened every time I was near one of the monarchs. Quinn's coconut and sugarcane scent sent my head spinning. If all of the Kings used the same fancy bath products, how come they each smelled so different, so *intoxicating*?

A low growl escaped from Quinn's throat as I traced my fingers through his hair. I didn't want the kiss to ever end.

Someone behind us made a gagging noise. Quinn tipped his head back, tearing his lips from mine. The air between us had become heavy, hot, sticking to my skin.

Out of the corner of my eye, I saw Courtney glaring at us. John had one arm around her, the other hand under the blanket they were sharing. He slobbered along her neck and tried to tip her head toward him, but she gave a growl of frustration and pushed him away.

"Courtney's watching us," I whispered to Quinn.

"Good." He kissed my earlobe. "Do you want to give her a real show?"

My heart hammered against my chest. Who was this person, and what had she done with Hazel Waite? Before I'd come to Derleth, the only thing I'd done was *try* to kiss a guy, and he hadn't even liked it. That was why it was so hilarious they all called me a whore – I'd lived with one for long enough that I knew all I ever wanted to know about sex. It was just another weapon that could be wielded against a woman, used to control and dominate, to keep her in chains. No, thank you.

And yet, put me in the hands of a Miskatonic King and I melted like butter. Probably it had something to do with the hunger of a Great Old God lurking over my head. In desperate situations, people did all sorts of crazy things. The Donner party ate each other. I made out with bad boys who were no good for me but tasted so damn fine.

Trey shuffled over and grabbed the box of popcorn from Quinn's hands. "Quit hogging the snacks," he growled.

Quinn hugged me to his chest. "Keep the popcorn. I've got the best treat right here."

"You don't get to keep everything to yourself."

My eyes widened as Trey lifted the corner of the blanket and slid in beside us. Quinn poked his tongue out at his friend, but he also shuffled me over to make room... shuffled me right into his lap, in fact. Between his legs.

Something hard rubbed against the crack of my ass. It took me a moment to realize what it was. *Quinn. He's hard.*

I jerked forward. Quinn tightened his grip around my torso.

"Feel what you do to me, Hazy," he whispered against my ear, sending a lick of fire down my spine. "You can't just leave me like this. That would be mean."

"Have you met me? I'm pretty mean," I whispered back, my throat tight. He was right. I wasn't going anywhere.

"Nope, you talk a big game, but you're a kitten." Quinn shifted, pulling the blanket tight around us. His hand slid up my thigh. "Let's make the kitten purr."

I kept my eyes facing forward, but I didn't take in a single frame of the movie. Quinn moved his hand along my thigh, sliding it slowly, achingly slowly, toward the source of the ache inside me, the point from which all fires blazed and sparked. He kissed a trail of fire along my neck, his teeth scraping against my skin.

Not to be outdone, Trey shuffled closer, pressing his body against me. "You like him touching you?" he asked. "If you're not into it, just say the word, and we can get out of here."

I opened my mouth, but I couldn't force sound from my

throat. Not when Quinn drew circles on my inner thigh and Trey Bloomberg's breath danced on my ear as he asked me.

"I think our Hazy really wants to see how this movie ends," Quinn murmured, his lips pressing against my hair.

"Very well." Trey's hand dropped to my other thigh, his fingers walking a path of fire up to meet Quinn's. "I expect it'll end in fireworks."

Their fingers met in the middle as they battled with the button on my fly. Quinn's lips trailed down my neck. "Hazy, Hazy, Hazy," he murmured. "You naughty girl."

"You want this, Hazel?" Trey's voice was hard, tight. He hooked a finger over the edge of my panties. Not daring to speak, I nodded.

"Good. Because I've been wanting to touch you like this for so fucking long." Trey turned my head toward him and crushed my mouth with his. He kissed me long and deep and slow, as if he possessed me, as if I was his.

This is such a bad idea, but I can't say no... not when they...

Fingers plunged between my legs, pushing aside my panties, resting softly on my mound. My breath hitched. *I can't believe we're doing this in here, where everyone can see.*

But no one was watching. Quinn had the blanket pulled up high, and no one cared, anyway. Everyone was distracted with their own blanket fumblings. This event was a wholesome veneer for a teenage Bacchanalian.

I gasped as a finger teased my entrance before slipping inside me. A second finger joined the first, pumping in and out with slow, measured strokes. Another finger pressed against my clit, rubbing me in my own juices in a languid circle, as if we had all the time in the world.

Heat rose through my body, starting in my core and radiating out, touching the tips of my fingers and toes. I was fraying at the edges, my whole body slowly falling apart under their touch.

A faint whimper escaped my throat. In front of me, Ayaz

turned around, his eyes blazing as they flicked to my face, to Quinn and Trey kissing me, to their hands under the blanket...

He scowled and turned away. My heart thudded, but then the finger on my clit circled faster, and I forgot all about Ayaz.

I don't know how they coordinated, but it was as if they had a natural rhythm together. As they moved, they took turns kissing me. Quinn's tongue darted into my mouth while Trey trailed sparks along my collarbone.

The fire inside me built into a ball of heat, hotter and hotter until it pressed against my skin, demanding freedom. I bent my head back against Quinn's shoulder, my muscles tensing. Another gasp escaped my throat.

Trey moved closer, his eyes half-lidded as he came at me. He pressed his hand lightly over my mouth. "Bite me," he whispered, holding a finger across my lips. "Make me *bleed*."

I bit down on his finger, my body jerking forward as a wave of heat coursed through my veins. The fire burst out of me, engulfing me in a heat so intense that red welts danced in front of my vision.

I flailed in the heart of the fire, losing myself in its wild hunger. When I found myself again, I'd collapsed against Quinn's shoulder. Trey trailed his fingers down my bare arm, raising the hairs on my skin. Both of them grinned like Cheshire cats.

"See, Hazy?" Quinn murmured. "I told you we'd make you purr."

No one but me noticed the small things. In homeroom the next morning, Courtney had plastered on her makeup much thicker than usual. The next day, both she and Tillie were back to wearing their hats. Amber didn't show up for class at all.

To the rest of the world, these things meant little. But to me, they were *everything*.

They meant my revenge plan was working. Which was nice, but I wasn't satisfied. I needed to do something bigger, something that tipped the balance of power in this school.

The only problem was, it was hard to think of ways to hurt the undead, to give them a taste of their own medicine. Especially without breaking my vow and revealing their secret to Greg and Andre. Unlike the scholarship students they tormented, the rich kids of Miskatonic Prep had nothing left to lose.

But maybe I could find the chink in their armor.

Two days later, I'd had to run back to my room for my history book, and I was late for class. I bounded back up the stairs just as the second bell rang. The last straggling students cleared out of the corridor, leaving me alone in the fancy dormitory. I took my time, scanning the notice-boards along the walls, searching for ghosts.

It didn't take me long to find them. Beside Amber's door was pinned a photograph of her with her arms around two identical smiling little girls, all three of them with perfect blonde pigtails. *Sisters.* On his notice-board, Derek stood beside an old man with a bushy grey beard, holding up an enormous fish. Creepy would-be rapist John Hyde-Jones had a picture of him and an older man wearing dirty overalls and sitting in the chassis of a car. Every board I stopped to look at held at least one image or note from the world outside, from a life before Derleth Academy.

How had I never noticed these before?

Because I'd been looking only at the guys. Trey never pinned anything on his notice-board. Occasionally, a girl would pin a love note there, begging for a date, but they never stayed there long. Ayaz had a rotation of drawings – mostly funny cartoons about the teachers and stuff that went on around the school, but sometimes dark things – visions I recognized from the dreams of the Great Old God. I'd never actually been inside Quinn's room, so I hadn't looked at his.

I paused in front of Quinn's door, running my fingers over the single image he'd hung there. It was his mother. She sat on one of those white Cape Cod porch swings with the ocean crashing behind her, a book open across her knee. She smiled a beautiful smile, but her amber eyes – Quinn's eyes – pooled with a sadness that reached out from the paper and punched me in the gut.

Voices echoed down the corridor. I wrenched myself away, turning toward the classroom wing, when I realized the voices were coming from Courtney's room.

I crept across the corridor on the balls of my feet and flattened my body against the wall. Courtney's door was open a crack. If I leaned out a little, I could see a sliver of the interior.

"It won't stop falling out," Courtney sobbed, lying across her bed with her head in her hands. Beside her, Tillie picked up a brush and pulled clumps of hair from the teeth.

Feeling bold, I leaned forward and gave the door a tiny push. It swung open another couple of inches, giving me more of a picture. Courtney rolled over, her face twisted in misery as she raked her fingers through her hair. She let out a strangled scream as her hand came away holding a clump of hair.

"Maybe we're sick," Tillie said, scratching at her cheek, where a large patch of hard, scaly skin had taken up residence on her face. She looked like she was transforming into a lizard person.

"Or maybe whatever they did to us is coming undone?" Amber offered up. She sat on the floor, her back against the bed, examining her own scaly arms. "Maybe it's like, our bodies returning to their natural state—"

"Don't say that!" Courtney sat up, her eyes ablaze. "I'm not going to be a walking corpse or going back to my grave. I refuse! They promised us everlasting youth and beauty – that was the trade-off for being trapped in this horrible place. Our bargain had no expiration date!"

"Do you think if we went to Ms. West, she'd let us out of the deal?" Amber asked, her voice hopeful. I wondered if she was thinking about those two twin girls in her picture.

"Of course not. You can't just un-dead-ify yourself. We are what we are, so we should at least get something out of it." Courtney scratched a patch of scaly skin on her arm. "Ow. I can't believe this. Why isn't this happening to anyone else?"

"Tell your mother," Tillie said. "Ms. West will have to care if she makes a fuss."

"I'm not talking to that bitch!" Courtney's shriek rattled the windows. I heard a thump as she slid off the bed. "I'm going to have another shower. Maybe I can exfoliate the skin away."

Tillie and Amber moved toward the door. I bolted for the main dormitory entrance, passing through onto the skyway just as they emerged in the hall. As I hurried to homeroom, I couldn't help the wide grin that spread across my face.

Greg had done a perfect job. The shampoo, face wash, and body lotion he'd created looked and smelled exactly like the real thing. Without laboratory analysis, there would be no way to know they'd been formulated to cause exactly this effect.

I had Courtney exactly where I wanted her.

It was time to move on to phase three. And I was beginning to understand what I had to do if I wanted these spoiled, rich, dead kids to pay.

CHAPTER EIGHTEEN

Under the library's stained glass window, I slid into a seat opposite Ayaz. He'd already spread several books across the table and had one open in front of him, a handful of notes jotted down. But he wasn't reading the book. Instead, he shaded a drawing of a girl in a flowing dress standing beneath a gnarled tree. I leaned forward, trying to get a good look at the picture. The girl had long, midnight hair. Was it meant to be Zehra—

Ayaz saw me looking and shoved his pad under one of the books.

"Hey," I said.

He grunted in reply.

"She wasn't wearing a dress. She had warm leggings and hiking boots. Much more sensible than what I'd been wearing," I added, remembering my ruined velvet dress and torn stockings.

Silence.

Rage radiated off Ayaz. I could practically see waves of it bending space-time around him, sucking all the happiness out of the air into a black hole of misery.

What's he so pissed about? This was the first time we'd spoken since the movie night when he'd seen me with Trey and Quinn.

Before that, we'd been reading through our stack of occult books together almost every evening, but Ayaz hadn't invited me to his room since. He avoided me in class and the dining hall. Finally, it was only when Dr. Morgan remarked that we seemed stalled on our research project about the Salem witches that he'd grunted out an invitation to study in the library during our free period.

If it was any other guy, I'd say he was jealous. But this can't be about Trey and Quinn. Ayaz has no claim on me. He only kissed me in the grotto so we could talk about his sister without anyone overhearing.

Besides, he's sleeping with the Deadmistress.

Even though it was an amazing kiss... it didn't mean anything. So what was he so pissed about? Was it about Zehra? We hadn't talked about her again since the grotto. Maybe he wished I'd got more from her, that I hadn't let her disappear so quickly?

"If we're going to study together, we have to actually speak," I said.

"Fine." Without looking up, he tossed a book across the table. "Dr. Morgan thinks we need to do some more work on the section of our project about the evolution of witchcraft. He suggested we look into the spiritualism movement. Here's a book. Make some notes."

"You don't want to—"

"Fuck no."

Fine. I flipped open the book and started reading, but I couldn't concentrate with Ayaz fuming across the table. I leaned across and tapped the top of his page until he emitted a low, warning growl.

"Are you mad at me about something?"

"Nope." He didn't look up from his books.

"So you woke up on the wrong side of the bed, or what?"

Ayaz slammed his book shut. "I want to get a good fucking grade on this project, and I'm not going to let some gutter whore scholarship student ruin it for me."

The comment stung. I bit back a retort. *Don't take it personally.*

He's doing exactly what you do, exactly what a bully does – lash out because he's upset.

Ayaz grabbed another book. Seizing my chance, I yanked the picture out from under his stack and thrust it in his face. "Are you angry about her?" I demanded. "Because I saw her and you didn't? I didn't ask her to rescue me from the cave."

He tore the paper from my hand. "Twelve years I thought she was dead," he growled. "She never bothered to let me know otherwise, but she seeks *you* out?"

"Maybe there's a reason she hasn't been able to get to you."

"I won't know, will I?" he said bitterly. "You never bothered to ask her."

Is he blaming his bad mood on me? "I was a little busy trying not to die. Maybe instead of sitting around moping, you go back to the cave and look for her. While you're there, maybe you could tell me about that sigil I saw and why it burst into flame?"

Ayaz glanced over his shoulder. Three tables over, a couple of juniors had their heads bent in their textbooks, no doubt trying to listen to every word we said. "We can't do this here."

"Fine." I flipped a page in the book and started reading about mediums and seances. I quickly discovered this book wasn't exactly a history of the occult. It was a history of the Spiritualism movement that started in the late Victorian era. The author exposed the frauds that had been used to trick people into believing they were communicating with the dead. Back in the 40s, there was a famous Scottish medium named Helen Duncan, who claimed to produce the spirits of the dead during her seances by excreting a slimy substance called 'ectoplasm' from her mouth and nose. The Secret Service started investigating her after she spoke with the spirit of a deceased sailor who revealed he'd been killed when a German U-boat sank the battleship *HMS Barham*. This statement was true – the *HMS Barham* had indeed been sunk by a U-boat. however for strategic reasons the War Office were keeping the tragedy a secret. They needed to know how this medium was threatening the war effort.

During their investigations, it was discovered Helen was swallowing cheesecloth and other items and then regurgitating them on command to create the illusion. In 1944 she became the last ever person to be imprisoned under the 1735 Witchcraft Act.

The book included pictures of Helen sitting in her seance chair, with what was very obviously bits of cheesecloth coming out her nose and mouth. One of the bits had a rubber glove stuck on the end, and sometimes there were also doll heads or cut-out faces from photographs stuck on the cloth. I couldn't believe people would fall for something so stupid, and yet according to the author, even now Helen still had her believers. The book stated:

> *In the darkened seance room, where attendees had already entered a state of mind where they expected to meet with strange visitations, where they longed to alleviate grief with news from the hereafter, and at the hands of a master manipulator, even the cheapest parlor tricks could appear supernatural...*

That gives me an idea...

I was trapped in this school with a bunch of revenants or edimmu or ghosts or whatever. I was well past the point where I thought any of this was faked. Sure, the boys could have planted those tombstones, but no one could have faked the hatred pouring from the Great Old God's hellish prison, or the horrific visions that haunted my dreams.

But these undead had ghosts of their own. I thought of Courtney's photograph burning a hole in the bottom of my bag, of Amber's sisters, of Quinn's mother and her sad eyes. I remembered all the scholarship students in the files in Ayaz's room, their faces crossed out with jagged marks.

I'd been looking for the perfect way to get revenge on all of them, to hit them where it would really hurt. Maybe, with the help of a few friendly ghosts, I'd finally found it—

"You don't need to study anymore, you already know everything," an insouciant voice interrupted my thoughts.

Trey's hand trailed across the page. I slammed the book shut and shoved it into my bag. I didn't want either of them to get an inkling of what I was planning. "I'm studying and Ayaz is ignoring me," I said. Trey's cruel expression gave nothing away, which usually meant he was about to throw down something brutal. "What do you want?"

"Get out of here," Trey said to Ayaz. "I need to speak to Hazel."

"We're busy." Ayaz didn't look up, but his voice dripped with acid.

With a sweep of his hand, Trey sent all the books flying off the table. *Thump, thump, thump.* They landed on the floor. The two junior students got up and rushed for the exit.

Ayaz flung his chair back and rose, shoving himself up in Trey's face so they were nose to nose. Fury flew between them as they hurled unspoken abuse at each other. At any moment I expected lasers to shoot out of their eyes. Finally, Ayaz shoved Trey in the chest, pushing him aside as he strode out of the library.

"What was that about?" I asked.

"Don't know. Don't care. Did you do something to Courtney?" Trey growled, slamming his palms down on the table, leaning over me in a way that would have been intimidating if he didn't smell so damn good.

"I haven't touched her, or any of the other Queens," I smirked, leaning back in my chair and flicking a pen between my fingers. It was technically true.

A vein in Trey's neck throbbed. "She hasn't left her room in four days. Apparently, there's something wrong with her skin."

"Woe is her."

"This isn't funny," Trey hissed. "If she finds out it was you, she could—"

"She can't touch me, remember?" I flicked my Eldritch Club tattoo at him. "Relax. Stop acting like you're about to go Kanye West on me. Just tell me what the problem is."

Trey's shoulders sagged. He moved to stand at the window, peering out one of the clear panels at the school grounds below. He looked like he was about to launch into another tirade at me when something caught his eye. He leaned forward, squinting through the glass. "Shit."

"What is it?" I joined Trey at the window. His hand snaked out to rest on the small of my back. The fingers sought my skin, trembling a little.

A black car circled the fountain out front before pulling to a stop directly in front of the steps. Ms. West stood ready to meet the visitors. Dark windows hid whoever was inside, but I knew from Trey's stiffened body that he knew exactly who it was.

The door opened. A dress shoe so shiny I could've done my makeup in it stomped on the cobbles, followed by a second. The driver slammed the door and I finally got a look at our visitor.

Vincent Bloomberg II.

CHAPTER NINETEEN

.

"What's he doing here?" I asked. "There's no Eldritch Club meeting."

From the back of the car, Damon Delacorte stepped out and held the door open. A woman slid out. I recognized her instantly by her slanted green eyes, the cascade of platinum blonde locks, and a feline body that looked ready to pounce. Gloria Haynes, fashion designer to the stars.

Courtney's mother.

Why was she here now, the new money fashion designer, with two of the most senior members of the Eldritch Club in tow? It couldn't be good.

Trey's face had gone bone white. I moved toward him, reaching out to touch his shoulder. He jerked away.

"Trey?"

Trey spun around on his heel and stalked out. I shoved my books into my satchel and followed him. He stalked down the hall, tossing a freshman against a locker when he didn't jump out of the way fast enough. He reached the atrium and pounded down the steps just as the three adults stepped through the main doors.

Closer now, I got a good look at their faces. Was it just the light in the atrium, or did they all three look a little older, a little saggier, with wisps of grey through their perfect hair?

"Dad." Trey stood in front of his father, his back rigid – a soldier standing to attention.

Vincent brushed past his son. "Go back to class, Trey. I'm not here for you. I have business with the headmistress."

"Class is over for the day." Trey grabbed his father's elbow, forcing the man to turn to face him. "Dad, what's going on? Why are you here? I wasn't told about any Eldritch Club business—"

Trey's dad yanked him forward, pressing his lips against Trey's ear. I leaned over the balcony, but I had no shot at hearing what was said. All I could see was the the definite streak of grey hair near Vincent's temple and the terror that flickered for a moment in Trey's eyes. He blinked, and they went back to being cold blue orbs.

Two thick arms wrapped around me. Quinn's tongue ran over my ear. "What a nice surprise," he whispered. "I was just coming to find you at the library. Are you done studying boring books? Do you want to study my cock instead—"

I shoved him away. "That line worked on Courtney? I didn't think my opinion of her could get any lower."

"You cut me, Hazy." Quinn leaned over the railing, just as the door to Headmistress West's office shut on the visitors. "What happened?"

"Courtney's mom, Trey's dad, and your dad are here."

Quinn's body tensed. "Where?"

"They arrived just a few minutes ago in the same car. We saw them from the window of the library. They've just gone into the headmistress's office." I couldn't tear my eyes from Trey's frozen figure, standing in the atrium, staring at the space his father had occupied only a moment ago.

Quinn ran a hand through his hair. "This is bad, Hazy. They

don't just show up here like this. Especially not Gloria Haynes. She's only been to the school a handful of times."

"Then we'd better find out why they're here." I tore my eyes from Trey and turned to Quinn. "You still know how to access that passage you told me comes out in the headmistress' office?"

"Of course."

"Then let's go."

I didn't have to tell Quinn twice. He led me back to the library, down through the stacks to an ancient computer station. Hardly anyone used these computers – there was no internet allowed at Derleth, so what was the point? Hopefully, it meant we wouldn't be discovered.

Quinn pressed a panel on the wall, and a small section sprung open, revealing a gap between just wide enough for one person to squeeze between the walls.

"It's a tighter squeeze than you're used to," he said, giving me a gentle push towards it. "Or maybe not. You're still a virgin, after all."

"I'm not a virgin," I snapped.

"Of course you are. The girl I fingered under a blanket had obviously never had an orgasm. If you aren't a virgin, then you need to kick the guy's ass because he clearly didn't do his job properly."

"I am so not having this conversation with you *now*." I glared at Quinn as I slipped into the passage, grateful the darkness would hide the flare of heat in my cheeks.

Quinn was right. It was a tight squeeze in the passage. I shimmied through the narrow space. One one side, rough stone scraped my arms. On the other, my fingers drummed against the drywall.

I crawled on my hands and knees, listening to snatches of conversation on the other side of the wall. Teachers talked in hushed tones. Coffee cups clattered together. We must have been somewhere in the faculty wing.

Quinn's arm crossed my shoulder, pointing to a t-junction in the tunnel up ahead. "Take the right turn."

I did. As I crawled along between the walls, Ms. West's voice echoed through the wood paneling. I stopped short. Quinn's head knocked against my ass.

"Ow." Quinn rubbed his head. "Give me a signal before you put the brakes on."

"Shhh," I hissed. I knelt on my knees and pressed my head against the wall.

"—you don't have control of this school, Headmistress." Vincent Bloomberg was saying.

"We're perfectly in control," West responded. I imagined her behind her oak desk, that satisfied smile playing across her lips.

"Then why is my board of directors demanding I hire a *woman* as my CFO? Why did Damon lose a council seat to a black man? Why is Gloria being eviscerated in the media for her use of rare animal fur?" Vincent's voice rose.

"Why do I have lines around my eyes?" Damon added.

"We're all seeing some signs of age. The creature's power is waning." Vincent again. "Four students a year is not enough."

"Mr. Bloomberg, Mr. Delacorte, Mrs. Haynes, with all due respect, we cannot afford to be imprudent. Our system has been carefully considered. What you're asking is impossible. Even finding four orphans who meet the criteria is becoming more difficult. Everyone is so connected these days – there's a social media trail to navigate. The students won't come with us until they've seen evidence. At some point, not even you will be able to keep what happens here a secret."

"Which is why we need to move on our grand design as soon as possible," Damon said. His voice had the same gentle cadence as Quinn's — easygoing and suave, but frightening because I knew it hid a monster. "We've been waiting twenty years, maneuvering the Eldritch Club into positions of influence. Surely by now our god has the power he needs to break free of his cage."

"We cannot be hasty with these things—"

"I've had enough of this," Damon sneered. "You've been pushing back on this for years, Hermia. According to you, we're never ready. I want to know why. I want a *timeline*."

"You don't commune with the god every day, as I do," Ms. West's tone was sugary and patient, as though she were speaking to a child. "I tell you, he is not ready—"

"It's that girl, Hazel Waite," Quinn's father snapped. "You said you'd removed her threat with your *agreement*, but it appears our stalwart Ms. West is under the little whore's spell."

"As I've *already* explained, the agreement stops Hazel from hurting herself, and by extension, our god. But I have not as yet determined what it is about her that causes the adverse reaction in our deity. She underwent the same processing as our other sacrifices, and yet the more her mind slipped toward oblivion, the more our god shrunk from her. She now knows this, which is unfortunate. She's wily and unstable. It's imprudent to make a move until we understand more."

"Have you really been trying?" Damon declared. "You've allowed her influence in the school. And we wonder why our power is waning — a crack whore criminal dares to wear *our* mark."

"I did not know this," Ms. West's voice was small. "Who told you that?"

"We have eyes and ears at this school, Hermia. What we've seen lately concerns us. The very fact that you bargained with this girl instead of destroying her shows just how weak your leadership has become." Vincent's curt tone gave me shivers. "I never should have agreed to a woman in a man's role."

"No man would have the stomach for what I do," Ms. West

said. For the first time during the conversation, her voice rose in volume.

"Then *do your job*. Find out what makes Hazel Waite different and get her out of our way. Damon and I saw her at the Halloween party, acting as though she was the Queen of this school. She's already found a way to cheat our god of two of his sacrifices. She needs to be put back in her place."

"I can't touch her when your son has taken a shine to her." There was a hint of triumph in Ms. West's voice.

"My son?" Vincent seemed genuinely surprised. "That makes no sense. He let her take the initiation and made that ridiculous show at the dance, but that was just for my benefit. Trey may act out but he would *never* demean himself by fraternizing with the likes of her."

"I can only confirm what I've witnessed," Ms. West said. "Your son has been doing a fair share of fraternizing. He sits with Hazel in class. She holds court at their table in the dining hall and attended Eldritch Club parties. She was even seen by one of the other students leaving your son's room late at night."

A fist thumped against something hard.

"And he's not the only one," Ms. West simpered. "Ayaz Demir has been working awfully hard on a history project with her. They've been studying in his room. Every night. With the door firmly locked."

Something made of wood splintered. *Geez, someone's having a tantrum.* "What kind of bordello are you running here?" Vincent boomed. "Ayaz should not have been paired up with her. This is ridiculous."

"I have it on good authority *Trey* was the one who allowed her and her two friends to take the initiation and wear the mark," Damon added. "There are students who wish to see the old order restored but are too afraid of Trey to cross him. Now, if Quinn were allowed to—"

"*Your* son is an even bigger problem." Gloria Haynes spoke for the first time. From her husky voice, I guessed she kept that slim figure of hers by eating nothing but drywall and smoking a couple of packs a day. "Quinn Delacorte has been telling other students this Hazel is his *girlfriend*."

"He wouldn't!" Damon's voice boomed. "I'll tear his throat out with my own hands."

Quinn tensed. I squeezed his hand. *Not if I stop you, you fucking abuser.*

"Silence!" Ms. West boomed.

A chair scraped back. I imagined the Deadmistress standing up to her full height, her black skirts sweeping around her ankles, looking every bit a villainous Morticia Addams. "I have been the steward of this fine establishment for twenty-three years. I gave my life to babysitting your spoiled brats in the name of our god, of our mission. I have sat in this very room more times than I can count and listened to you undermine my every decision. I must ask, when am I to receive *my* reward?"

"You of all people know the greatest reward is service to our deity," said Damon.

"I do, and I've been serving faithfully inside this prison while you've all been enjoying your power in the outside world. I was promised that after ten years I would be able to leave this place," Headmistress West leveled. "That deadline has come and passed, and yet I am still here, still repeating the same infernal lessons and chaperoning inane Halloween parties. What good is this power if I am cannot wield it?"

"You'll have no reward if you don't rein in the students," Bloomberg said. "Starting with my son."

"And mine," added Damon. "And sort out the Turk while you're at it. He never should have been allowed here in the first place. If I'd known my son would be schooling with a terrorist—"

"Watch your mouth," Vincent warned.

For once, I agree with you, Vinny Boy.

"What's up, Bloomberg? Can't deny you've got the Middle

East on your payroll?" Damon smirked. "But back to the topic at hand — those boys cannot be allowed to ruin this for all of us because they can't keep their dicks in their pants. I expect swift and decisive action."

My fingers tightened around Quinn. He squeezed back.

"As much as I hate to admit this, the boys are not the problem," Gloria Haynes said. "It's the girl, Hazel. She's a boil infecting this whole school. Hermia, I demand that something be done or I'll be removing my generous patronage from Derleth Academy."

"Good. We don't want your kind here, anyway," Vincent snapped. "This place turned to the dogs as soon as we let in *new* money."

"My money is just as good as yours, Vincent," Gloria shot back. "In fact, it's better, since *my* heir hasn't squandered my fortune on a failed startup."

"You take that back!" Vincent thundered. "It wasn't Wilhem's fault the market shifted—"

"Sit down, Vincent. Now, Gloria," Ms. West cooed. "Let's not get carried away. We greatly appreciate your donations to this school, and—"

"*I'll* deal with Hazel Waite," Vincent's voice dripped with menace. "I'll find leverage. She'll fall into line."

Ms. West snorted. "You're not equipped to deal with this. She's an orphan. She has no family. Over the first quarter she has shown remarkable resilience to the torments of her fellow students. She has no attachments, no weakness to exploit."

"You underestimate my resources. There's *always* leverage. You just haven't been looking in the right places." I imagined Vincent standing up, buttoning his immaculate suit jacket and indicating the meeting was over. "You focus on regaining control of this school and making sure those boys of ours toe the line."

Chairs scraped. The Eldritch Club members left the office, murmuring their secret plans to each other. Quinn and I remained in the dark tunnel, clinging to each other as the weight of their words locked us in place.

Vincent Bloomberg was coming for me, with the entire force of the senior Eldritch Club behind him. How the fuck was I going to deal with that?

CHAPTER TWENTY

I found Trey in an empty locker room, the same place he went to collect himself after his father yelled at him on the lacrosse field the day he'd injured Quinn's eyes. He sat on the same bench, staring at a row of empty lockers, his cruel mouth set in a firm line, his hands clasped so tight the knuckles had turned white.

I sat down on the bench beside him. "Hey."

He grunted.

"I saw your father whisper something to you. I'm guessing he wasn't inviting you on a fishing trip."

"He wants me... nay, he *commanded* me to remove the three scholarship students from the Eldritch Club," he said. "Or I will be removing myself."

"Can he do that?"

"He's a senior member."

Vincent's cruel words echoed inside my head. "Are you going to do it?"

"All my life I've tried to please him," Trey said, still staring ahead. His voice sounded far away. "Nothing is ever enough. I'll always be a failure in his eyes. My brother, Wilhem, he can do no wrong. Quinn would say the sun shines out his asshole. Even Ayaz

– the poor Muslim kid my father only brought to this country for PR reasons – gets more respect from him than I ever did."

"I don't know what that's like," I said. "My mom was happy with anything I did."

Almost anything.

"You're lucky," he said.

I snorted. "Is that *the* Trey Bloomberg, heir to the Bloomberg fortune, telling me that I'm lucky?"

"I'm not the heir anymore," he muttered.

"But you're the oldest. You share his name. Isn't that the way it's supposed to go?"

"I can't be his heir. I was the oldest once, but I'm stuck here and my dipshit brother passed me by. He got to drop out of university, become a founder, run his tech startup into the ground, and get a job and a corner office at Daddy's firm. And as far as the outside world knows, I'm dead." Trey rubbed his head with his hands. "It's so fucked up, Hazel. All the kids who go here... it's too convenient. Dad got me out of his way so he could groom Wilhem to take over the business. Damon Delacorte got rid of the only person standing between him and his sadistic tendencies toward his wife, Tillie's parents saw her as a chess piece they could maneuver into a better social position. She's been promised to me since birth."

"Your parents arranged your marriages for you?" Trey nodded. "That's medieval levels of bullshit."

"You don't know the half of it." Trey laughed without mirth. "*All* the Miskatonic students are more valuable to their parents dead than alive. And Courtney..."

"What about Courtney?"

"I think her mother saw her as a threat. Courtney was younger and hotter and she had a talent for design. She had a huge following on LiveJournal. She would have become one of the earliest online influencers. Then the next thing, she's tragically killed in a fire."

My heart hammered in my chest. "Spell it out for me, Bloomberg. What are you saying?"

Trey glanced toward the door, as if checking we were alone. He reached across and grabbed my hand, knitting his fingers in mine. "No one else knows this. No one's ever talked about it. Maybe they all think it, but I doubt that. That's the whole point. Everyone is far too wrapped up in their own shit to see."

"To see what?" I whispered.

"That *we* were the first sacrifice," Trey choked on the words. "That it was no accident we were killed in that fire."

My stomach twisted. If that was true... Their parents sent them to this school knowing they'd be sacrificed, all so they could get their hands on the power of the god. They did all this to keep their place in the world.

Fuck.

If what Trey said was true... I literally *stared into the face of hate itself*, and nothing that Great Old God had thrown at me compared to the horror of what their parents had done.

Good old human evil tops interdimensional cosmic deity yet again.

If it's true.

I knew a thing or two about trauma, and dying in a fire then being brought back from the dead wins the prize in the 'who's more fucked up' lottery. This cruel, remote King was still processing that dark shit. No wonder Trey was so detached, so driven to keep repeating the same year with the same result. If he kept pretending he was King of Kings at this school, then he didn't have to face what was really going on.

I remembered those words he'd scrawled across the college prospectus in his room. NO FUTURE. NO HOPE. NO TOMORROW.

I rested my hand on Trey's, squeezing his shaking fingers. "I believe you, but do you think there's a possibility that you've convinced yourself this is true because you hate your father that much?"

"You're right about one thing," he spat. "I *do* hate him."

"And with good reason. Quinn and I just snuck through that secret passage and listened in to their conversation." I told Trey everything I remembered of what we'd overheard, about how the god's powers were waning outside the school, how Ms. West was getting impatient for what she saw as her *reward*, and how his father was going to find leverage on me, whatever *that* meant.

Trey rested his head in his hands. "Fuck."

"My thoughts exactly."

"Hazel." He turned to me, and his amber eyes swam with tender regret. The Trey Bloomberg who gripped my fingers like he was holding on for dear life wasn't the same as the cruel King who'd tormented me. Soft heat glowed in my chest. For the first time, he lowered his perfect rich bad boy facade, and behind it was the same chaos that lurked inside me.

"I'm here."

Trey rubbed a finger over my knuckles, and it was one of the most tender things I'd ever felt. He let out a long breath. "I'm so sorry they chose you. I'm sorry because I let you make that stupid fucking deal. Mostly, I'm sorry for making your life here so miserable before."

Whoa. An apology. I didn't expect that. "Were you that cruel to all the scholarship students?"

"I learned from the best." Trey looked away again. "No, I wasn't. At the party... I was holding you over the edge. I wanted the others to think I was going to drop you, but I made sure I held you tight. I was never going to drop you. We knew that hurting you hurt the god. Ms. West told us to lay off, but we thought if we pushed a little further, we might be free. But then your body went limp. You *wanted* to die and I..." he gulped. "I know I did that. I broke your spirit. It was what I was supposed to do, but I hate myself for it and I know I can't ever make it up to you, but..."

"Don't do that," I choked out.

"I'm trying to apologize to you."

"Yes, and you didn't do a bad job, for your first time. But don't be sorry for them choosing me. You had nothing to do with it, and besides, *I'm* not sorry. It seems to me I was exactly what this dump needed." I stood up and brushed off my skirt. "And as for making it up to me, I know what will be a good start."

"What?"

I beckoned him with my finger. "Dry your eyes, rich boy. Follow me."

CHAPTER TWENTY-ONE

We went back to my room and waited until dark. It was strange seeing Trey Bloomberg sitting on the edge of my shitty bed, his gorgeous ass sinking into the broken springs as he tried to pretend he wasn't freaked out by the scritch-scritch-scritch of the rats in the walls. Surprisingly, we found a lot to talk about – books we enjoyed, movies we hated, dreams we gave up on.

When the clock struck eleven, I hauled him to his feet and shoved him out the door. Trey trailed after me as we crept across the atrium into the classroom wing. Our feet padded against the polished stone floors. At the end of the hall, I stopped outside the door to the art suite. Neither Trey nor I were taking art as a subject, but I'd spent enough time in the art suite at my old school with Dante that I figured they'd have what I wanted.

Annoyingly, they didn't. After picking the lock on the studio door, I searched all the cabinets but couldn't find any spray paint. Apparently, rich kids spent their time trying to copy the masters instead of experimenting with street art. Never mind. I found some thick square-headed brushes and two cans of red paint. I shoved them into Trey's hands.

"Why do we need these?" He asked.

"You ask too many questions, Bloomberg." I threw the door open and beckoned him to follow me. "Come on, spoiled King. Keep up."

"Hazel, what are we doing here?"

Trey and I stood opposite the gym, staring up at the dressed stone facade of the building.

I gestured to the wall with my brush. "I thought it was obvious. We're going to graffiti that wall." I shoved the edge of the palette knife under the rim of the can and popped off the lid.

Trey's eyes bugged out of his head. "We can't do that."

"Why not?" I grinned.

"*Why not?* Because that wall has stood for over five hundred years. Parris laid the first stone himself. It's *historical*."

"So? It will continue to stand. It will just be a little... decorated." I swirled my brush around in the paint. "Come on, Trey. You said yourself, there's no future behind the walls of this school. The only reason people don't do shit like this is because they're afraid. But what's there to be afraid of when you're already fucking dead?"

"Plenty." A shudder ran through Trey's body.

"Okay fine, so that star-gobbling deity could devour your soul or whatever. But if it's so all-powerful, it's got better things to do than worry about a couple of kids slapping some paint on a wall. Here, I'll show you."

"Hazel, no!" Trey grabbed for my brush, but I darted around him and slapped a long diagonal line across the stones. Red paint dribbled down the wall, like rivers of blood.

"And look, I can make it into a dick," I smirked to myself as I turned the line into an enormous cock, complete with a huge set of balls. "Because this school is full of dicks. Consider it a class portrait."

Trey made a choking noise. His shoulders trembled with suppressed laughter.

"Come on, rich boy. Your whole life you've done everything that's been asked of you. And where's it got you? King of a school of reanimated corpses, that's where." I slashed my paintbrush across the wall, painting a tic-tac-toe board. "Go on, it's cathartic, I swear."

Trey's hand trembled. Red paint splattered on the starched collar of his shirt as he raised the brush. His shoulders tensed. The earth wobbled on its axis.

He pressed the brush into the stone, pulling away to leave a small red dot.

"Bloomberg, you rebel." I slapped him on the shoulder. I could practically see the adrenaline surging through his veins.

A wicked grin spread across Trey's lips, a smile that skipped stones across the river of my soul. He stared at the brush in his hand. After what felt like an eternity, he dipped it in the paint.

With two lines, Trey slashed a red cross into the tic-tac-toe board. Giggling, I placed a circle. He won, hooting and hollering as he enacted a dorky victory dance that was more appropriate for a major lottery win than a kid's game that was rigged from the start.

An accurate metaphor for life.

I'd never imagined Trey like this, giddy with childish joy. He laughed and whooped as he slapped the paint as high as he could reach. We covered the wall in immature drawings, then collapsed on the grass to relish our orgy of rebellion. The historic wall was completely covered in dancing dicks, stick-figure representations of teachers involved in all manner of lewd activities, and some wonderfully poetic curse-words.

"Jizzwizard?" I pointed to a word Trey had just finished. "Where'd you come up with that?"

"Quinn said it to Ayaz once. It has a certain permeance."

"Of course. And who's that?" I asked, pointing to a caricature of a man with his mouth open, ready to suck on the enormous cock I'd drawn.

"My dad," he replied, placing his hands behind his head and grinning up at his creation. "He thinks he's this powerful leader, but really he's just doing the bidding of his god. He's a pawn, just like me."

"You don't have to be a pawn. Do you think when we're free of this place, you'll go to college?"

Beside me, Trey's body stiffened. "You keep saying 'when,'" he said, his voice straining. "But it's never going to happen."

"Have a little faith. I'm clever. Ayaz isn't too bad himself. We're going to crack this."

"I know you're clever. And you're stubborn and strong, too. But you can't stubborn your way out of this. The Great Old God has been trapped in that void for over five hundred years, drawing power from despairing souls. No one's even come close to defeating it."

"That's because no one *wanted* to fight it."

"We don't know that. Maybe there were people in Parris' circle who tried to stand up to him, and—"

"We *do* know that, because we know the people who are attracted to its power are exactly those who can't resist it. Think of who your father might be if he was free from this need to control everyone and everything around him," I touched my hand to his. "Think of who *you* might be."

Trey shuddered. It was like he was shrugging off a heavy cloak that had been dragging him down.

"People who are truly free... they would never come to a place like Derleth Academy in the first place. They don't need it."

"Then why are you here?" he whispered, turning to me, his amber eyes burning.

"Isn't it obvious?" I whispered back.

Trey's lips brushed mine, not hot and needy like they had been before, but soft and warm and searching, brushing against mine with a featherlight touch.

This was the guy who'd been my tormenter from the moment I arrived at this school. He'd been specifically *selected* to unleash my own personal hell, and he'd done an admirable job. He'd broken me down, very nearly destroyed me. But in the process, he was destroying himself, and in this kiss we started to rebuild the broken walls—

"Is someone out there?" Professor Atwood called. I jerked my head up. Trey swore, rubbing his lip.

Two shadowed figures stepped out from the side entrance. Flashlight beams crisscrossed over the tennis courts.

"What do we do?" Trey looked terrified.

I grabbed his hand, yanking him to his feet. "We run!"

I took off toward the trees, Trey hot on my heels. I threw a glance over my shoulder. Light darted across the field only a few feet behind me. I dived into the rose bushes. Thorns snagged at my uniform, scraping my skin and probably putting runs in my last good pair of stockings. I ran on, listening for Trey's heavy breathing in my wake. The roses widened out into a small clearing. I pulled Trey down into it, the pair of us crouching in the fallen leaves and rosehips, clutching each other as we listened hard for our pursuers.

"I thought I saw a couple of students out here," Atwood said, his voice loud and clear in the still night.

"You sure it wasn't one of the aberrations?" I recognized Doctor Halsey's voice. "They've been more active lately."

"It must've been. They're gone now. I just... look at that, on the wall!"

Halsey swore. "Those rotten kids. Hermia isn't going to like this."

"With the Eldritch Club breathing down her neck? That's the understatement of the decade. We'd better go tell her."

I waited for what seemed like forever. When my injured leg

could no longer stand the pain of crouching down, I stood up, casting an eye across the field. It was empty, for now.

"Come on." I grabbed Trey's hand, dragging him out of the bushes. We emerged further west, closer to the dormitory building. Flashlights started to appear near the gym. I linked arms with Trey and the two of us flew to the fire exit, which we'd propped open with a piece of broken masonry.

I slammed into the door, shoving it open. The two of us dived inside, sprawling across the marble tiles, fighting to catch our breath.

"That was..." Trey struggled to his feet. He pulled me up and we leaned against each other, holding tight as we half gasped, half cackled with laughter. "My heart's beating a mile a minute. Is this what life in the hood is like?"

"Oh sure," I grinned back. "White graffiti artist like you, you'd fit right in."

"You know, I think this is the most fun I've ever had." Trey bent down, his lips inches from mine. I leaned forward and pressed my lips to his, eager to continue what we started before. Trey's lips brushed against mine, his tongue yielding. I reached up to touch his cheek.

He tore himself away from me, clutching his head in his hands.

"What?" I demanded. "Don't want to kiss the charity case anymore?"

"That's not it," he growled, backing down the corridor. "I promised myself I wouldn't do this to you."

"Wouldn't do what?"

"Hazel, I treated you like *shit*."

"I remember," I said darkly. "I was there."

"Right. So I can't do this. I don't deserve it. I don't deserve *you*."

I rubbed my lip. A part of me wanted to say, *what about what I want?* But he was right – I wasn't going to beg Trey Bloomberg for anything, even if my body still surged with heat, with *need*.

I shrugged. "If that's what you want."

The look on Trey's face said what he wanted and what he thought he deserved were a universe apart. "Yes," he said, and then louder, more definite. "Yes. It's what I want. I want to earn you."

"Fine."

"Fine." He sucked in a breath. "Okay then. Goodnight."

"Yeah." I watched him turn, walk away from me. His body disappeared into the darkened corridor, cloaking himself in the night. A ghost retreating into the spirit realm, leaving behind only a cold spot and a shiver down the spine.

My spine was tingling all right, but not from cold. I pressed my finger to the scar on my wrist as a sick feeling crept across my chest. I thought about the revenge I was plotting. Of all the monarchs, Trey was the one who most deserved my punishment. His relentless cruelty had nearly broken me. When he held me over that cliff, something inside me snapped. I'd *wanted* him to let go.

I had to make these rich kids understand that they couldn't treat people like that. They needed to be punished. So why did I feel so guilty about what I was about to do?

Was it because Trey Bloomberg was already punishing himself?

CHAPTER TWENTY-TWO

"Psst." Nancy pretended to drop her books beside my desk in History class. I bent over so we could whisper to each other. "There's an Eldritch Club meeting tonight."

"Oh?"

"It's probably best you make an appearance. There's going to be a vote about the leadership of the Club. Courtney's hoping you guys don't show up."

"So Trey and Quinn and Ayaz don't know about this?"

"Trey knows," she whispered back. "I think he's trying to protect you by keeping you away, but I believe you deserve the chance to stick up for yourself."

I was touched. Nancy had never been one of the worst bullies, but she had laughed along with the others when Trey and Courtney filled my locker with rotting meat and Ayaz had tossed maggots in my breakfast. She was guilty, too, but she seemed to be trying to make amends. I felt a familiar stab at the idea that if I could make my revenge happen, she'd be hurt by it, too.

"Thanks, Nancy."

"No worries. See you at the bloodbath."

After class, I grabbed Greg at his locker. "Eldritch Club

meeting tonight," I whispered, casting my eyes around the corridor, hoping Courtney or one of her minions weren't keeping tabs on us. "Can you tell Andre?"

"If I see him." Greg stacked his books inside his locker. "He didn't come back to our room last night."

"Shit." He hadn't sat with us at breakfast or lunch, either. "But wait, I saw him in class today. English Lit."

Greg nodded. "Yeah. He was in my chemistry lab. But he didn't say anything to me."

"He never says anything."

"You know what I mean." Greg slammed his locker. Hard. The metal banged, making him jump. "Sorry. I'm still not sleeping well. I'm a little jumpy. I just wish I knew why he's avoiding us."

Andre's disappearances played on my mind as I made my way back to my room after dinner. If he was seeing a girl, that was awesome, but I wished he'd talk to me or Greg about it. Especially Greg – that guy needed one less thing to worry about. I closed my bedroom door, turned around and—

A fist swung out and slammed into my face.

"Ow!" I staggered back, cupping my hand over my nose. I tasted metal.

A figure stepped out of the shadows. The light clicked on, blinding me momentarily. "Hello, gutter whore," Courtney snarled. Behind her, John Hyde-Jones grinned maniacally.

Shit.

How did they get into my room?

Adrenaline pounded behind my eyes. My fight-or-flight response was permanently set to *fight*. I swung my fist, whooping with delight at the satisfying thwack it made when I connected with Courtney's jaw.

Her head snapped back. She staggered and tripped over the bed, going down in a tornado of shrieking and flailing limbs. Unfortunately, that only created space for her goon squad to close in on me.

John leered in my face as he reached out to grab me. I ducked and got one good, solid kick between his legs before someone pinned my arms behind my back.

"Fuck... her... up!" John gasped, dropping to his knees. His face twisted in agony as he cupped his balls.

"With pleasure." Tillie surged forward, an evil smirk on her face.

I kicked and screamed and struggled with everything I had. My foot slammed into Tillie's stomach and she doubled over. But there were six of them and one of me, and not a lot of space to move. Derek swiped my legs from under me and slammed me on the floor. My jaw cracked on the bare stone. Stars danced in my vision. My ears rang and for a moment I forgot where I was.

Scritch-scritch-scritch. The rats circled overhead, roused by the smell of blood.

Then the group started kicking me, drawing me back to my body and all the trouble I was. Pain rained down on me – a flurry of feet and fists and foul words that shattered the adrenaline so I felt every blow. My mind struggled to process what was happening, what I should do in this situation. I tried to go for the shard in my sleeve, but someone kicked it out of my hand. Heavy boots crushed my fingers, pinning my wrist to the ground.

As the blows rained down, the god – *their* god – cried in its prison. Vile visions forced their way into my head as it lost another sliver of control, as its power waned and its grip on our world slid even further. I wondered vaguely why the students couldn't feel it, but then a swift kick to the stomach slammed the air from my lungs and I didn't wonder about anything.

I curled into a ball, protecting my face with my hands as I tried to lash out with my feet. They grabbed my ankles, held me down. "Spread her legs," I heard John say. Dimly, I knew this was bad, but I couldn't force my body to move as fast as I needed to.

"There's no time," Courtney leaned over me. She hocked a wad of spit into my face.

Her spittle rolled down my cheek, hot and humiliating. I'd never wanted to hurt anyone as much as I wanted to hurt this bitch, but she had me over a barrel and she knew it.

"You got lucky, whore. You were late showing up to this party, so you miss out on the punishment you deserve. But we've got to run. We have the reputation of the Eldritch Club to save." Courtney stepped back, and Derek came forward, holding a length of rope. Fresh panic surged inside me. I bucked, trying to roll away, but Tillie still had her foot on my wrist, crushing my hand.

"The guys will notice I'm gone," I gasped, as Derek wrenched my arms behind my back, lashing my hands together.

"No they won't," Courtney sang in a singsong voice. "Dear Trey is trying to keep you away from us, so he hasn't even told you about tonight's meeting. They won't know anything is wrong until after the meeting, and I'm sure there will be so much to discuss that by then it will be too late. You're a disgrace to everything the club stands for, and to the name of our school," she hissed. "You've been warned, but still you insist on tainting everything with your filth. We're here to clean house."

Courtney held up a clear glass bottle with a screw top – one of the cleaning liquids the maintenance staff used to polish the marble floors. "Open wide, *Hazy*." Quinn's nickname grated in her nasal voice.

I jerked my head away. Tillie slapped my cheek so hard tears stung in my eyes. John grabbed my jaw and wrenched it open. I bucked and struggled, but there were too many of them. The bottle came closer, closer...

I tried to picture flames engulfing my body like they had in the cave, pushing out in a giant fireball and burning Courtney fucking Haynes to ashes. But nothing came except a spasm of fear. I was too far gone, too wrapped up in the god's visions and the pain and humiliation. I couldn't find the flames. I couldn't even save myself.

Burning liquid hit the back of my throat. I squeezed my eyes shut. Panic seized my body. I tried to spit the stuff back out, but they kept pouring in more and more. It burned all the way down, searing my insides with a pain so intense I knew I had only moments before I passed out. I could even *smell* burning – an acrid, chemical odor that drove my panic to new heights.

Inside its void, the god howled.

Emptiness burned behind my eyes – a sickening black fog that started in my brain and spread through my whole body, taking away the pain on a cloud of oblivion.

Darkness took me.

CHAPTER TWENTY-THREE

"She drank poison. Quick, you have to help her!"

My insides are on fire.

I bounced in someone's arms as a panicked voice called over my head. I was being carried into the school infirmary. Old Waldron leapt up from her desk. The person carrying me dumped me on the bed, rolling me over onto my side, placing me in the recovery position, stroking my cheek with tenderness.

"Please." His voice cracked. "I don't know what to do."

Quinn. He was here. He'd come to save me. My arms ached to reach out and hold him, but no matter how many messages my brain sent out to my limbs, they wouldn't move. The inferno inside me raged against my skin. My vision swam. Quinn grew three heads that all spoke in unison.

"Hazy? Hazy? *Hazy.*"

I tried to tell him what had happened, but my lips were tendrils of flame. As they moved through the air they turned to ashes. Three Old Waldrons leered over me, three warts bobbling in my vision as she lifted my eyelids and poked around inside my mouth. "You said she *drank* poison? Why would she do a thing like that?"

"You have to do something!" The three Quinns were crying.

"Maybe it's for the best," a calm voice spoke from the door.

The temperature in the infirmary dropped. All I could make out was a shadow moving around the bed, trailing black robes across the floor.

"Hazel Waite has become increasingly paranoid and erratic," Ms. West's voice boomed through the room. She knelt down beside me, her long fingers stroking my hair. Three pale faces with red slashes for lips wobbled in my vision. "I've had reports from other students she's been picking fights, tormenting others, defacing school property, experiencing hallucinations. Given her history, I suspect she's suffering from a type of delayed psychosis."

"What would you know about it?" The Quinns demanded.

"I used to work in the health sector," she replied, leaning over my bed. Her fingers felt like knives slicing through my skin. "I've seen cases like this before. Patients who've lived with years of neglect and abuse who experience trauma often fall into a pattern of paranoid psychosis. When coupled with a persecution complex, as Hazel demonstrates, we have a profoundly disturbed student who is a danger to herself, and to others."

"They tried to kill me!" I managed to choke out. I rocked my body, trying to throw myself off the bed.

Ms. West threw me back. "Fancy drinking floor polish and then trying to blame it on another student," she tsked. "This must stop, Hazel. I'm giving you one more chance to get this under control, because I know how much you want to be here at Derleth. But if I hear of one more incident like this, I'll have you sent away, somewhere you can get professional help."

Then her head exploded into a cloud of black shadow. My skin sliced open, and everything went dark as the pain dragged me under.

I woke with a start. I wasn't in the infirmary, but on a hard stone floor with my stomach heaving. *If that was a dream, then where am I now?*

My body convulsed as a spasm of pain shot through me. I lay in agony, waiting for the convulsions to ease. I tried to push myself off the cold ground, but my arms wouldn't move. Something sharp dug into my wrist.

"Who is that?" A voice called out, muffled in the gloom. "Hazel, is that you?"

"Greg?" I choked out, rocking on my stomach. The smell of rotting flesh hung in the air, sweet and fetid. My stomach heaved, and I dissolved into a coughing fit.

"Yeah." Greg broke down into a hacking cough of his own. "Did they make you drink..."

"...floor polish? Yeah. I can't—" I bent over as my stomach was seized by a violent spasm. Tears rolled down my cheeks as I threw up the contents.

Across the room, Greg was also making retching sounds. I spat on the ground and tried to roll away. My wrists ached from being tied behind me. The stench was so thick here that it felt like the smell had form, that it draped over me like a blanket. I couldn't even wipe my mouth.

Greg's arm brushed my back. "Sit up if you can," he said. "Perhaps if we move close enough, one of us could untie the other."

"Good idea." I rocked onto my side, curling my legs up to force myself into a sitting position. My body screamed in protest. Every movement was agony, but I managed to pull myself up. I shuffled backward until my spine pressed against Greg's. After a little more fumbling we clasped our fingers awkwardly.

"I'll try you first." Greg curled his fingers under the rope that bound my wrist. It dug into my skin, pressing against the bruises from the beating and the scar on my wrist until red welts appeared in front of my eyes. I was dimly aware of the god's pain, but it held nothing to my own. Greg grunted as he wiggled and tugged, but the bonds didn't loosen.

"It's no good," he sighed, sliding out his fingers. "I can't bend the way I need to pull the ropes through."

"Okay. I'll try you." I dug my fingers into Greg's ropes, feeling out the knot. Immediately, I ran into the same problem. I could tug a bit of the rope, but then I couldn't pull it under and out. My fingers just wouldn't bend that way. Nothing on my body worked right. But I wasn't going to give up.

"Maybe there's something in this room we can use," I said. "Like an old nail or a super handy knife. We could cut the ropes. Where are we, anyway?"

Scritch-scritch-scritch.

For the first time, I focused on the space, aware not only of the odor but of the vastness around me, and the noise. We were in a large dark room, with rats circling behind the walls.

Scritch-scritch-scrrrrrrritch. They seemed to be growing in number.

"I've had a little crawl around. I think it's a disused classroom. There's an old blackboard on the wall and a bunch of desks stacked up."

"Any windows?" Maybe we could smash the glass, use it to cut the ropes, and then crawl outside.

"They're boarded up. That's why it's so dark in here."

Damn, knew that would be too easy. "Okay, that's something. If the boards are old, maybe we can get some of the nails out and use those—"

"Hey!" Greg sounded bright. "You don't happen to still have that glass shiv on you?"

I felt around my sleeve, then remembered. "No. I lost it in the attack."

I tried to twist my feet under my body so I could lever myself up. Halfway there, my stomach heaved, and I broke down into another coughing fit.

When my stomach stopped convulsing, I pulled my wretched body to my feet and stumbled around the dark room. My face smacked into a wall. *Right, found the blackboard.*

Greg groaned as he pulled himself up. "The windows are over here," he called out. I stumbled through the darkness, heading in the direction of his voice. "How long do you think we've been here?"

"If I had to guess, I'd say long enough to miss the Eldritch Club meeting," I said darkly.

"They made us drink poison," Greg's voice shook. "We could have *died.*"

"I know," I whispered. "I know."

Apparently, the tattoo on my wrist meant nothing. The senior members of the Eldritch Club knew about the agreement I'd made. But Greg and Andre were supposed to be off-limits, which meant that maybe Courtney didn't know about the agreement, or that she was deliberately going against it...

Greg and Andre...

"Greg," I choked out. "Were you with Andre when they caught you?"

"Oh, shit," Greg breathed. "No, I wasn't. He was off somewhere. Hazel, what if he's..."

What if he's somewhere in this room with us, unconscious... or worse? My thighs smacked against metal chair legs. "Andre," I yelled, kicking around the floor, hoping and not hoping I'd find his body. "If you can hear us, make a noise. Kick something if you can. Andre, please..."

"Andre! Andre!" Something metal clattered and Greg swore.

A bright shaft of light fell over the room. I squinted into the brightness. *What the fuck now?*

A shadow moved across the beam of light. "Hazy? Are you in here?"

CHAPTER TWENTY-FOUR

"Quinn?" I choked out, my knees buckling.

"Hazy?" The shadow moved toward me. A warm hand circled my arm. I lurched myself toward him. My foot caught the edge of a metal chair. Without my hands to break the fall I went down hard, sprawling across the ground at Quinn's feet. A spasm of pain rocked my body.

"Owww," I moaned, rolling over and curling my legs to my chest.

Quinn pulled me into a sitting position. "Hazy, what have they done to you?"

"I'm fine," I cried. "Can you see Andre anywhere? Greg's here too but we can't find Andre... They made us drink cleaning liquid. He might be..."

I couldn't make the word pass my lips.

"I'll look." Quinn circled the room twice, coughing as he kicked aside the metal chairs and checked under every table and behind every box. "Fuck, it reeks in here. Greg, mate, you need to lay off the beans. Nope, he's not here. What the hell's that noise in the walls?"

Relief flooded through me, to be replaced a moment later by

fear. If Andre wasn't here, where was he? Had they done something else to him?

"We have to find him," I murmured, trying to force myself to my feet again.

"Get back here," Quinn growled, grabbing my arms. He tugged at the ropes. My hands dropped free. I flexed the fingers, wincing at the red welts where the rope had dug in, while Quinn freed Greg.

"Can you guys walk?" Quinn leaned under my shoulder, practically dragging me toward the door. "We've got to get to that meeting. Trey needs our help."

"I... I think so." I tried to stand under my own weight, but my knees buckled. Quinn looped my arm over his and half dragged, half carried me out of there.

Halfway up the stairs, I had to stop to throw up again. Greg fell on the landing, his face deathly pale.

"Shit, man, you don't look good." Quinn slid his arms under Greg and hoisted him over his shoulder. "Hazel, I'm going to carry him the rest of the way, but I'll be back for you."

"It's fine." I hauled myself to my feet. "I'll manage."

Quinn shot me a desperate look, but he continued up the stairs with Greg. I dragged my wretched body up behind them as fast as I could. We were on the main staircase that led up into the atrium, which meant the classroom we'd been in was deep beneath the school, near the gymnasium.

That explains the horrid smell and the scritching. And that's why I had that vivid dream about being in the infirmary – because we're near the god's prison. His influence is stronger here.

Quinn raced for the open doors that led from the atrium down onto the quad. He had to stop there to set Greg down while he emptied his stomach again. I pitched myself across the quad, trying to ignore the pain shooting up my legs. *We're almost there. We're so close...*

The dining hall doors swung open. Courtney strutted out like a catwalk model, Tillie, Amber, Derek, and John flanking her. "Hazel, Greg, Quinn, so nice of you to join us," she smirked. The doors swung shut behind her as she descended the steps toward us.

"You poisoned us," I choked out. I pooled saliva in my mouth and spat at her. I was so weak it landed on the cobbles a foot in front of me. There was blood in it.

"Nonsense, silly. I can't do anything to harm fellow members of the Eldritch Club. You can't use that as an excuse for your own tardiness. Unfortunately, you're too late. We've just adjourned the meeting after a very exciting vote." Courtney twirled a string of blonde extensions around her finger and flashed a villainous smile. "You're looking at the new president of the Eldritch Club."

CHAPTER TWENTY-FIVE

"I'm sorry, Hazy. I should have been faster." Quinn collapsed on Trey's couch. For the first time since he'd rescued us, I took a good look at him.

What I saw made my stomach churn.

Quinn's eyes had swelled up. His right one was completely shut, and the left was already coloring. Sweat clung to his brow and plastered his shirt to his torso. A long cut along his jaw had leaked blood onto his collar. He clasped his hands in his lap, like he didn't know what to do with them anymore.

"Does anyone know where Andre is?" Greg asked. He gripped the edge of Trey's counter, looking like he was about to keel over.

"Nancy says she overheard Courtney talking to John about him. He was scheduled into one of the music rooms, but when they went there to find him, the room was empty. So it looks like he saw them coming and hid." Trey paced in front of his plasma TV. "He's cleverer than the rest of us. Quinn, what happened?"

Quinn tried to smile, but his mouth wobbled. "My dad showed up at school. He wanted to have a conversation."

I fell to his side and wrapped my arms around him. He winced.

"What is it?" I grabbed the edge of his shirt. Quinn tried to stop me, but he was too slow. I yanked up the fabric and recoiled in horror.

Long, red welts striped Quinn's back, from his shoulders right down to just above his ass. Blood leaked from several of them, and his flesh hung in ribbons where the lines overlaid each other.

Those are whip marks.

I clamped my hand over my mouth, but I had nothing left inside me to throw up. My stomach churned painfully, and the sting in my throat burned.

"Shit, dude."

I jumped at the sound of Ayaz's voice. I hadn't realized he was here, but then the trip from the quad up to Trey's room was a blur of pain. Every breath tore at my throat and burned in my lungs.

Ayaz slid into the chair opposite, his dark eyes sweeping over Quinn with concern and disgust. His gaze flicked to me, and he instantly looked away.

I can't worry about Ayaz now. Quinn's hurt.

"Your dad did this to you?" My hand reached for the welts, but I couldn't bring myself to touch them. I didn't want to hurt him anymore. "And *then* you carried Greg up the stairs? You must've been in agony."

"Yeah, well." Quinn's single eye rolled back. "Did I impress you? Will you be my girlfriend now?"

Tears sprung in my eyes. My friend Dante had been in and out of abusive foster homes most of his life. My mom had abusive boyfriends. I knew what people who were supposed to care for you were capable of. But I'd never seen anything this... *barbaric*.

We may be dead, Quinn had said. *But we can still bleed.*

He'd endured all that, and yet he still came to save us.

"We have to get you to the nurse," I said. Just saying the words made me think of that weird dream I had, and I shuddered. But this wasn't about me. I was fine... sort of. Quinn was a mess.

"*You* need the nurse," Quinn shot back. As he said it, my throat stung. I broke into another coughing fit.

"No." I choked out. I had a bad feeling that going there would make that nightmare come true. "I won't go there. But you can hardly move, Quinn. I can't even imagine how much it must've hurt to drag yourself this far."

"Do I get a vote?" Greg coughed violently. "Because I think we should *all* go—"

"No." Quinn circled my arm, pulling me back down beside him. "If I go to the infirmary, word will get back to my father and he'll do something worse to me. Or to you, Hazy."

"Me?"

"Yeah." Quinn winced again as he leaned forward, pointing at the wounds. "I'm supposed to take this punishment silently. I got these because I wouldn't agree to stop seeing you. I'm not putting you in front of him for anything."

Shit. My stomach churned, and I almost threw up again. *I don't want to be the cause of this. I don't want Quinn to be hurt.*

Trey set down a carton of milk on the table. "Drink that," he said. "I read that if you swallow poison, you can use milk to help protect your stomach lining."

I swiped it out of his hands and took a long gulp. It felt like a cloud floating down my throat. Cow lactation had never tasted so good. I finished half the carton before I passed it to Greg.

"Trey, do you have a first aid kit?" Greg asked, accepting the carton from me and taking a long sip. "At the very least, we should put some dressings on Quinn's wounds."

"Yeah, I do." Trey went into the bathroom and returned a moment later with a white box. He sat down on the other side of Quinn and pulled out dressings and antiseptic.

"This is going to hurt like a motherfucker," he said as he started to clean the wounds.

"You weren't kidding," Quinn hissed through gritted teeth. His fingers crushed mine as Trey finished his gruesome job, taping dressings over the worst of the wounds. Pain shot up my arm as the hand Tillie had stomped on endured more pain, but it only made the god weaker and meant Quinn kept holding me, so it was worth it.

"What happened in that meeting?" I demanded.

"Exactly what I expected would happen," Trey said. "Courtney had already got to all the other student members. She gave a speech about how the sanctity of the club was in jeopardy, that I had been in charge for too long, and that we needed new leadership to usher in a new era at Miskatonic. She had a stack of support letters from senior members, including my father. That basically sealed the deal. I had a few votes – Paul and Nancy and a couple of others. Quinn and Ayaz might've been able to swing things around, but neither of them was there."

"Ayaz wasn't there?" I swirled around to face him. Ayaz dropped his gaze again, avoiding me, avoiding all of us.

"No… I didn't even know about the meeting. I skipped out on afternoon classes. I went out to—" he shook his head. "It doesn't matter where I went. The point is, I wasn't there when you needed me. I'm sorry, bro."

"It wouldn't have mattered." Trey's voice was flat, emotionless. He was doing what he always did – holding all the darkness inside, keeping it to himself. It was the only way he could retain control.

"I tried to get there, but Courtney…" I coughed, gripping Quinn's shoulder. "I could have done something."

Quinn winced again, but he wrapped me in his arms, pulling me against his chest, so my head rested on his ruined shoulder. He let out a long, slow breath as his fingers stroked my hair. He didn't try to kiss me or lighten the mood with a dumb joke. He just held me and I held him, in a way I hadn't been held since my mother was alive.

This isn't your fault.

"I hate that you're getting beat up because of me," I murmured.

He coughed. "Don't do that. Don't blame yourself, Hazy. Dad doesn't need you to give him a reason."

"Why was your dad even at school today? Doesn't he have a *job*? Why do all your parents care so much about this stupid club and about what you guys do here? They're the ones who—" I tried to say trapped, but my tongue wouldn't form the word. I reminded myself that Greg was in the room, and changed what I was saying. "—*sent* you to this school in the first place."

"Because we represent our family honor." Trey grabbed the first aid kit and started rooting through it. He pulled out a sachet of burn relief cream and another dressing. "Even though we're—" *dead*, I finished for him in my head "—*invisible* to the world, we are supposed to make this school a miniature representation of the world order. I thought that as the King of Kings, I had the power to decide who would rise and fall, but I miscalculated. I'm just as expendable as the rest of you. We can't count on the protection of the Eldritch Club any longer."

Gritting his teeth, Trey rolled up his sleeve. I gasped. Where his Eldritch Club tattoo had been, there was now an ugly patch of charred flesh.

CHAPTER TWENTY-SIX

"Look what Hazel did to my hair!" Courtney screamed, waving a bottle of doctored shampoo in Ms. West's face. "She put chemicals in my shampoo and now my hair is falling out!"

"Is this true, Hazel?" Ms. West steepled her fingers and leaned over her desk, eyes sweeping over me with a mixture of curiosity and disdain.

"You can't prove anything," I shot back, leaning back in the hard chair that faced Ms. West's desk. I was no stranger to the chair. It had cradled my ass many times since I arrived at Derleth.

"I can so." Courtney grabbed my bookbag. I yelled and grabbed for it, but she dumped it out on the floor. Books, pens, and Turkish Delight candies I nicked from Ayaz's kitchen scattered across the floor. Courtney grabbed a bottle of shampoo and dropped it on Ms. West's desk.

"Get one of the chemistry nerds to test that." Courtney folded her arms and smirked at me. "I bet it's got all sorts of weird stuff in it."

Ms. West pushed her glasses down her nose, regarding the bottle with interest. "Hazel, is this true?"

I shrugged. I didn't care if they knew. What were they going to do to me? What was a little detention when they already planned to feed me to their god? "She got what she deserved. I only did it because she poured tar all over my hair," I shot back. "I was nearly sick from the fumes and I had to cut off all my hair. Personally, I think she got off lightly."

"That's not true," Ms. West said. "The first week you arrived on campus I took you to Old Waldron. She cut off your filthy dreadlocks. They were a health risk for the student body – we couldn't have a lice outbreak."

"No, *Courtney* and Trey broke into my room and put tar in my hair."

"Do you mean Trey, your boyfriend?"

"He's not my boyfriend. And she filled my locker with rotting meat and—"

"Stop," Ms. West snapped. "I've heard enough of your baseless accusations, Hazel. I don't need to remind you that *you* were the one reprimanded for throwing meat around in the halls. You admitted that you put that meat in your *own* locker so you could deliver it to Courtney's dorm."

"Her bullying is out of control." Courtney folded her arms and stuck out her lower lip. "I just don't understand why Hazel hates me so much."

"You being a vile, manipulative bitch might have something to do with it," I pointed out.

"*Hazel*, that's enough." Ms. West stood. Her black skirts swirled around her feet as she held open her office door. "Thank you for bringing this to my attention, Ms. Haynes. Please, return to class. Derleth Academy has a zero tolerance policy for bullying. You and your parents can rest assured we will be dealing with this issue."

Courtney flashed me a pitying smirk and flounced out of the room, leaving me alone with Ms. West.

I expected the headmistress to yell at me. Instead, she knelt down beside me. Her eyes swam with this weird look that someone who hadn't seen her try to throw a student into the void might mistake for kindness. "Hazel, I'm concerned about you. All your teachers are. You've been lashing out ever since you arrived at this school. I've had many scholarship students arrive at Derleth with a chip on their shoulder, and none of them had your history of trauma. Derleth could be a turning point in your life, a chance to cast off the cards you've been dealt and make a fresh start. We want to help you, but we can't do that if you fight us at every turn."

"What is this shit?" I narrowed my eyes at her. "Drop this concerned teacher act. This school isn't a 'fresh start,' it's a death trap."

"I don't know what you're talking about, dear." She placed her icy fingers over my hand. "You're clearly still dealing with unresolved trauma from your mother's death. I think you may need to speak to a professional. We can arrange that—"

I flung myself out of bed. My feet tangled in the sheets, trapping me under the blankets as I fought to wrap my hands around Ms. West's neck and choke the life out of her. It took me a few moments to realize that I was no longer in her office, but in my own bed in my cold dorm room, and that the whole altercation with Courtney had been another strange dream.

Scritch-scritch-scritch. The rats in the walls circled overhead. I smiled. That sound had become a comfort. It centered me, brought me back to where I belonged.

The dream haunted me as I swung out of bed and gathered my things for the shower. I closed my hand around the bottle of shampoo I'd stolen from Courtney's room when I'd replaced hers. *That was weird. It was like I'd entered another reality – one where I was the bully instead of Courtney. Except that it was all kind of true.* Hearing my own actions thrown back at me like that gave me a sick feeling in my stomach.

Or maybe that was just the residual impact of being *poisoned*.

I can't believe I'm thinking this, but if you're listening to my thoughts, Great Old God, I'd like to go back to the hate-filled nightmares, thanks.

Or maybe the dream was telling me something else. I bent down and checked the gap between the desk and the wall, where I'd hidden the things I'd collected so far for my final punishment plan. I was building a decent stash. All I had left to do was set a date.

I needed an event involving the whole school. But the second quarter was drawing to a close, which meant exams were starting next week. There were no school dances or parent days until next quarter. Could I wait that long?

Would I survive that long?

CHAPTER TWENTY-SEVEN

When Trey and I reached the library during our free period, we discovered his 'usual' table had been usurped. Tillie flashed us a satisfied smirk as she opened out her books, and Derek cracked his knuckles, daring us to make a scene.

Trey's back stiffened. He stepped toward them, but I yanked him down into a nearby chair. "What are you *doing?* Derek is eighty percent neck. He'll smash your pretty face into a pulp."

"This is a direct hit on my power," he hissed. "I can't show weakness."

"It's a *table*," I said, the words burning my damaged throat. "Get over it."

Trey glanced over his shoulder. Tillie laughed at something Derek said. She went in for a hair-flip but seemed to forget she was wearing a beanie to cover her ruined hair, so all she succeeded in doing was looking like she had a neck cramp. I started to laugh, but that hurt my throat even worse.

"You've got to stop thinking like a monarch," I said to Trey. "You're not one of them anymore. Ninety-nine percent of people don't have a special table in the library, and you don't see them crying about it. We've got more important things to worry about, like what's up with Ayaz and where he went the other day when he should have been at the vote."

"I talked to Ayaz. He isn't a problem." Trey slid his math book across the table and lowered his voice. "Did you find Andre?"

I let out a sigh of relief. "Yeah, he came back to Greg's room that night. He said he'd been hanging out with someone and hadn't even heard about the meeting. So that's a relief. I hope they don't—"

A huge book slammed on my desk, startling me out of thought.

"Fuck!" I threw my pen at Ayaz. "Don't just throw books at people without warning."

"I found something." Ayaz slid into the seat beside Trey and started flipping through a dusty book. "I went back to the cave where you saw Zehra, but I couldn't find—"

"Whoa." I held up my hands. "Back up the Ayaz-wagon. Are we talking again?"

"We were always talking," he snapped.

"No, we weren't. You flounced out of the library the other week and haven't spoken a word to me since. We lost a week of study because you've got your head stuck up your ass. So what gives?"

Ayaz and Trey exchanged one of their meaningful glances. "I had some shit to work out." Ayaz softened his voice, his words like velvet. He tapped the book in his hand. "Do you want to hear what I found?"

"Yes. But first... you said you went to the cave. Was this during the Eldritch Club meeting?"

His eyes darkened. "Yes. If I'd known they would pull that stunt, I never would've—"

"It's fine," Trey said quickly. His hand cupped his wrist, where his tattoo had been burned off. "It would've happened even with you there."

Another meaningful glance between them. I wished I could be

inside their heads. I bet it was a real circus in there. Ayaz met my eyes, the intensity of his stare starting a fire blazing across my chest. "Hazel, I couldn't find any trace of that sigil you saw."

"It was there, I swear it. And it lit up when the fire started."

"I believe you, but I didn't see it. And that made me wonder why." Ayaz turned the book toward me and pointed to a symbol on the page. "Is what you saw something like this?"

I squinted at the circular sigil. It did look familiar – seeing it in the book made me realize that it had been different to the others I'd seen around the school. The shapes and lines inside it were a unique style. "I think so? Honestly, I might not remember all the details perfectly, considering that at the time I was a little bit busy *running for my life*."

But Ayaz wasn't listening. "It wouldn't be exactly like this one, because it's unlikely what you saw was ever written down. We never found a sigil like this in Parris' book because it's not one of his sigils. It's the sigil of another magician. Rebecca Nurse. She used to be part of Parris' inner circle, but she later became one of his biggest detractors. She went on to study medicine, even though she was forbidden to practice as an African American woman, and she became an early agitator for abolishing slavery."

"What does it mean that her symbol is drawn in a cave on Parris' land?"

Ayaz threw up his hands. "I don't know. I have a theory, but you're not going to like it."

"It's got to be better than long division," I slammed my text-book shut and leaned across the table, running my hands along the edge of the image. "Hit me."

"Parris doesn't detail what caused his falling out with Rebecca, but I'm willing to bet they argued over the Great Old God. We know Parris wanted its power, but maybe Rebecca wanted to send it back where it came from? Anyway, I think that maybe Rebecca was using her sigils to plant some kind of weapon – something that could destroy the god or bind it so Parris couldn't use its power. If she did, then she might have placed some spell on the sigils so that no one in Parris' inner circle could see them."

"Sigils? You think there's more than one."

"From what I can make of this, there has to be." Ayaz ran his hand over the book. His fingers brushed mine, and a surge of heat ran up my arm. "My guess is she didn't finish whatever spell she was trying to work, because otherwise, the god wouldn't still be here. But maybe that sigil you saw is all that's holding the creature in its prison."

"That's a whole lot of maybes. Get to the part I won't like."

Ayaz cleared his throat. "One of two things happened – either someone destroyed the sigil, or there's a reason you can see it and I can't. It might be because you weren't yet a full member of the Eldritch Club, because you hadn't completed the initiation, and neither is Zehra. But there's only one way to find out."

"Oh no, no way." I jerked my hand back. "I escaped that once. I'm not going back."

"It's our only choice."

"Take someone else. Take one of your grotto girls. You could have a little party on the way."

He shook his head sadly. "You know that I can't. It has to be you. For all we know it has something to do with your power."

"Power?" I feigned innocence. "What power?"

"Come on, Hazel." An edge cut through Ayaz's voice. "I read your file. I know you're lying about the fire."

"I don't know what you're talking about." I folded my arms across my chest. My thumb found the scar on my wrist, pressing into it so hard it hurt. I faced off against Ayaz and Trey, who both tried to stare me down – one with eyes of ice, the other with a fire blazing inside him.

"Really?" Trey smirked. "Because you told the police that your friend went to find your mother to tell her you were being hurt by a gang, but the gang followed him and threw a molotov cocktail through a window in the apartment complex. And yet, the police found accelerant on your hands."

No.

That's my secret. And I'm not giving it to either of you. I'm not trusting anyone, ever again.

"I don't have to listen to this." I stood up and slammed the chair back into the table. "I have to go."

For the rest of the day, I fumed in silence. My final class was English Lit. I sat with Andre but he ignored all my notes asking him about where he'd been disappearing to. That was one of the advantages of being mute – you got to keep your secrets.

The bell rang. I gathered up my things and walked toward the door. Tillie stuck out her foot and tripped me up. I went down hard, books flying everywhere. My knee cracked against the marble floor. Tillie's friends tittered. Well, all except for Loretta, who packed up her books without a word.

"Look at her, down on her knees," Courtney smirked. "Where she's most at home."

So we're back to this then.

After classes, we had another rehearsal for the school production. I met Greg at his locker and we walked over together. Safety in numbers. He'd been tripped up in one of his classes, too, and someone had squeezed some kind of cooking oil through the vents in his locker, ruining his books. He didn't tell me what people had been saying, but the barrage of insults hurled at us as we walked through the halls gave me a fair idea of what he was enduring right now.

"Well, popularity was fun while it lasted." Greg plastered a fake smile across his face as we made our way into the auditorium and up to our usual seats.

"I'm not sure we were ever really popular." Ayaz's eyes burned into my back as I sat down and flipped through a script. Courtney had been making lots of changes lately, mainly involving shrinking down my scenes and giving herself more stage time with Trey. I sighed as I noticed another of my numbers had been cut.

"Ayaz is giving you serious puppy eyes." Greg grabbed the script out of my hands. "Go talk to him."

"They're not puppy eyes. More like a rabid dog." I lunged for the script, but Greg held it out of my reach. "I'm not speaking with him right now."

"Sure you aren't. Go. It'll be here when you come back."

Sighing, I made my way down to the front row, where Ayaz and Trey sat together, their heads bent in whispered conversation. Courtney glared at me from on stage, but she couldn't stop me talking to them without making a fuss that Dr. Halsey could see. I slumped down beside Ayaz, catching a whiff of his honey and rose scent. My head spun as the two of them looked over at me – a pair of icicle eyes swimming with pain, and two dark orbs that churned with a rising storm.

Over the course of half a year, they'd gone from my bitter enemies to my allies to... something more. They'd both kissed me until I was breathless, turned my insides out, and danced on the edge of insanity with me. They'd both sacrificed so much and I... I didn't know what to do with all the emotions that swirled around inside me.

But I did know that we needed answers.

"I'll meet you both in the pleasure garden after lights out," I said. "Don't make me regret this."

"You owe me big time," I muttered, pulling my collar up around my neck as I jogged toward the three figures emerging from the rotunda. "I'd rather be tucked up in bed with my rats for company."

"If I can destroy the demon before you're due to give him your eternal soul, will that fulfill my debt?" The corner of Ayaz's mouth tugged up ever so slightly, and my heart pattered against my chest. One day I'd get a full smile from that guy, and it would probably heal the world.

"Add a giant stack of tacos to that, and I think we could call it even." I bit into a salmon tart I'd nicked from the dining hall. We'd been kicked off the monarchs' table, and I didn't feel safe eating there anymore, so Greg and I just ran in, stuffed food in our bags, and ran back out again. "All this rich-people food is giving me indigestion. I'm desperate for some orange cheese and processed meat."

"I'm with Hazy on that," Quinn bent over my shoulder and gobbled my last bite. "This food is *awful*."

I swatted his hand. "That was mine!"

Quinn grinned, which wasn't a rare occurrence, but it made my heart skip every time. He leaned over and pressed his lips to mine, giving me a taste of my lost salmon tart along with the distinctive sugary sweetness of his kiss.

Why wasn't this guy my boyfriend again?

Oh, that's right. He's dead.

"Can we stay focused on the task at hand?" Trey snapped. "We need to get back to school as soon as possible. We're being watched."

"Right now?" Quinn swept his eyes along the treeline. "Because we could give them a show—"

"Not *right now*, obviously. But if they notice all of us out of our rooms, they'll swarm this area looking for us. My dad will probably call in a SWAT team. Hazel, you sure you weren't followed?"

I shook my head. "Not even Greg and Andre know. Andre was carrying his sheets up to the laundry chute when I left, and I could hear Greg snoring from behind their door."

"Why would they follow us?" Ayaz said. "They've never cared about students roaming the grounds after dark before. They know we can't leave the school, and Hazel made it clear she wouldn't run and leave Greg and Andre behind."

I'd noticed the guys were finally calling my friends by their first names. They'd acknowledged that Greg and Andre were people worthy of fighting for. That was one of the things I'd sworn to do this year, and it had happened. They'd shown that they could change.

But what about the other things I'd sworn to do? Tonight, we might be one step closer to lifting the god's hold on the school, but if all that meant was people like Courtney would be free to exercise their cruelty in the wider world, then that wasn't a win at all. I knew that I still had to make her understand, make them all understand what they could and couldn't do. But the guys... what I was planning would hurt them, maybe even break them, and I didn't think I could do that anymore.

But then, just because they called Greg by his first name and their touch make my heart flare with fire, didn't mean they'd actually learned anything about being kind. Could twenty years of unchecked cruelty be undone in a few short weeks? If they were finally free, would they be the boys I'd come to know, to care about? Or would they be monsters?

"If you're so worried about our little field trip," I said to Trey, "you don't have to come."

"I know that." Trey kicked a loose rock over the edge of the cliff. It was a long time before he spoke again. "Yet, here I am."

Yes, here they all are trying to help me break this spell, even though they think it's hopeless, even though success may mean they pass over and I never see them again.

And I was still plotting to punish them. It felt wrong. I hated it. But not doing it felt wrong, too. Everyone in this school needed to learn a lesson. I shouldn't spare them just because I... because I...

I bit my tongue, not ready to finish that sentence.

Ayaz spun around, the compass held against his chest. "This

way." He pointed off into the trees. We started walking. A cold shiver ran down my back as I remembered the last time I walked this same path with a blindfold over my eyes.

Trey and Quinn strolled with insouciant ease, like they knew the fun never started until they arrived somewhere. Ayaz hopped ahead, consulting his map and compass and searching the treeline for landmarks. I kept a pace or so behind him, lost in my own thoughts.

"Are your parents part of the Eldritch Club, too?" I asked Ayaz as he helped me down a stone ledge.

Ayaz snorted. "Unlikely. I don't think 'our' kind are welcome. Vincent Bloomberg and his circle still think my people live in caravans in the desert."

"*You* were allowed," I pointed out.

"Only because Trey spent a year building my reputation at Miskatonic. I had to wait for permission – for one of them to anoint me. The Eldritch Club members never wait for permission. They believe the whole world belongs to them, ripe for the picking."

"Why do you think I have some kind of power?" I blurted out.

"Huh?"

"In the library, you were trying to imply that I had magical abilities."

"From everything that's happened, I can't see any other explanation. Unless you're a pyromaniac."

"Don't say that," I growled, my throat stinging. I tore away from him, leaping down the stones. The burn on my leg tugged as the healing skin stretched over the muscle.

"Hazel, wait up."

Yeah right. Because I always do what other people want. Especially when they try—

"Argh!"

Ayaz leapt off a stone ledge and landed in front of me, cutting off my path. I swatted him on the shoulder. That got one of his rare, earth-shattering smiles.

"You're going the wrong way." Ayaz pointed further along the ledge. "It's over there. Also, I'd like to point out *you* were the one who asked about your power."

"I don't have any power," I grumbled. *I wish they'd just drop it.* "I'm just a poor gutter whore with a heart of gold. *I've* never summoned a deity from a cosmic dimension."

Ayaz shrugged. "Fine. You're completely normal. Guess we're walking in silence."

"Guess so."

He was as good as his word, staying beside or behind me as we clambered over rocks and jogged between towering trees. Every now and then, his arm would brush against mine, his heat licking my skin.

I hated to admit it, but I'd missed him. We'd been spending so much time together this quarter, studying Parris' book and working on our witchcraft project. I loved watching Ayaz work – he had a singular focus and a vast intellect that could pick out seemingly insignificant details and put them together into a fully-fledged story. He saw patterns in everything, from the shapes of letters on a page to the configuration of panels on the stained glass windows. And just when he set my mind spinning with facts and details, he'd unleash his wicked dry humor and leave me laughing so hard I'd gasp for air.

"While we're asking difficult questions," I blurted out. "Why were you angry at me?"

"I thought we weren't talking."

"Was it really about Zehra? Because I'm sorry I didn't think to ask her more, I was just so desperate to get back in time and I honestly thought I'd hallucinated her—"

Ayaz looked away. "It wasn't about Zehra."

"Then why?"

"Because of the movie night," he whispered. "Because I saw

what Quinn and Trey did with you."

My cheeks flushed with heat. "I don't know what you thought you saw, but nothing happened."

"Really? Because it looked to me like they were fingering you until you came, and I have it on very good authority from half the girls in this school that's not *nothing*."

"I am so *not* talking about this."

"All I want to know is who you've chosen." Ayaz whirled around to face me, a storm raging in his eyes.

"Who I've...?" I rolled my eyes. "I haven't chosen *anyone*. I'm *not* choosing. I'm *trying* to survive this fucking school. So for a tiny fraction of a moment, I got to pretend I was someone else. I wasn't the gutter whore defined by what I didn't have, but one of those perfect girls who guys like you fall over to make happy. So yeah, it happened, but we haven't talked about it. Quinn thinks it was all fun and games, and Trey has probably been scrubbing my smell out of his skin ever since. Why does it matter?"

"Because..." Ayaz screwed his face up. He caught sight of something, and quickened his pace, pulling away from me and shoving his way through a patch of brambles. "I see it just up ahead," he called back.

Way to avoid the conversation. I hit the top of the ridge and saw it – the outcrop of rock on the slope of the hill, the crescent-shaped scar in the landscape that marked the place where I'd emerged from the cave.

The tremor started in my feet, shuddering up my legs so I staggered off-balance. I reached out to steady myself, but my fingers refused to grip the stone and I collapsed on my knees. I pressed my fingers into the scar on my wrist as a spark of fire licked behind my eyes.

"Hazel?" Ayaz spun around, his voice rising with concern.

"I can't," I whispered.

Ayaz knelt down beside me. "Then you're going to die."

"Maybe not," I joked. "You didn't."

Ayaz narrowed his eyes, ignoring my comment. "Courtney and Ms. West and Trey's dad are all going to win. You're going to be swallowed by the god of the void, and be stuck at this stupid school until the world ends, and do you think they'll let up on you once you're one of us? No, they'll devise grander tortures for you, kill you a hundred times and then bring you back just to kill you again. Is that what you want? Is that—"

Gritting my teeth, I shoved him aside and launched myself down the slope.

"Yay, Hazy!" Quinn yelled after me as I leapt over rocks and skittered around fallen branches. My feet kicked up dirt and rocks as they churned toward the entrance, even as my heart leaped into my throat and blood pumped in my ears.

I didn't stop until the crescent of the cave swallowed me into its stygian gloom. Inside the entrance, sound bent in odd ways, bouncing off the rocks and making the space twist and contort. In the distance, water dripped. I pressed my fingernail into my scar in a vain attempt to stave off a flashback to the last time I was here.

The boys slipped down into the cave after me. Trey and Ayaz clicked on flashlights, the beams illuminating rows of stalactites like sharpened teeth guarding the mouth of the beast.

"It was this way." I slapped my hand against the wall, leaving a handprint so we could find our way back. The guys fell into line behind me. No one spoke. I focused all my energy on not dissolving into a terrified heap.

Somewhere out there in the darkness lurked the slithering creature Courtney summoned to hurt me. Last time, it had tasted fire. If I were it, I'd be out for revenge.

After a time, we emerged into the sloping tunnel where the Eldritch Club had sprung their trap. In the wide beams of Quinn's and Ayaz's flashlights, it now appeared less sinister – an almost cozy space where the rocks formed small pools that trickled into the narrow ditch.

I shuffled along the slick rocks to reach the far wall. A large circle was drawn on the stone, with multiple lines and shapes inside it. It might not have been identical to that one Ayaz had shown me in Rebecca Nurse's book, but it was definitely her style. Even though water channeled through the cave, the image was crisp and unbroken.

"See? It's exactly where I remember it," I called back to the guys. "You must've looked in the wrong place."

Ayaz came up beside me. He frowned at the wall. "There's nothing there."

"Yeah, I don't see anything," Trey said.

"Whatever you're smoking, Hazy, you should share." Quinn's arm snaked around my waist.

"You really can't see it?" The sigil was almost the span of my outstretched hands, and very obvious.

Ayaz ran his hands over the wall. Where he touched the lines of the sigil, they rippled, the mark bending away from his fingers.

That's impossible. Stone doesn't move. I swiped my finger through the black line. It was like touching stone, because that was exactly what it was.

So then why did it move when Ayaz touched it?

Ayaz studied my face. "There's nothing on this wall. I can't even feel a trace of magic in the stone."

"I'm telling you, there is an enormous sigil right *here*." I traced the outline of the circle. "Did you bring the picture?"

Ayaz dug out the torn page from Rebecca Nurse's book and smoothed it against the stone. I compared the details. "Yeah, it's like ninety percent identical to the one in the picture."

"You're not bullshitting?" Quinn's eyes widened. "You really can see something on that wall?"

I rolled my eyes. "Dude, I don't kid about cosmic deities."

"She's telling the truth," a woman's voice said from behind us. "I can see it, too."

CHAPTER TWENTY-EIGHT

I whirled around. The woman who'd saved my life jumped down from a rock ledge, landing in a crouched position. She stood up to her full height, hands on hips, that waterfall of midnight hair rippling over her shoulders.

"I thought I told you not to come back here," she shook her head at me. "Instead you bring my brother and his two annoying friends."

Ayaz. I whirled around to check on him.

He'd frozen in place, his mouth hanging open. The book page fluttered from his hand. "Zehra?"

"My brother!"

They fell into each others' arms. Tears rolled down Ayaz's cheeks as he held his sister's face in his hands.

I stepped back, feeling like I was imposing on something private and precious. Trey fished the page out of a puddle, but the ink had already run. I leaned against Quinn, averting my eyes and waiting until the waterworks were over.

"Why did you come back?" Ayaz choked.

"I told you I would, you silly goose." She tweaked his nose, and the pair of them burst into laughter.

"How are you alive? We found the boat broken up on the rocks..."

Zehra swatted him around the ear. "It's all your fault. You never taught me how to row! It was so hard – no matter how much I tried I couldn't get away from the rocks. The tide pulled me in and I managed to climb out before the boat broke up on the rocks. I swam to shore, ran through the forest, and made it into Arkham. I used that money you gave me to take a bus down to New York City, where I got myself a new name, new ID, new life." She grinned. "I went to veterinary school."

Ayaz laughed. "Mom and Dad said you weren't allowed to be a vet. Last we talked, you were going to study business at Harvard."

"Well, what Mom and Dad don't know won't get them murdered." Zehra tucked a strand of hair behind her ear. "Besides, I'm a much better vet than I am a businesswoman."

Ayaz seemed to be struggling for words. "Did you... how did... You didn't tell Mom and Dad about me and the school, did you?"

"What do you think?" Zehra slapped him around the head. "Of course I did. I called them from New York with the whole story. They thought I was just making things up, telling one of my stories. Of course they didn't believe you were a resurrected spirit trapped in a creepy school where they sacrifice students to an ancient god who wanted to eat my soul. They thought I was acting out, and called Vincent Bloomberg to see if he could return me to the school. That alerted him to the fact I was Ayaz's sister, and so instead of truancy officers, he sent assassins after me. So I've been in hiding ever since."

"My dad has *assassins?*" Trey's face looked pale.

"Oh yeah. Real nasty ones, too." A wicked grin spread across Zehra's face, which quickly turned into a wince as she tried to wriggle out of Ayaz's suffocating embrace. "They shot at me, once, from a black car. It was *thrilling*. I gave them the slip a few years ago, so I've just been traveling around, seeing a bit of the world, trying to find something that will bring you back from the not-so-dead."

"How did you give trained assassins the slip?" Ayaz gazed at his sister with a mixture of awe and horror.

"Yeah. If my dad really was trying to kill you, he'd never give up without a body," Trey added.

Zehra rolled her eyes. "Duh. I faked my own death."

"What?" Ayaz looked so stricken, I burst out laughing. Zehra laughed too, and kissed his forehead.

"Don't worry, dear brother. All I did was take a little vacation to the Philippines. I came back with a killer tan, a fake birth certificate, and a photo of my gravestone in a local cemetery. I feel bad about Mom and Dad finding out, but they did send me to this hellhole in the first place even after your death, so Allah can smite their asses for all I care. Plus, being dead has awesome benefits. I haven't had to pay tax in ten years, and all my old friends back home posted super nice things on my Facebook wall."

"Your sister is awesome," I grinned, holding up my hand for Zehra to high five.

"She's *insane*," Ayaz growled, wrapping his sister in another protective hug. "Don't you two go being friends now. You're a bad influence on each other."

"Too late." Zehra wrenched out of his grasp and threw her arm around me. I leaned against her shoulder and grinned.

I'd never had a girlfriend before. I hung out with a couple of the strippers at Mom's club, but they didn't have enough between their ears to be worth the effort. In this crazy place, I needed as many friends as I could get, and I wasn't about to turn down a crazy Turkish chick who could teach me how to fake my own death. I hugged Zehra back.

"I hate to break up the reunion," Trey hissed. "But we need to get back to school before we're missed."

Zehra's face swung around, seeing the rest of us for the first time. "Trey Bloomberg, you haven't changed a bit. I still remember the first day I came to this school. You had Ayaz steal my diary and you read my poem aloud to the entire dining hall. You made me want to die. Guess the joke's on you."

Trey's smirk froze. *I dig this chick so hard.*

"He did something similar to me," I said, offering my hand for her to shake. "We didn't formally introduce ourselves last time, friend. I'm Hazel Waite, scholarship student, currently one of only three living students at Derleth Academy."

"Zehra Demir." She shook my hand with a firm grip. "I know all about you, Hazel. That was a hell of a deal you made with the devil."

"I'm told that we're not supposed to call the Great Old God a devil or demon," I said. "Apparently, it upsets him."

"I meant Headmistress West," Zehra grinned. "She's the devil incarnate."

"No argument." I grinned back.

"I'm not sure why we're still hanging out in this cave." Zehra led me back towards the entrance. Trey protested, but I was only too happy to ignore him. "So, tell me, if you're a scholarship student, how did you end up with my brother and the two biggest dicks in the school?"

"I actually don't have an answer to that question." I shrugged. "I guess they're trying to help me."

"Hazy's my girlfriend." Quinn came up behind us and tried to throw his arm over my shoulders. I shoved him. His foot slipped and he skidded back, landing on his ass in a puddle of brackish water. He winced and I ran to help him, knowing that must've hurt with his injuries.

"Fuck!" Trey growled as Quinn splashed filth up his trouser legs. "Thanks a lot, Quinn."

"You're welcome," Quinn said, deliberately splashing Trey again as he let me help him stagger onto his feet.

"I amend my previous statement," I said to Zehra. "Trey and Ayaz are helping me. Quinn is trying to get into my pants."

"Why are you back here, Little Turk?" Quinn asked as he slipped into step behind us, keeping a bit of distance this time. "Surely there are better things to do with your freedom than hiding out in caves and spying on us?"

"Well, *Quinnanigans*, I'm trying to get your life back," Zehra punched him in the arm. I smirked. *Quinnanigans – I'll have to remember that.* "All the time I haven't spent escaping assassins and learning how to surf, I've been trying to figure out exactly what happened here. I've tracked down a woman who used to work with Headmistress West, back when she was plain old Dr. Hermia West at Arkham General Hospital."

"So?" Trey demanded.

"So... didn't you read those articles I left for you?" Zehra's eyes flashed, just like Ayaz's did when he was frustrated.

The articles... I remembered the stack of old newspaper clippings in the storage room. They weren't there now. "There was one about the fire. I went to show it to Ayaz but then I got waylaid by some shadows and next time I looked they were gone."

"Waylaid by shadows... jeez." Zehra rubbed her forehead with her hand. "I thought you were the brains of this lot. Guess it's going to have to be me, as usual. All the answers you needed were in those articles, and if someone at that school has their hands on them..."

"You'd better catch us up," Trey said. "What did you find?"

"Three years before the fire at Miskatonic Prep, Hermia West was fired from Arkham General after it was discovered she was experimenting on bodies in the hospital morgue."

"If that's true, how did she get the job as headmistress at a prestigious school? Surely that would've come out in the media?"

"The hospital would do anything to avoid litigation by the families of the deceased. According to my source, West had a wealthy benefactor who swooped in and offered a generous donation to the hospital if they kept the story out of the papers. By the time Hermia West appeared in front of the school board, she had a glowing recommendation from one of their own."

"Let me guess," Trey said darkly. "Vincent Bloomberg II."

Zehra shot finger guns at Trey. "This guy's cleverer than he looks."

"You're the one who's brilliant." Ayaz squeezed Zehra so tight I thought her eyes would pop out of her skull.

"That's not even the full story. Before the morgue incident, there were two cases of mysterious patient deaths. In both cases, someone punctured the patient's IV drip and administered a concoction of drugs – none of which were doctor prescribed or listed on that patient's chart. Both patients died in agony while their bodies were in complete paralysis – they couldn't call out for help. Also, a bunch of medications and chemicals went missing from hospital stores. Neither the thefts nor the deaths were ever connected to Ms. West, but the other nurses and the internal hospital risk manager suspected she was the one behind them."

"What does this have to do with the school?"

Zehra's eyes flashed. She hadn't forgotten the things Trey had done to her, and hearing the impatience in his voice brought that all back. When she spoke again, her voice had an edge to it. "You think it's a coincidence West got the headmistress job even though she's not exactly qualified, and then three years later a whole bunch of students die in a fire, and those same students then end up as reanimated corpses, confined to the walls of this very school?"

"You're saying it wasn't the deity that brought us back from the dead?" Ayaz frowned.

"Correct." Zehra threw her dark hair over her shoulder. "I think it was West. *And* my source believes that if we can get the formula for the chemicals she uses, or even research notes on how she does it, then we could find a way to..." she stopped.

"To do what?" I asked.

Zehra squeezed my hand. "Sooooooo... it's unclear. Maybe we could restore you guys to life, give you the ability to age, to step over the boundaries of Parris' home, to *live*. Or maybe all we can hope for is to lay you to rest and set your souls free."

"We don't have souls any longer," Trey muttered.

"I'm not sure *you* ever had one to begin with, Trey Bloomberg," Zehra said, swiping her hair out of her face. "But yeah, I can't promise what's going to happen, so if we're going to do this you have to be prepared that..."

...that the guys might die for real.

All three of them looked to me, their faces a mix of anger, of horror, of regret. A sick feeling churned in my stomach. Even though I'd seen their gravestones, it was still so hard to think of them as dead — not when they laughed and fought and held me and kissed with lips that burned.

But they *were* dead, and for twenty years they'd been trapped inside bodies frozen in time. The torture they'd undergone at the hands of Ms. West and the Eldritch Club had robbed them of their chance for a future... and a vital piece of their humanity. No wonder they were capable of such cruel bullying — they'd known only cruelty themselves, their abuse baked into their skin.

The thought of them dying for real hadn't occurred to me. I always expected that if we lifted the spell, they would return to life. But Zehra was right — they already had one foot in the grave. They *died* in that fire twenty years ago — whatever unnatural process Ms. West had subjected them to had trapped them in this half-state, this life-that-was-not-life. To set them free, to truly break the curse of Miskatonic Prep, I would have to say goodbye. Forever.

Shit.

I fucking hate goodbyes.

Tears sprung in the corners of my eyes. I swallowed hard, forcing them back. Quinn met my eyes and flashed me a wobbly smile, and they almost spilled over. But no fucking way was I crying in front of the monarchs. I wasn't giving them that power over me, of knowing how much they meant to me now.

"Personally, I think we're owed a shot at life." Quinn flexed his biceps. "I can't die without unleashing all of this magnificence on the world."

"We have to try," Trey agreed.

"This isn't about us, anyway. If we could stop this happening to others, then I want to find out, even if that means..." Ayaz sucked in a breath, unable to finish the sentence. "Where would we find research notes?"

"My source says that Ms. West must have a lab somewhere in the school. It would have to be cold, or have some kind of cold storage for any bodies she collects. That's where you'll find your evidence... ow, lay off, you're crushing my ribs."

A lab, like a mad scientist from a stupid horror film. I knew that this lab was where she planned to take me at the end of the school year, when my end of our bargain came due. She'd cut me open and experiment on me, trying to figure out why I hurt the god. I doubted I'd survive the process.

Ayaz didn't loosen his grip on Zehra. From the haunted look in his eyes, I knew he'd realized that if his soul was freed, he'd be leaving her behind.

Trey glanced at his watch. "Ayaz, we should go."

Zehra untangled herself from her brother's grasp. "I'll walk you to the entrance."

Ayaz's eyes bugged out. "You're not... living in this cave, are you?"

She laughed – a musical sound that filled my head with light. "Of course not. Right now, I'm living out of an RV on the edge of the village. I can't get the bloody thing up this road, so I hike up here as often as I can to search for Rebecca's sigils, and to check up on my older brother here. I've gotten pretty good at using the caves and tunnels to sneak around without being seen."

My gaze flew back to the sigil on the wall, forgotten in the thrill of meeting Zehra. "So you know about Rebecca Nurse, too? And you can see the sigil?"

She nodded. "But none of the guys can. Either because they're edimmu, or because of some other reason. It's the only one I've found so far, but I believe there must be others. I also gave you an article about Rebecca Nurse, but I'm assuming you didn't read that, either."

I sighed. "Nope. Although someone at the school has had some interesting night-time reading."

Zehra shuddered. "I hope those articles haven't fallen into the wrong hands."

"Me, too." As we walked to the entrance, I asked Zehra how she ended up at Derleth. "Surely the school wouldn't be so stupid as to accept a student who already had a sibling at Miskatonic?"

"Yeah, they only accept orphans for that reason. Basically, everyone fucked up. The political situation between Turkey and the United States has changed since Ayaz went to live with the Bloombergs. My parents were so desperate for me to come here and get the same education that when they heard there was a scholarship program for orphans, they sent me here to apply with a different name and a different history. They didn't even care that Derleth was on the same grounds where Ayaz had died. I played my part so well that the school didn't connect that I was Ayaz's sister. So of course, when I show up here and see my brother who is supposed to have died eight years ago, I'm a bit suspicious."

We emerged above ground. The rising moon peeked through the trees, throwing an eerie pale light over the landscape. Zehra threw her arms around me. "I won't go any closer to the school, in case you're being watched. I'm relying on you to look after my brother and his two idiot friends. But you have my permission to kick his ass if he ever bullies another person."

"Deal." I didn't want to let Zehra go. I wanted to cling to this dark-haired fireball of fury and hope forever. I wanted to follow her down the peninsula to her RV and drive as far from this fucking school as we could get. But she was right – the guys needed me here, and it was dangerous for all of us if they discovered her. We had to say goodbye.

Zehra took a phone from her pocket, but then frowned at it. "It would be nice to find some way to communicate that doesn't involve you having to walk all the way out here. I forgot that you're not allowed phones."

"Whoa," Quinn peered over her shoulder as she swiped the screen. "They've changed a lot since we last had them."

"If we could find where Ms. West keeps the ones she confiscated, maybe we could take one." I thought of all the pictures on mine – mostly selfies of Mom and Dante and me – memories I'd brought with me to Derleth to remind me of what I'd lost. It hadn't even occurred to me to try and steal the phone back.

Zehra took a scrap of paper from her pocket and scribbled a number on the back. "This is my phone number. If you ever manage to steal one of the confiscated ones, you can contact me on this. Otherwise, I'll be in the entrance of the south tunnel – the one that leads from the forest by the pleasure garden into the god's cavern – in a week's time. If you want to see me again, be there."

"We will." Ayaz embraced his sister again. Trey grabbed his shoulder and dragged him away. Zehra stood by the cave entrance and watched us until we submitted the crest of the hill. When I looked back one last time, she was gone.

Ayaz walked in a trance, frequently having to stop to re-orient himself. "I can't believe she's alive. All these years, I'd convinced myself..."

"Not only that, but she might have a way to save you." My mind churned with the possibilities. For the first time, we had a direction, a cause. "If what's been done to you is a scientific process that happened under Ms. West's knife, then there could be a way to reverse it."

"I can't believe it," Quinn kept saying. "All this time they'd been telling us it was the god who brought us back to be its servants. But really, it was Ms. West."

Trey walked in silence. I knew what he was thinking – that this tied in perfectly with his theory that the senior Eldritch Club members planned this, even before the fire.

"Do you guys remember anything from after the fire?" I asked. "Any details you can recall might help us find the lab."

"I remember pain," Quinn said. "A fuckton of pain."

"It was the night of the annual alumni dance," Trey surprised me by speaking up. I waited for him to continue. He didn't.

"Can you say more? I want to understand."

"It's a big event for the school, to celebrate the year coming to a close. We'd eaten in the dining hall, and afterwards the school had organized a dance in the gymnasium for parents and students. The parents went first for one of their private meetings, while we all went back to our rooms to get ready and drink and get high. By 8PM every student was in the gym, hitting the dance floor in their finery – Tillie wore this glittering gown that..." Trey cleared his throat. "We were dancing when I noticed something odd. The parents started leaving – first in pairs and threes, then it seemed as if there was a great exodus. I went to find my dad, but just before I could get to them, both gym doors slammed shut."

Angry tears burned in the back of my eyes. I couldn't believe their parents – the very people who were supposed to protect these kids, to love them unconditionally – could have knowingly lured their kids into this trap. Was that how far they would go for more power?

"I remember..." Trey's eyes flickered. "I remember carrying Tillie across the gym, heading toward the doors. Her sparkly dress caught fire and she screamed and screamed. I couldn't see anything through the smoke and there was this *scritching* noise, like rats running across the floor. Smoke burned in my lungs. I couldn't breathe. My mind went white – I fell into this deep sleep punctured by brutal dreams. The next thing I knew, I woke up screaming, trapped in the dark, buried in a tiny box where the air was growing stale.

"They'd buried us, alive but not alive. I could hear the priest's voice overhead, the sound of parents and families sobbing. The earth above groaned with the weight of their pain. I banged my fists on the lid, but it wouldn't budge. For hours I wrestled alone with the dark, screaming and begging for release. The air in my coffin must've run out, but I didn't suffocate. The next thing I remember was the scrape of a spade on wood, the lifting of the weight that bore down on me, a bright rectangle of pale moonlight as the lid was lifted and I peered out of my grave. Quinn helped me up. Everyone was there, climbing out of the ground or helping to dig the others out. We all looked alive, felt alive, but we weren't. Our burns had healed, our lungs good as new, our minds wrung out of good memories and tender dreams. If there was a lab, they made sure we didn't remember it."

Beside me, Quinn shuddered.

There was no talking after that, nothing to say that could lighten the horror of Trey's story. Ayaz fell in step beside me. His fingers brushed mine, raising the fire along my arm. I entwined my fingers in his, holding his hand all the way back to school.

We emerged in the pleasure garden, finding it empty except for Nancy making out with a guy under the rotunda. I assumed it was Paul but when he turned his head, I realized it was Barclay, another guy from Trey's lacrosse team. Nancy raised her eyebrows when she saw the four of us, but she didn't stop us or call out. I guess she figured we all had to keep each other's secrets.

Trey went in the tunnel first. I followed behind Quinn, my mind racing as the dark closed around me again, the embers of the fire stoked by Ayaz's touch still flickering inside me. So many things had happened tonight, so many secrets revealed and emotions laid bare. I didn't know what would happen next, only that all options ahead of us were terrifying – but I *did* know that unless the guys did something awful to me, there was no way I'd be able to inflict my punishment on them. Not anymore.

I also knew that right now, tonight, I was barely holding it together, and I didn't want to be alone.

As Ayaz emerged from the mirror behind me, I reached out and took his hand, feeling the fire roaring to life inside me. "You doing okay?"

He shook his head. "I don't fucking know. It's a lot to wrap my head around."

"Sure is. Ayaz?"

"Mmmm."

"Stay with me."

CHAPTER TWENTY-NINE

I have no idea what the fuck I'm doing.

As silently as I could, I inserted my key into my door and swung it open, pulling Ayaz inside. The last thing I needed was Greg or Andre waking up.

The door clicked shut and I was alone in my dorm room with my scritching rats, Ayaz Demir and my pounding heart.

"This used to be Zehra's room," he said, running his fingers along the peeling paint on the wall. His silky voice raised the hairs on my arms. "I cried when I saw it for the first time. She deserved so much better than this. So do you."

"This is a palace compared to where I grew up." I stood at the foot of my bed, frozen in place by the sight of him – those broad shoulders dominating the narrow space, that strong chin pointing directly at me like a dare, a challenge. His warm scent filled my nostrils, curling tendrils of sweet honey and rose through my brain, smoothing out any last traces of doubt. I stepped toward him, feeling the room contract, the pull of need tugging us together. "Didn't you sleep here when you first came to Derleth?"

Ayaz shook his head. "They didn't have the official scholarship program then. I was a charity case here on Vincent's dime, but he still gave me a nice room. No, this madness started after the fire, when they needed the sacrifices. It was all the Eldritch Club's idea."

"Why keep the new scholarship students down here in the dungeon, then?"

"All of this is supposed to put the charity cases in their place. It's supposed to be the beginning of what breaks you. But you..." Ayaz closed the space between us in one long stride, his body inches from mine. My skin tingled with heat as his eyes swept over me, his jaw tight with need. "You've never stayed where you were put. You've never been broken."

"I don't know about that," I whispered. My arms ached, heavy in their sockets, desperate to hold and to be held. I leaned forward, a moth to my flame, seeking the heat only his touch would provide.

"This is so fucked up." Ayaz's breath fluttering against my lips. "You're not supposed to want me. Not after everything I did."

"Stop being so fucking tempting, then," I growled.

We fell against each other, mouths clashing, tongues hunting for the flame. My heart raced ahead, and I clung to him - the only thing keeping me upright. As we fought for purchase against each other's warm bodies, Ayaz watched me through narrowed eyes – two shards of obsidian between tangled lashes.

I'm really doing this. Tonight. With a dead boy. With my bully.

Yes, I fucking am.

Ayaz's hands gripped my shoulders, shoving me toward the bed. I bent down to the nightstand, grabbed a condom, and thrust it in his face. "Here."

He caught it between his fingers, his eyes wide. "Hazel, what is this?"

"It's a condom, obviously. People throw them at me all the time, since I'm the resident whore," I said. "This is me being sensible."

"I'm an *edimmu* – you can't get pregnant from someone who isn't alive."

"My mother told me I'm never supposed to take a guy's word on it."

"Don't you trust me?"

I hesitated. *Trust.* I never trusted anyone, except Greg and Andre. You didn't trust in my world. Trust got you beaten up or left for dead. Trust left you with debts to pay and only one way to clear them. Trust got your heart stomped on and your hands covered in blood and fire. The only two people I'd ever trusted before were dead.

After everything I've been through, do I trust Ayaz?

"Yes." The word was a whisper, a promise. It said a hundred things I couldn't articulate.

More than any of the others, Ayaz understood how hard that was for me to say. His trust had been broken, too. He'd been bought and sold between families to further his parents' ambition. He'd been used by Vincent as a way to torture his own son. He'd been kept from his sister. All his life, he'd been taught that cruelty was the only way to stay on top, to stave off the darkness.

"I trust you," Ayaz whispered. His next kiss was soft, accepting my trust and giving his own in return – a broken fragile thing, like a bird with a broken wing. He gently pushed me backward, giving me every chance to break the kiss, to stop this before it went further. But I didn't want to stop.

"I still want the condom."

"I know."

My legs brushed the side of the bed, and I sat down, curling my fingers around his school tie and dragging him down with me. The broken springs groaned under our combined weight. The bed was only wide enough for one body, so Ayaz laid on top, fitting me beneath him like two puzzle pieces slotting together.

He leaned me back against the pillow, his eyes studying me. The room filled with his intoxicating scent. I breathed deep, drowning in him, losing myself in those fierce eyes. My thighs tightened around his leg, and a moan escaped my lips. We ground our bodies together in all the places that mattered, teasing the flame higher and higher, until my skin seemed to be made of sparks and ashes.

I popped the buttons on his school shirt, pressing my hands to his chest, tracing the tattoos the way I had done in the grotto. Ayaz peeled back my hoodie and t-shirt, revealing my breasts nestled inside my good black bra. He moaned as his hand cupped my breast, his finger grazing my nipple through the fabric. "Fuck, I've had dreams about this bra."

I snorted. "You have not."

"You've been spying on my dreams, have you?" His lips tugged up into one of those rare, heart-melting smiles. "Ever since I saw you get into that pool with Quinn, I've been seething with jealousy. And then at the movie night, he got to have his hands all over you; him and Trey. And they *knew*..."

"Knew what?"

"Knew that I had a thing for you," he whispered, his silky voice catching on the words. There it was, that vulnerability I'd wanted to see in him for so long.

"How could you have a thing for me? You're sleeping with Ms. West. And you threw maggots in my breakfast." A shudder ran through my body at the memory of it. My muscles tightened as the horrible realization dawned on me that he could be about to spring another torment on me, that he might have seduced me on purpose to get me into this position and—

Ayaz stroked my head, and the broken look in his eyes made my body relax. "Can I tell you something I've never told anyone except Quinn and Trey before?"

"Sure."

"I don't *want* to fuck her. I hate it, in fact. But she made it quite clear that if I didn't drop my pants for her, she'd find new and interesting ways to torment the few people at this school I actually care about. So that's why I tried so hard to fight what I felt for you – I didn't want her to use you against me. And I did the maggot thing because I'm a fucking asshole. But the day I did that, the creature's power waned as it had never before. Tillie's father lost his seat in Congress. And Trey and I realized that maybe you were key to burning this whole motherfucking thing down."

"How do you gather that?"

"Everything that happens in this school is just a smaller version of the real world. The Great Old God manipulates behind the scenes. It makes sure the Eldritch Club members remain in power. For every scholarship student sacrificed, it makes the world more unequal, a little more weighted toward keeping power with the powerful. And for every heart that breaks, every student we've broken, they get closer to their endgame. We thought resistance was hopeless... until you." Ayaz shook his head, squeezing his eyes shut. His arms tightened around me like he was afraid to let me go. "Forgive me, Hazel. I was so fucking wrong. This place had me all twisted up inside. I thought... we thought, that if we pushed you harder, if we drove you right to the edge, then it would break the god and we'd be free."

Even though I'd known that already on some level, hearing him say it still sent a jolt of shock through me. "And then Trey held me over the cliff," I whispered.

"Yes. And then we realized that we'd gone too far, that we'd done to you what we'd done to others. That our own evil had cost us everything..." Ayaz struggled to breathe through his confession. He rose up onto his hands, tearing the bond between us as he shoved his body away. His face twisted in wide-eyed horror – not horror at me, but at himself. "I should go. You can't want me after this—"

I grabbed his shoulder and slammed him down, crushing my mouth against his. I poured everything I had into that kiss, feeding him from the fire that burned inside me. He'd done a shitty thing, but he was far from the only one. My punishment plan felt completely ridiculous now, needlessly cruel. Ayaz wasn't a monster. He didn't need to be shown right from wrong. He knew already, he just didn't have a choice. We were all pawns on this board – we did what we needed to stay in the game. Right now, I needed him.

"You didn't break me," I said, trailing my fingers over his dusky skin. "I was forged in steel and fire. Now shut the fuck up and kiss me, because I'm probably dying in this school, but I'm not going out a virgin."

"But why me? Quinn or Trey—"

"Because…" I touched my hand to his hair, curling my fingers through the silky strands. "We're the same."

"I'm the luckiest fucking edimmu on earth." Ayaz cupped my cheeks in his hands, bringing my face to his to sear me with his kiss. His body shifted to cover me, his hardness digging into my thigh. Clothes flew in all directions as we pawed at each other, hungry to close the space between us, to press hot skin to skin. My nails scraped his back, clawing for purchase as we slid together, trying to crawl inside each other's fire.

Ayaz bent back and flung my feet out on either side of him. He plunged his head between my legs. I gasped as his tongue found the spot where my fire burned brightest – the source of the flame. Ayaz dug his nails into my ass, lifting me off the sheets so he could taste more of me.

My whole body throbbed, crackled, *blazed* with fire. I trembled as flames tore down my arms and circled my chest.

And then, the rush came – the fire burst out of me, pushing me over the edge and outside my body. I floated somewhere in the world of spirits, lost to everything except Ayaz's lips on mine, his hard body shielding me from the nightmares that threatened to overwhelm us both.

"You're beautiful," he whispered as he reached between us, guiding himself inside me.

You're beautiful. No one had ever said that to me before.

"You're..." My words dissolved into a moan.

A condom wrapper tore.

When Ayaz entered me, fire danced on my eyeballs. There was a sharp jolt of pain. My flesh burned up. He moved inside me, slow at first, then faster as my body adjusted to his size, to the way he scorched me from the inside out. In between the flames, my mind left my body again, and I saw a flash of the cavern below the gym. The chains jerked and rattled against the trapdoor, and the creature in its void cowered in fear and rage.

What we were doing right now hurt it more than anything else. That knowledge made me shift my hips up to meet Ayaz's thrust, driving him deeper, driving out the demons that had infected us both.

I needed him, in a way I'd never needed another human being before in my life.

We drove out the darkness with our bodies, burning up in an inferno of our own creation. Our limbs tangled together, hearts beating in unison against our chests. For once the darkness wasn't a place where nightmares waited to creep up on me. I *was* the darkness, and it felt fucking good.

Ayaz cried out as the fire burned through him, as he released his own demons into the flames. His muscles contracted around me, his body growing stiff then collapsing against me, panting as sweat rolled down his back.

We held each other as the sun rose, as the inferno we built died back to embers, as my eyes fluttered shut. I slept, and Ayaz's warm fire kept the nightmares at bay.

CHAPTER THIRTY

I dreamed that I'd aced all the upcoming exams, that my name flashed from the very top of the merit points chart. I'd crawled to the top of the rankings, and now I owned the school. Until Ms. West called me into her office and accused me of cheating and stealing points from other students...

I woke with a start, my forehead slick with sweat. My head lay across Ayaz's bare chest. He wrapped his arms around me, holding me close, while the rats *scritch-scritched* above our heads.

Ayaz slipped out early after planting one last, languid kiss on my lips. I lay in bed, curling my toes under the sheets and tracing the map of fire his lips had traced across my body. His honey and rose scent clung to my skin and lingered in the air. As light from the high window pierced the room, I lifted the covers off my knees, noticing for the first time the damp patch on the sheets between my legs, speckled with a few droplets of blood.

Gross.

This was one of the things about sex they never told you in class. *Great.* Now I had this big wet patch in the middle of my bed. I used tissues to clean myself up as best I could, pulled on some jeans and Dante's old basketball tank, took the tank off again because it felt weird for some reason, and shrugged on one of my rumpled uniform shirts instead, and gathered up my sheets.

There was a laundry chute on the dormitory floor, near Quinn's room. Us scholarship students had to lug our linen up the stairs in order to send it down to the laundry. We didn't get room service the way the rest of the student body did.

As I lugged the ball of sheets down the hall, students jostled me on either side. "Getting ready for your life of servitude," Amber sneered as she elbowed me in the ribs. I didn't dignify her with a response.

As I neared the chute, I noticed Andre was already there with a pile of his sheets, scribbling something on his pad.

"Are you a neat freak or something?" I grinned at him as I threw my sheets into the wide chute. "I just saw you up here the other day and..."

I remembered why guys might need to change their sheets all the time and snapped my mouth shut. Andre shifted his weight to his other foot. But his expression wasn't one of embarrassment. He looked like he was trying to decide something.

"You okay, dude?"

Andre's pen flickered across his pad. He handed me a note.

"Do you trust me?" he'd scribbled.

"Of course I do."

Andre lunged at me, planting his huge hands on my shoulders. He shoved me with all his might. I slammed into the wall and toppled headfirst down the chute.

CHAPTER THIRTY-ONE

I landed in a soft pile of white clouds. The smell of stale sweat and... other bodily fluids invaded my nostrils, followed a moment later by the overwhelming whiff of bleach and lemon.

I swam my arms through the mass of linen, fighting my way toward light and air. A heavy object flopped down beside me. *Andre.* He grabbed me under his powerful arm and dragged me to the surface. I gasped for breath as my head emerged from an enormous pile of dirty sheets, but the air around me was humid and stale.

"What did you do that for?" I demanded. Andre just kept on grinning as he swam to the side of the tub and pulled himself out.

I tried to put my feet down, but they were tangled in the sheets. Andre grabbed both my hands in his and dragged me out. I fell over the side and collapsed against him, grateful to be back on solid ground again.

I peered around me, trying to figure out where we were. I was only able to make out faint outlines through the haze of steam. My eyes stung from the bleach that permeated the air.

All around me were tubs of steaming water. Figures in grey smocks bent over the tubs, stirring them with large wooden paddles and rubbing the linens on wooden washboards. It looked like a literal sweatshop. Above the noise of sloshing water and gushing steam and wet fabric splashing was the constant *scritch-scritch-scritch* of thousands of rats swarming inside the walls.

"This is barbaric," I yelled to Andre over the din. "There are industrial electric washing machines for exactly this reason."

Andre tried to scribble a note. He got as far as, "Keeping them busy stops them from reb—" before the dampness ruined his pen. He shoved it into his pocket, shaking his head. He grabbed my hand and dragged me between the vats.

Already the bleach stung my eyes. I had to squint to see through the steam as Andre yanked me through a low door into another room. Bleach still clung to the air in here, but it was less noticeable. Instead of the oppressive heat of the washroom, frigid air from a vent on the far wall blasted the workers as they placed the sheets under a large steam press before folding and stacking them on a central stainless steel table. All of this under constant supervision from the rats in the walls.

Andre marched straight up to a girl who worked on the assembly line, folding sheets into neat squares. He took her hand in his, and I was shocked at how cracked and calloused her skin was. Andre pointed to me. The girl's eyes widened, and she staggered back.

I recognized her. I was certain she was the girl Andre had been signing to at the Halloween afterparty. But I felt as though I'd seen her face somewhere else, in a photograph or something. I knew it was important, but I couldn't connect the dots.

"It's okay." I tried to give her a reassuring smile. Andre shook his head at me and I quickly wiped the smile away. Smiling wasn't really in my repertoire. "I promise I won't hurt you. I'm Andre's friend. You like Andre, don't you?"

Andre turned her head towards him, gesturing in a series of hand signs in front of her face. She slapped his hand down and made her own signs in return. I could tell from the few signs

Andre had taught Greg, Loretta, and I that this was not ASL. It was an altogether different language.

The pair of them signed back and forth, before Andre turned to me, shrugging his shoulders as if to say, "she's all yours."

"Hi." I gave a dumb wave to this girl. She glared at me through narrowed eyes. She had been beautiful once, with dark eyes and brown hair in tight curls. Now, the skin around her eyes and mouth had shrunk and pocked, there were patches of dry skin flaking off her neck and hands, and her eyes betrayed too many unspoken horrors. My throat closed up as the taste of those chemicals still burned on my tongue. "My name is Hazel. I'm a scholarship student here."

Andre tried his pen again. This time it worked. He handed me his paper.

"This is Sadie. She came here as a scholarship student nineteen years ago. They imprisoned her here."

My stomach turned. Sadie was a scholarship student. So why was she down here in this hellhole, instead of part of the student body...

And then I *saw*.

I glanced around the room at the rest of the maintenance staff. The tough conditions had aged some of them prematurely, but they were all clearly young people.

They're all scholarship students.

And then I remembered where I'd seen Sadie before. She had a file in Parris' book, a picture with a slash through it – she *had* looked so different then – bright and full of hope.

This is what the faculty and alumni do with the sacrifices. This is why they deliberately choose orphans from poor neighborhoods and ethnic communities, so they can reinforce this idea that in life there are masters and servants.

Bile rose in my throat. Just last night I'd thought that I'd come to terms with what Trey, Quinn, and Ayaz had been a part of, but that was before Andre opened my eyes to the darkest secret of

Miskatonic Prep. All these people down here had been bullied by them over the years, and now they were *slaves*.

This was *sick*.

Sadie moved her hands in a series of quick signs and Andre scribbled down another note. "She says that the Kings took her to a dark cave under the school and lowered her into a dark hole where something attacked her. She hasn't aged since. She can't leave the school grounds. She can't escape, and every day she has to cook and clean for the students who did this to her. Hazel, what's going on?"

"What's going on is—" but I couldn't say any more. The words dried on my tongue. I couldn't break the agreement I'd made.

Instead, I turned to Sadie, anger surging inside me for what had been done to them. How *could* they? How could Trey and Quinn and Ayaz and all the others swan around upstairs while this injustice went on? Why did it take them twenty years to finally try to stop this?

There were so many people down here. They could outnumber the students, overwhelm the faculty. They could have done something about this years ago, so why hadn't they? What did Ms. West and the Eldritch Club have over them? "Why do you meekly follow what the faculty wants?" I demanded, struggling to contain my rage. "Why don't you try to warn others so they could spare themselves the same fate?"

Staring at me with grave defiance, Sadie opened her mouth. I gasped as she revealed the ugly scar and frightful stub where her tongue should have been.

CHAPTER THIRTY-TWO

I gulped back my revulsion at the barbaric wound. "Who did that to you?"

But I didn't need to ask. I *knew*.

Sadie signed frantically at Andre. His hand whirled as he signed his reply. They signed so fast that even if I had known the language, I couldn't have followed them. Finally, Sadie stepped back, folding her arms. She swept her accusing gaze over my body.

"You're right," I told her. "There's something at this school that isn't of this world. I've seen it. But I'm beginning to understand that it's not the true evil here."

She nodded.

"We're going to destroy the people that did this," I said, pointing to Andre and I. "Once and for all. We're going to find a way to give each and every one of you your life back. *Real* life, not this wretched servitude."

Sadie's eyes widened. She shoved me hard in the chest. I stumbled back against the conveyor belt. "What was that for?" I demanded, but then I heard it. An old-fashioned bell tinkling. A girl rushed through the room with the bell in her hands, sprinting towards the washroom with it.

A signal of some sort? Or a warning?

Beckoning us to follow her, Sadie disappeared behind the steamer. In the corner of the room was a low, narrow door. Sadie yanked it open, revealing a tiny platform and a rope pulley and a wooden stake to jam the brake. An old-fashioned dumbwaiter. She leaned inside, grabbed Andre's collar, and pressed her lips to his in a brief, searing kiss before pulling away and slamming the door.

Dayum, Andre. He had been busy this quarter.

Inside, it was pitch black and barely small enough for us both to fit on the platform. "I should have guessed you had a girl," I whispered to Andre, squeezing his hand. "Now I know how you managed to get that key for me."

He didn't reply, of course, but he did squeeze my fingers back.

A cramp shot up my leg – an old sting from my burn scar. But I didn't dare shift. Neither of us made a move for the winch. I didn't want the sound of the dumbwaiter to give us away. And also, I wanted to hear what was happening outside.

"What's going on down here?" a harsh voice demanded. I recognized Professor Atwood. "Why are you away from your station? It's not your break time for another hour."

Of course, there was no reply.

"Two students are missing." Atwood's voice moved closer to us. "They didn't show up in homeroom. They *cannot* find their way down here. I want three of you to stand guard on the staircases, turn anyone back you see. If you find the students, you are to restrain them and wait for me."

The door rattled as someone tugged on the handle. I grabbed the bolt and braced my foot against the frame, holding the door shut.

"Quick," I whispered. "Pull us up."

Andre grunted as he yanked on the chain. I winced as the dumbwaiter creaked and the chain scraped against the pulley. We jerked off the ground. Andre yanked again. Another jerk and we sailed upward.

"What's that noise?" the voice demanded. "Is someone in the dumbwaiter?"

A thin shaft of light appeared along the edge beside our feet as Andre gave the rope another jerk. I caught a glimpse of Professor Atwood's cruel eyes before he disappeared below the edge of the platform.

It's dark in here. He couldn't have seen you.

The dumbwaiter shuddered as we reached the top of the shaft. Andre shoved the brake into place. We pressed all over the platform and walls, searching for some way to exit the shaft. Finally, I found a small handle in the lower right corner. I lifted it and the door popped open. It was so small I had to get down on my knees to climb out. Andre had to angle his shoulders diagonally to squeeze through.

I scrambled to my feet, grabbing Andre's arm. We were standing in a narrow corridor of bare, undressed stone, flanked with locked doors, a glass window in each one. My boots scuffed a dirt floor. The air was so cold our breath came out as puffs of steam.

I peered into one of the windows, but a layer of ice obscured the glass. All I could make out was a couple of shelves, upon which sat long containers like meat lockers. Cold smoke curled under the door.

"Is that… dry ice?" I asked. Andre nodded.

"I think I know what's behind these doors." I shuddered and grabbed Andre's hand. "Let's get out of here."

Our feet pounded down the hall as the dumbwaiter groaned and cranked behind us. Professor Atwood yelled something down the corridor, but like fuck we were stopping for him. We rounded a corner and crashed into another girl wearing the uniform of the maintenance staff.

She grabbed my arm and dragged me into a dark corner,

pushing us into a small tunnel, just as Atwood came around the corner. "Where did they go?" he demanded. "Did they look in the freezers?"

The girl, of course, didn't answer, and we didn't stick around to find out what Atwood did next. We followed the narrow tunnel down, down, down, until we finally emerged into the sunlight, crawling out from a small warren hidden beneath a towering oak near the tennis courts.

I threw my arms around Andre, trying to force my heart rate back to normal. "Fuck. Fuck."

He nodded, his own breath coming out in ragged gasps.

I pulled away, for the first time in a long while taking a hard look at my friend. In the set of his jaw and the kindness in his eyes, I saw the risks he'd been taking all quarter, the time he'd spent learning the sign language Sadie and the other maintenance staff used to communicate, the truths about Derleth Academy he'd started to put together for himself.

And I saw something else. Strength. Defiance. Love. Exactly what we needed to win this. I wrapped my arms around him and dared a smile. "Congratulations, Lothario. I wish I could tell you more right now, but I can't. What I can say is that you might have just discovered a way we can help your friend Sadie and everyone else at this godforsaken school."

CHAPTER THIRTY-THREE

I stood outside Ayaz's door, my hands in fists at my side, my blood practically *boiling*. I'd trusted them. I'd fucking *trusted* them and they hadn't told me the whole truth.

As Andre and I snuck back into the school and made our excuses to the teachers, feigning a make-out session in the quad that got out of hand (I was the gutter whore, so that was easy for them to believe) I turned over what I should do next. My palms burned – I knew what I *wanted* to do. We walked into the atrium and two of the trash cans caught fire.

What I wanted was to burn the whole fucking place down. But they'd done that once before. Miskatonic Prep wouldn't stay dead.

Andre placed a hand on my shoulder. His steady eyes calmed me, brought me back to center. I had to focus on what I'd set out to do – free my friends, free the edimmu. Although now I wasn't doing it for the monarchs but for all the scholarship students who'd come before me, the voiceless who deserved a voice.

The mission hadn't changed. That meant I had to keep up my friendship with the Kings, even though the thought of seeing them made me sick. And that brought me back to Ayaz's closed door. Behind it were the three guys who flipped my life upside down and shown me that nothing was what it seemed. Now I had to throw myself in there like Daniel in the Lion's Den and pretend everything was fine, because I needed them if I was going to make this happen.

Would that some angel would take pity on me and wire the lion's jaws shut. Or maybe I'd just punch them. I hadn't decided.

I sucked in a breath and knocked.

"You think you've found Ms. West's laboratory?" Trey glanced up at me from his spot on the designer sofa, his icy eyes narrowed in suspicion.

"Yep." I pretended to toss my hair over my shoulder and struck a classic Courtney pose. My jaw clenched, but I managed to turn it up into what might've passed for a smile. "Frankly, I'm disappointed you've been here twenty years and never noticed it before. It's so obvious."

Quinn shuddered. "Don't do that, Hazy. You're giving me flashbacks."

"So is it actually obvious?" Ayaz was on his hands and knees, hunting through one of the compartments under his bed. He pulled up a series of plans and maps.

I snorted. "Maybe? It's big, and it's around the main school buildings, but I'm not sure exactly where it was because we accessed it from a rickety dumbwaiter from the laundry. There weren't any windows inside and it was freezing cold, so I believe it's underground."

Ayaz dropped his maps on the coffee table. He tried to brush his hand against mine, but I jerked away. I sifted through the stack and unrolled one that gave a three-dimensional cutaway of the dormitory building, showing details of underground servants quarters and storage rooms. "It's around here, but... this isn't accurate. None of these spaces have a curved roof."

"You mean like an icehouse?" Ayaz asked.

"A what?"

"Some old houses would have a cold room or icehouse. Ice would be chipped from freshwater sources and shipped around the country, where it would be packed in special ice houses along with insulation like straw. For Parris to have one up here, the ice would have to be shipped from the nearest freshwater lake, which is a good hundred miles away. It would have been a real talking point among his circle of friends." Ayaz swept his eyes over the drawings. "It would make sense to have it around here, near where the old kitchens were. There's probably an entrance above-ground, too – where the workers would pack in the ice and straw without traipsing through the house."

I bet that was the tunnel we crawled out. I squinted at the lines, but couldn't see anything that resembled the complex I'd seen. "Is it strange that it isn't on the map?"

"I honestly don't know. This map wasn't made during Parris' tenancy, but about a couple hundred years later, when the building was being renovated to turn into a school. It's possible there were rooms underground the workers and architects never found. But an icehouse would be the ideal place to have a laboratory – it would be naturally chilled, and being underground, it's insulated from sound."

"There were all these smaller rooms, with what looked like giant freezers inside," I remembered. "But they were locked. She must keep a key somewhere."

"She's not going to let that key out of her sight," Ayaz said. "It's probably on her person."

"We have a very easy way to get under her clothes, right?" A knife twisted in my gut at the thought of Ayaz with the Dead-mistress, but I had to remind myself that I couldn't care now. Not knowing that Ayaz had been a part of ·what was going on downstairs.

Ayaz's face darkened. "I don't think that's a good idea. She doesn't tell me anything."

"I'm not surprised. You're not exactly a pillow talker. Isn't that right, Hazy?" Quinn looked at me. A hot blush crept over my cheeks. If Quinn only guessed at the truth about me and Ayaz, he knew now. And his expression...

He looked *hurt*.

But why would he even care if I slept with Ayaz? Quinn didn't care about me, not really. He was all about living in the moment, about chasing the next big thrill, without a care for who got hurt in the process. And I was the ultimate thrill – the forbidden fruit. I thought all this, and yet seeing those amber eyes look away tore me up inside in ways I didn't understand.

I wanted badly to trust them. Part of me still did, but... but... the stub of Sadie's ruined tongue burned into my skull.

"She hasn't... called on me since the first quarter," Ayaz muttered, avoiding my eyes.

I hated how relieved I was to hear that.

"So?" Quinn crossed his feet on the table, putting a giant crease right through the middle of Ayaz's map. "Go to her. Work your Turkish mojo and riffle through her pockets when she's in the bathroom."

"Don't you think I've already done that?" Ayaz gritted his teeth. "She's too smart. She doesn't trust any student, especially not one who'd sleep with a teacher."

"But she'd have a spare key, right?" I said. "Evil geniuses don't accidentally lock themselves out of their lairs because they left the key in their other bra. Especially not Headmistress West. She wants a second copy of *everything*, just in case."

"And we have a secret passage that leads right to her office," Quinn declared, uncrossing and re-crossing his feet, screwing up the maps even worse. Ayaz balled his hands into fists. "And the most perfect distraction to lure West out of her office."

"This isn't a good idea," Trey said. "If we locate this key, we risk West finding it missing and figuring out we're trying to get into her lab. She's going to know we want to destroy the god. Hazel's deal will be off and all the charity cases will be fair game."

At the words 'charity cases,' a chill ran down my spine.

"I agree with Trey," Ayaz said. "There are risks."

"You're just saying that because you don't want to put your dick into her again," Quinn said.

"This might be our only shot," I said. "I can't believe you're both chickening out. You know what's at stake."

Trey held up his hands. His cuff slid down, revealing his burned-off tattoo. "If we get caught, I can't protect you anymore."

"You've never protected me," I shot back, the anger flaring inside me. "You hurt me. You tried to throw me off a *cliff*."

Trey's jaw clenched. He stood up without a word and stormed off. A moment later, the wall shook as he slammed the door.

Quinn and Ayaz exchanged a look. I glared at them. "What?"

"Nothing." Quinn shrugged. "Trey hates being called out."

"Or, an alternative explanation is…" I hedged.

Quinn put his feet down and leaned forward, his amber eyes gleaming. "See, the thing is, Trey won't admit it because… well, because he's Trey. But he's been protecting you from the start."

I snorted. "That's bullshit."

"Nope. All those things he's done, he did to stop something worse from happening."

"That's completely fucked up."

Quinn shrugged. "This is Miskatonic Prep – it's where you come to get a first-class education in fuckedupitude."

"Why can't he just find a less shit way of protecting people?" *Why couldn't he save any of those poor people downstairs?*

"Because he's Trey. He doesn't think like that." As Ayaz stood up to gather the maps, he glanced over his shoulder at the door.

"Trey believes that the only way to prevent someone worse from taking over this school was to be the big bad wolf. And his greatest nightmare has just come true – the wolf has been dethroned, and a panther is in his place. Her fangs and claws are sharp and deadly. Honestly, he's not taking this whole being kicked out of the presidency position with grace and decorum. But we can't worry about him now. We've got a key to find."

Wah wah wah. At least Trey still has a tongue.

"Yes. Which means that Ayaz is going to get his booty spanked." Quinn slapped Ayaz's ass.

"Don't be foul," Ayaz growled. "It's not like that."

"Better lube up, Ataturk."

Ayaz locked eyes with me, and I saw the pain lurking in those obsidian orbs. I knew now that he'd been coerced into sleeping with Ms. West, but Quinn didn't know I knew that. He was deliberately trying to lower Ayaz in my eyes.

"Hazel, are you asking me to do this?" Ayaz asked, his voice tight.

I shrugged. "You don't have to do anything you don't want to. Maybe you can find a way to draw her away from the office without..."

...without bending her over a desk and fucking her roughly from behind. I didn't need to finish.

Ayaz gave me a sad smile. "For you, I'll do anything."

"Good. Ataturk is in the game." Quinn dragged me out of the dorm room before I could say anything else. He led me down to the library. Courtney and her friends were studying under the stained-glass window, lording it over Trey's old table like feudal lords. They shot us filthy looks as Quinn led me into the stacks.

"You don't think they'll follow us?" I whispered.

"Of course they will." Quinn slammed the stairwell door shut and jammed a chair under the handle. "Now, let's get into that passage. Without his magical dick in play, I don't know how long Ayaz will be able to tempt Ms. West from her office."

"Do you have to be so mean to Ayaz?" I demanded as Quinn shoved a computer desk out of the way and slid open the secret panel.

"What's wrong – your boyfriend can't stick up for himself now?"

"He's not my boyfriend, Quinn," I snapped. "And not that this is the time, but it shouldn't matter to you if he was. I know you don't really want to be my boyfriend, so what's the big—what the hell are those?"

Quinn passed me three brand new bars of soap.

"Have you ever read about the escape from Alcatraz?" Quinn asked. "They made a copy of a key by pressing it into a bar of soap. You can put the key back and we can use the soap mold to create a cast of the key. That way, West never has to notice the key missing and we can get into the lab as many times as we need to."

"You're cleverer than you look." I took the soaps from him and shoved them in my pockets. "Stay here and guard my exit."

"You got it." Quinn gave me a boost into the tunnel. I was about to shut the door when he shoved his head into the opening. His eyes widened. "Hazy?"

"Yeah?" I lifted my head. Quinn mashed his mouth against mine. The kiss knocked my breath from my lungs. Slow and soft, it built inside me like a tidal wave crashing over me, pulling me under.

This wasn't Quinn the joker, desperate for distraction. This was someone who craved salvation, who kissed because he was holding on by a thread that was fraying away and he needed a lifeline. He cupped the side of my face, his thumb trailing across my cheek. His eyes remained open – those amber pools flecked with light, tinged with tenderness and regret.

Wow.

I knew I should pull away, I should keep my distance because this was a guy who'd let a great injustice continue and didn't even see it. But I couldn't make my body obey. It was Quinn who drew away and gave me a wink. Just like that, the old Quinn was back. "I just want you to keep your options open."

My mouth was still hanging open as he swung the door shut behind me. *Where did that come from?*

Is he trying to tell me that he actually cares about me? That I'm more than just a distraction to him?

My lips still burned from Quinn's kiss. I couldn't wrap my head around him, so I shoved that aside to deal with later. I crawled through the tunnel, trying to stay as quiet as I could. The soaps dug into my hip as I rounded a corner. Stale air scratched at my throat. Somewhere above my head, I heard the faint scritching of the rats. *Please don't come any closer. I don't mind you guys in the walls, but I don't want to meet you in the dark.*

My knees ached from crawling by the time I found the place where Quinn and I sat listening last time. I pressed my ear against the wall, but I couldn't hear anything except the pounding of my own heart. *How will I know if Ms. West is out of her office, or if she's just working in silence? We should have organized this better. We should have had a signal or—*

There was a knocking noise, and then a sultry voice said, "Enter."

I backed away from the wall, my heart hammering. Good thing I hadn't opened the panel.

"Headmistress," it was Ayaz's voice. "I wondered if you could come with me for a moment? There's something I need to show you."

"I'm busy, Ayaz."

"It's very important," he said. There was a strain in his voice.

"I see." A chair pushed out. "Is this a problem that you have, in your trousers?"

I squeezed my eyes shut, wishing I didn't have to listen, didn't have to imagine. *He's doing this for me. He's doing this for me.*

Fuck. This not caring about the guys anymore was harder than I thought.

"Yes." That voice. So soft, so silken. The same voice that told me I was beautiful. *I fucking hate this.*

"Why do we have to go somewhere?" the Deadmistress purred. "I've a perfectly serviceable desk right here."

Because we need you out of your fucking office.

My stomach lurched. If she made him do it here, and I had to listen...

"Miss, I have a surprise for you. But I can't bring it to you. I have to take you to it..."

"You're sweet," she purred. "Very well. I'm amenable to being surprised."

I heard the pair of them talking quietly to each other, their voices fading as they crossed the room. The door to West's office swung open and shut again. The lock clicked shut.

As soon as I heard their footsteps fade away, I slid the panel aside and stepped into the room. Ms. West's office had a one-way window that looked out at her secretary's desk and waiting room, but as it was the weekend, the secretary wasn't working today. The room was thankfully empty. I was on my own.

Where would she keep a key?

I tried the desk drawers. Luckily, none of them appeared to be locked. Most of the drawers contained stationary – pens, pencils, a leatherbound date-planner. One held a stack of alchemical drawings. I wanted to take them to show Ayaz, in case he could make sense of them, but that was a bad idea.

The next drawer was stuffed full of cell phones. *A-hah!* I riffled through until my hands closed around my phone, and I tucked it into my pocket. She'd never notice one was missing amongst all those others.

A shudder ran down my spine as I realized that every phone in that drawer belonged to a student just like me who was now walking the halls as the living dead with their tongue cut out.

The bottom drawer contained a bottle of alcohol and a block of expensive Belgium chocolate. Ms. West's private stash. But not a key in sight.

As I was pushing the drawer shut in frustration, the bottle rolled along the bottom, and the sound it produced sounded weird, muffled. Leaning down, I pressed my fingers on the bottom of the drawer, tracing the height against the outside wall. The drawer was a good one-inch shallower than it should have been.

Gotcha.

I set the bottle and chocolate on the rug and ran my hands along the edges of the wood, searching for a spring. I didn't find one, but at the back there was a small finger hole. I inserted my finger inside and tugged up the false bottom, revealing a black velvet ribbon holding two keys.

Keys in hand, I rushed back to the panel, where I'd set down the blocks of soap. I pressed the keys into two of the blocks, careful not to move them around. When I lifted them out, I had a perfect impression of each key. I used the edge of my blazer to wipe off any excess soap, then dropped the keys back in the drawer, replaced the false bottom and bottle, slid the drawer back into place, and locked it.

I checked over the desk to make sure everything looked exactly as I left it. As I pushed the chair back in so it sat in the same position on the rug, my eye caught a colorful flyer on the desk. Gingerly, I pinched the corner between two fingers and held it up to the light.

The flyer looked like it had been made using 90s clipart, which meant it definitely came from inside the school. That software suite hadn't been updated since the Miskatonic fire, and none of the teachers seemed to have the latest equipment.

It invited students to a formal dance in the third quarter, to be held in the newly refurbished gymnasium. A chill ran down my back as I remembered that eerie, deserted gym with the shadows flitting beneath the bleachers. The flyer promised a night of magic and wonder and encouraged students to 'dress to impress' in their most lush formal attire. One couple would be voted king and queen. Weirdly, instead of the Derleth Academy crest with the strange star, this flyer showed the old Miskatonic crest.

My first thought was, *this is the perfect opportunity to have my revenge. Students and alumni gathered together in one place, on the site of the fire that started this madness.*

But how can they be refurbishing the gym? Why hold a dance on the very site where all these students lost their lives? And why use the Miskatonic crest if it's supposed to be a secret from the scholarship students—

Voices sounded outside. A door slammed. I jerked my head up in time to see the secretary shuffle over to her desk, followed by Ms. West dragging a protesting student by the ear. *Quinn!*

Shit.

If Quinn was here, that meant Courtney got into the computer lab at the other end. I had to hope that she hadn't found the tunnel entrance. My only chance was to get inside and wait it out.

I dropped the flyer, but it fluttered off the desk and landed on the rug. I scooped it up and placed it back on the stack of papers, hoping she wouldn't remember exactly where it had been.

I raced for the panel. As I swung my leg over to get inside, I accidentally kicked the lever that held the door open. The panel slid shut with me on the wrong side, still in the office. I yanked my leg out of the way just in time.

Shit, shit.

I pressed around the edge of the panel, but no amount of pushing or jiggling made it swing open again. I spun around to search for a hiding place just as Headmistress West walked into the room.

"Miss Waite, what are you doing in here?"

CHAPTER THIRTY-FOUR

"Oh, hi, Headmistress," I breathed, my hands behind my back, tugging my blazer down over my pockets in the hopes she wouldn't see the phone I'd shoved in there.

"Why are you in my office?" she demanded.

An excellent question. I scrambled for a probable reason. "I was looking for some notes Dr. Halsey left for me. She said she'd drop them into the main office, but they weren't there and I saw the door was open and I thought I'd just check if she left it in here…"

"Is that so? Because I distinctly remember locking this door behind me. I've just had to unlock it again."

"It… er, swung shut and locked behind me. But it was definitely open when I came in."

"I see." She dragged Quinn inside and flung him into one of the chairs facing her desk. He met my eyes, his face creased with concern. "It would be very odd for Dr. Halsey to leave notes for her students in my office, since she has an office and cubby hole of her own."

Damn. "Oh, well… I must have misheard."

"Indeed." The headmistress' lip curled back into a smile that had no heart to it. "Or perhaps you were attempting to break in here to find the answers for your upcoming exams."

"Why would I do that?" I glared at her, overwhelmed with rage. Was she *really* still going to pretend she was a normal principal at a normal school? "I'll never go to a university. Come the end of the year I'll be dinner for your god. I'm only acing classes right now to keep up appearances, so Greg and Andre don't suspect anything's amiss."

"Then explain to me why only minutes before this supposed meeting with Dr. Halsey in *my* office, Courtney Haynes saw you and Quinn Delacorte disappear into the computer lab under the library and barricade the door. And yet, when John Hyde-Jones broke down the door and they entered the room, only Quinn was in there."

"I wish I could explain, Headmistress." She moved around the desk toward me, her black skirts swirling about her ankles. As casually as I could, I shifted my weight to my back foot. "But the truth is, Courtney Haynes isn't exactly trustworthy. She's saying that I was with Quinn, even though I wasn't. Right?" I glanced over at Quinn and he nodded vigorously.

"I broke up with Courtney last quarter," he said. "Ever since I've been hanging out with Hazel, she's been acting jealous, trying to hurt Hazel. She even beat—"

As soon as Ms. West's attention was diverted, I bolted around the other side of the desk and flung open the door. Headmistress West boomed after me. "Hazel Waite, get back here. I'm not done with you."

But I'm done with you. And now I've got a way to prove something's wrong at this school.

I sprinted through the atrium, shoving aside kids as I barreled up the stairs. "Watch it, gutter whore!" Tillie snapped as I slammed my elbow into her ribs.

"Eat me!" I yelled in return, sprinting through the locker corridor and onto the walkway that led to the dormitory. With every step, my phone slapped against my thigh. *My phone. A link to the outside.*

There was only one person who could keep me safe while I used it. I pounded my fists on the door. To my relief, it flung open.

"What happened?" Trey demanded.

"The headmistress caught me in her office." I sagged into the sofa. Trey sat down beside me, his leg brushing mine, warm and reassuring.

"Where's Quinn and Ayaz?"

"Quinn's still there. I just ran past her and came here. I think he'll try and hold her in there for a bit. I got the imprints of the keys. And I got this." I held up the phone. "Only the soaps are still in the passage. And I have no idea where Ayaz is."

Trey's blue eyes shone with concern. "You'd better tell me the whole story. Is the headmistress about to storm in here and hurt you—"

As if on cue, fists pounded on the door. My heart leaped into my chest.

"Trey, let me in, you bastard!"

I sagged in relief as Trey got up to open the door. Quinn slammed it shut behind him and flopped onto the chair. "That's 50 demerit points for me. Whatever will Daddy say?"

"What happened with West? Is she looking for me?"

"Of course she is. She'll be here any minute. And for the real icing on the cake, our parents just arrived."

The color drained from Trey's face. "Your dad? My dad?"

"Never a dull moment." Quinn's face broke out in a reckless grin as he slapped the soaps down on the table. "Oh, I did manage to nab these from the tunnel while she was out greeting the senior Eldritch Club. You did a great job, Hazy."

"We did a great job." I turned on my phone, whooping with joy as it beeped to life. The battery light was still flickering, but it had enough juice to send a message. My heart jolted as the screen-

saver came on – me and Dante making duck-faces at the camera. I
flicked past it as fast as I could and typed a message to Zehra. I'd
memorized her number.

*I've got the key and location to Ms. West's lab, but I need to get them to
you, now. Shit's going down.*

A moment later the phone beeped with a reply. *I'm on the
eastern side of the grounds. I'll be at the cave in half an hour.*

"Fuck, where's Ayaz?" Trey demanded, pacing across the room,
rubbing at the burn on his wrist. I turned off the phone and
threw it down on the table and touched my fingers to my own
burn.

Quinn shrugged. "Dunno. He wasn't with the headmistress
when she dragged me in. Maybe he couldn't pull his pants over his
giant cock in time—"

There was a brisk knock on the door. "Open up, Trey," Headmistress West demanded. "Your father is here. We need to speak
with you."

Shit, shit. I remembered what Vincent Bloomberg had said
about 'taking care of me.' So far, he hadn't tried anything, but I
knew this visit wasn't out of familial duty. He'd found his leverage.

From the shattered glass of Trey's eyes, he knew I was in
danger. He stalked across the room and threw open one of the
windows. "Get out," he whispered.

"Huh?"

"There's an old tree right beside the window. Use the drainpipe to swing over and get down. I've used it hundreds of times.
Take these," Trey shoved the soaps into my hand, along with a
lighter. "Get them to Zehra."

"Trey, are you in trouble?"

"It's not important." Behind us, fists pounded on the door.

"It's important to me. You've got to get out of here."

"No."

"We could all go in different directions, confuse them, hide in
the pleasure garden tunnel."

His aristocratic features remained hard, resolute.

I pounded my fist against the window frame. "Why won't you save yourself?"

"Because I'm cut from the same cloth as my father. I'm a monster, Hazel. I need to be controlled." Trey pressed his lips to mine, stealing a breathless, desperate kiss. Wood splintered as someone rammed the door. He tore his lips from mine and shoved me out the window. "Go. Now."

CHAPTER THIRTY-FIVE

I swung my leg over the glass panel and stepped out onto the ledge. The stone sloped sharply away. I strangled a scream as my foot slipped off. I grabbed the drainpipe running alongside the window and hugged it as my body swung out over thin air. I was three stories up. If I fell, I wouldn't have to worry about what Vincent Bloomberg would do to me, cuz I'd be splattered across the cobbles like a life-sized Rorschach test.

Oh well. At least it would hurt the god.

The drainpipe groaned under my weight. I tried to kick out my foot to snag the nearest tree branch, but all that succeeded in doing was swinging me around so I was facing into Trey's dorm room. The door cracked down the middle and fell open. Ms. West stood in the corridor, flanked by Courtney, Tillie, John Hyde-Jones, and a circle of senior Eldritch Club members.

They stormed into the room. Vincent grabbed his son by the throat as Ms. West lunged at Quinn.

Go. Now.

My stomach lurched and shoulders screamed as I swung my body around the pole. Mom would probably be good at this. Pole dancing was always her specialty. I flung out my hand and grabbed the nearest branch, swinging myself into the tree like a cartoon monkey.

SNAP. The branch broke just as I slammed into the trunk. I wrapped my free arm around the tree, dropping a few feet before I was able to slide into a fork. My breath came out in ragged gasps as I leapt down the branches, ignoring the pointy bits that dug into my flesh. I jumped onto the lawn and raced past the visitor lot, now filled with cars, and across the field.

Cold wind whipped around me. My legs burned, but I didn't slow down until I hit the rose bushes at the bottom of the fields. Thorns snagged on my stockings, tugging at me like claws, trying to drag me back. The soaps jabbed against my legs. I hoped they hadn't broken.

Fuck. I left the phone on the table. It was out of battery, anyway. I had to hope Zehra didn't need to message me again.

Blood whooshed in my ears. My chest heaved but I kept on running, running, running. I didn't even care anymore what they did to me. Let them toss me into the void. I'd fight that fucking Great Old God all the way down to hell. But if I could stop this happening to others...

This ends with me. I will be the last.

...if only I could do more. If I could give the students of this school a chance to live their lives again... Faces from Ayaz's files flashed in front of my eyes, all those voiceless scholarship students, chosen because they had no one to fight for them.

Until now.

Trees flew by in a blur, the ocean rising up between them as I neared the edge of the cliffs. The ground rumbled beneath me, rolling and pitching under my feet. *The god's wrath?* I didn't stop to find out. I skidded to a stop as the rock ledge came into view, the same one the guys had used to shelter me from the club all those weeks ago. I dived behind the stones and slithered between the crack, fumbling in my pocket for the lighter. I flicked it on, illuminating the edge of the entrance. I turned myself around and slid backward into the hole. My foot slipped on the edge. My fingers lost their grip, and I half leapt, half tumbled onto the shelf below.

I landed hard on my side. The lighter flew from my hand, bouncing on the stone and flickering out. The cavern plunged into darkness.

No. No. No.

I couldn't be *here* in the dark. The darkness hid the shadows, the oppressive weight of hatred, the call of the god that wanted to have me all to himself.

Panic rose in my chest. I felt around me, searching for the lighter, begging the darkness for some solution. Fear crept through my veins. A strange heat pooled in the palms of my hands, zigzagging across my fingers. I held up my hand, running the tips together, trying to make sense of the burning, living heat that scorched the inside of my skin.

The heat bubbled against the surface. I cried out as my hands burst into flame – orange glowing orbs piercing the gloom.

Light flared, then died back. I held up my hand, watching with awe and horror as flames rippled over the surface of my skin. The heat warmed my face and yet my hands weren't burning. All I felt was a faint sizzle through my veins – the kind I got when I kissed one of the guys.

Or when I started the fire that burned the slithering creature.

From the darkness, a tall flame darted in front of my face, sending me reeling. *The lighter!* I stared as the flame from the lighter fell, becoming a small orange pinprick.

What? How is that possible? How is the lighter burning without me touching it? How are my hands on fire?

I must've spilled lighter fluid on myself. I've gone into shock. Any moment now that'll wear off and the pain will begin.

But it didn't. Instead, as I watched, the flames on my hands shrunk away of their own volition, seeming to dissolve into my skin, leaving only the flame of the lighter.

I really am doing this.

Or maybe not. A tiny, hopeful voice echoed in my head. *Maybe you just had a hallucination. You hit your head in the fall. The lighter must have had a spark left. You blew air on it when you exhaled. That's a much more sensible explanation than you summoning fire from your fingers.*

Nope. That wasn't true.

I can't pretend any more. I really do have some sort of power.

Well. Fuck.

But I couldn't worry about that now. I needed to find Zehra. Groaning, I rolled over on my side and grabbed the lighter, holding it up as I pulled myself into a sitting position. Pain stabbed my hip. I held the lighter down, admiring the fresh tear along the seam of my Derleth Academy blazer and the scrape visible through my ruined stockings. From somewhere deep in the recesses of my mind, the god groaned with pain.

It doesn't matter. I'm here. I made it.

I dug out the soaps and inspected them under the light. They were completely undamaged, the tiny impressions of the keys packed inside. I didn't have the map, but if I told her what to look for, I knew Zehra would figure it out.

The cave felt different somehow, changed and oppressive, the stones closing in on me. A fine dust wafted in the air, rippling and curling around the flame. The dust stuck to my lungs, scratching the back of my throat. I coughed loudly.

Something clattered against the stones. My heart pounded. I called out into the gloom. "Zehra? Are you here yet?"

The only answer was darkness. Clamping one hand over my stinging hip, I crept down to the next shelf. I held up the lighter, but I could only make out a couple of feet in front of me.

"Zehra?" I moved to descend to the next step. "I hope you're not waiting too far into the cave—"

My words caught in my throat as the light illuminated a rock protruding vertically from the edge of the shelf, blocking my way. *I don't remember that from last time...*

I ran the lighter along the surface of the rock, searching for a reason. The flame caught something dark etched across the stone. I recognized the symbol anywhere – the sign of the Eldritch Club.

What's it doing here? I ran my fingers along the edge of the rock, searching for a way around. The eerie veins pulsed as they criss-crossed at the edge of my vision. My nails scraped the edge of a second rock. Confused, I stood back and thrust out the lighter.

What I saw made my stomach turn.

The stones seemed new to me because they *were* new. There was a hole above the stones. The cave groaned as another piece of rock slid out and cracked on the shelf next to me. The roof of the cave had fallen in. That must've been the rumble I felt before.

The cave-in completely sealing the tunnel. No one was getting in, or out.

CHAPTER THIRTY-SIX

I clawed at the stone, shoving it with all my strength until I managed to topple it onto its side. I dragged out a second stone, opening a tiny gap in the wall. Blackness rushed at me. "Zehra?" I called into the gloom. "Are you in there?"

No reply.

Get help. Get the guys. She could be trapped on the other side.

If that was true, there was only one way she could go – deeper into the cave, closer to the god's cavern.

I clambered back up to the entrance and crawled out from under the ledge, pausing to listen for the sounds of a search party. No one was out looking for me. I don't know whether that was a relief, or a warning. I sucked in a deep breath and ran toward the pleasure garden stairs.

My feet skidded on the damp stone as I took the path as fast as I could. The pleasure garden stood empty, eerie now that it was devoid of life – the crumbling rotunda appearing otherworldly, the angles bent all wrong. I located the path behind it that wound up toward the tunnel entrance and ducked inside.

Once inside, I flicked on the lighter, but this time it had well and truly fizzled out. I squeezed my eyes shut. *Focus. Stop panick-*

ing. You won't help Zehra if you panic. I knew the tunnel like I knew the burn on my wrist. I walked slowly, keeping one hand on the wall and the other on the low ceiling. The familiar scritch-scritch-scritch of the rats powered me onward, drawing me back to—

My body slammed against something hard.

Huh?

I reeled, my head spinning. I staggered back and thrust out my hands. *I must've disoriented myself in the darkness. The tunnel runs practically straight, so I can't have run into—*

My fingers scraped stone. I felt around, my hands sliding over dressed blocks, mortared in place. A wall of stone that filled the entire tunnel, without space for even a rat to fit through.

The tunnel had been blocked up.

CHAPTER THIRTY-SEVEN

This can't be a coincidence.

I felt around the edges of the tunnel, but whoever had bricked it up had done an excellent job. It wasn't moving. I couldn't wiggle any of the stones free.

With nothing else to do, I re-emerged into the pleasure garden. The twisted statues mocked me from their plinths – *she will die down there because of you.*

Our one chance was slipping away. I couldn't let that happen.

I raced back to the school. I didn't need to check the doors to know they'd be all locked up. They didn't want me to escape this time. Quinn had said there were at least two other passages into the school, but he'd never shown them to me, and even if I did know where they were, I had no way of knowing if they were bricked up, too. I counted windows along the dormitory block, stopping beneath Quinn's. I tossed pebbles at his window, but no one stirred. I peered into the dining hall and many classrooms, but they were all deserted. *During the day? What's going on?*

I clambered back up the tree and tried to peer into Trey's window. But the room beyond was cast in darkness. I couldn't see a thing. I rapped on the glass but no one came to the window.

Where are they? What are they doing to my boys?

The Eldritch Club cars were still in the parking lot. I briefly considered hotwiring one and taking off. But I couldn't abandon Zehra, or Greg and Andre, or Trey or Quinn or Ayaz. For someone who swore she'd never trust another human being again, I sure had a lot of reasons tying me down to this demented place.

I circled the building, hoping by chance there would be a first-floor window open. I even tried the lock on the maintenance shed so I could find some tools to dig out the stone. No such luck. The thought started to nag at me, that maybe I'd reacted too hastily. What if Zehra wasn't trapped inside, but it had just taken her longer than expected to make it to the cave? What if she was waiting for *me* while I was running around out here?

So I dragged my broken, tired body back to that freezing cave and waited. I waited until the sun fell below the horizon, and then I kept waiting through the long and bitter dark night. I sheltered under the ledge, hugging my knees and biting my lip to keep my teeth from chattering. Nightmares tugged on the edge of my consciousness, but I refused to give over to them. Not here. Not so close to the god's subterranean prison.

From the cave, the oppressive darkness watched me, waiting for its chance to strike. I refused to give it that chance.

Zehra never showed up.

Sick with cold and worry, I waited until the sun rose high enough that I could see a fraction inside the cave. I felt around for the metal box the guys kept there and shoved the soap molds inside. Then I trudged back through the trees, heading to the school.

The bell rang just as I limped toward the main entrance. Shit. Mid-year exams started today. I hadn't studied. I hadn't showered. I didn't even know what my first exam would be. But I needed to find the guys, so I joined the crowd of students pouring into the dining hall, which had been converted into an examination room.

I searched the crowd for one of my friends, but couldn't see any of them.

Something was wrong. Nothing was adding up. What had the Eldritch Club done to them?

Numb with worry, I took a seat at one of the desks. At the front of the room, Dr. Halsey barked instructions, but I didn't hear a word. All around me, students whispered about my torn clothes and disheveled appearance.

Finally, I saw two figures I recognized – Greg and Andre were escorted in by Professor Atwood and deposited at the front of the room. Within moments, Greg had two spitballs stuck to the back of his chair. I turned around and scanned every face. Neither Quinn, Ayaz or Trey were anywhere in the room. There were no spare desks.

Where are they? Quinn, I could almost understand skipping class. But Trey would *never* miss an exam.

And when I thought about it, Ayaz had been missing ever since he'd gone off with Ms. West. A knife twisted in my stomach. *They're in trouble. I know they are.*

"Hazel, eyes to the front of the room," Dr. Halsey said, not unkindly. Professor Atwood handed her a note. She unfolded it, pushing her glasses up the bridge of her nose. When she looked at me again, her gaze was hard.

"Hazel Waite, report to the headmistress' office."

CHAPTER THIRTY-EIGHT

I thought about running as soon as I exited the dining hall, but Ms. West must have anticipated that, because she'd sent Professor Atwood. Mr. Dexter waited in the corridor to escort me as well. The two of them flanked me as I trudged across the quad and through the atrium to the headmistress' door.

I dragged my feet, rubbing mud into her plush carpet. The headmistress sat behind her desk, her fingers steepled together in a pyramid in front of her. Atwood and Dexter moved to the back of the room, talking in low voices to a man I didn't recognize. Behind Ms. West, one arm leaning casually against the fireplace, a pair of icicle eyes stared at me with the detached fascination of a serial killer. Vincent Bloomberg.

"Miss Waite, please, have a seat." Ms. West shuffled some papers.

"Why have I been pulled out of my exam?" I demanded.

"There's no need to take that tone with me. After your behavior in my office yesterday and then absenting yourself from the dorms last night, this disciplinary matter demanded immediate attention. We're concerned about you." She peered down her nose at my uniform. "I see you spent the night camping in the forest like an animal. Students caught sleeping outside their own rooms receive an immediate 20 point demerit."

"Since you didn't catch me sleeping, I guess we're fine." I slammed one shoe against the rug, digging the heel into the deep pile. It squelched. Ms. West's mouth puckered.

"Despite your destructive behavior, you're not in trouble, Hazel. We're here to help you." She leaned across her desk, her grey eyes swirling with something that might've passed for concern if I didn't know she resurrected students in her Frankenstein lab. "Is there anything you want to tell me? Anything weighing on your mind?"

Just the fact that you're going to feed me to a cosmic deity and then reanimate my body in your heinous lab and trap me in this school for the rest of my life so that your precious Eldritch Club can control the world. I guess you might say I'm a little preoccupied.

"Thanks for your concern," I said through gritted teeth. "But I'm fine. Can I go now?"

"Not just yet." Ms. West shuffled the papers in her hands and laid them down in front of her. "Your behavior ever since you arrived at this school has been erratic and disruptive, and it's only getting worse."

"*My* behavior—"

"You have been implicated in some serious incidents of bullying and blaming other students for your cruel actions. You broke into my office, and your interactions with other students are starting to cause alarm."

"What bullying incidents? You mean how I've been the *victim* of bullying by your beloved class president?"

"Miss Haynes tells me that several students had their toiletries spiked with chemicals that made their hair fall out and damaged their skin. We searched your room and found empty bottles from the products in question. What a nasty, dangerous thing to do! If they'd got those chemicals in their eyes, you might've caused permanent damage."

erortn

"I only did it because Courtney poured tar all over my hair," I shot back. "I was nearly sick from the fumes and I had to cut off all my hair. Personally, I think she got off lightly. Why isn't she being hauled in here for all the bullying *she's* done?"

"Because you're not telling the truth," Ms. West said. "You're trying to cast blame on an innocent student in another attempt to torment her. The first week you arrived on campus I took you to Old Waldron. She cut off your filthy dreadlocks. They were a health risk for the student body – we couldn't have a lice outbreak."

"That's not what happened! *Courtney* and Trey broke into my room and put tar in my hair."

"Do you mean Trey, your boyfriend?"

"He's not my boyfriend. And Courtney filled my locker with rotting meat and—"

"*Stop*," Ms. West snapped. "I've heard enough of your baseless accusations. I don't need to remind you that *you* were the one reprimanded for throwing meat around in the halls. You even admitted that you put that meat in your *own* locker so you could deliver it to Courtney's dorm."

I snapped my mouth shut as a cold unease settled in my chest. This whole conversation felt like deja vu. *This is a lot like my dream. In fact, it's exactly like my dream. But why? What does that mean?*

"After some careful consideration, I decided to speak with some of your classmates and get the full picture of what's been going on with you. What they've told me is concerning." Ms. West shifted a paper to the top of the stack. "According to Ms. Fairchild, you have called them insulting names like 'rich bitch' and spread rumors about them to turn their friends and boyfriends against them."

"Tillie is another bully who has been torturing the scholarship students since we arrived—"

"Tillie Fairchild and Courtney Haynes are two of your class leaders. They've proven themselves trustworthy and responsible.

Miss Haynes has also become close with Loretta Putnam, so I know you're not speaking truthfully. Why would Courtney pay for a room in the dorms for a girl she was bullying?"

"Because... because she's brainwashed Loretta. It's probably something to do with sacrificing her to your demon god and then bringing her back to life."

The words flew out of my mouth before I could stop them. To my surprise, the god let me speak them. Either the stranger in the room knew all about the agreement or the spell that stopped my tongue had lifted.

Ms. West didn't react how I expected. She looked down at the file on her desk and sighed. Then she turned to the teachers and the strange man. "See? This is what I'm talking about."

My fingers started to tingle as rage bubbled inside me. I stared down at that paper under her hands, my picture pinned to the front. A file about me, just like the one Ayaz had kept in Parris' book.

I hocked a wad of spit right in the center of it.

Ms. West didn't flinch. She picked up the paper, folded it in half, and slid it into her trash can.

That was when I knew I was in deep fucking shit.

"You've made wild claims about things at this school," she said, her voice all concerned and soothing. "Human sacrifices, rats in the walls, a cosmic god living under the gym, students raised from the dead to torment their classmates. You have quite the imagination."

I folded my arms and glared at her. *What are you playing at?*

"These wild stories have us concerned. We love our students to exercise innovation and imagination, but when you start to blur the world between fantasy and reality, you become a danger to yourself and others." Ms. West reached across her desk with taloned fingers, like she wanted to hold my hand or some shit. I folded my arms across my chest and shoved my hands under my elbows. "Quinn Delacorte brought you to the infirmary after he found you passed out with a bottle of floor polish in your hand. After emptying your stomach of the poison, you claimed it was Courtney who forced you to drink it."

"I never went to the infirmary!" I said. "And she *did* force it down my throat. And down Greg Lambert's throat, too. Ask him if you don't believe me."

She turned a page on another file. "I've already spoken to Mr. Lambert. He was at rehearsal for the school production at the time of this alleged attack, as was Ms. Haynes and her friends."

I rubbed my head. *This isn't real. She's trying to mess with my head. She knows we're getting closer to destroying her.*

The strange man spoke up. "I've read the file. This young lady believes she took part in a cultist ritual, and that delusion allows her to justify her behavior within her own reality. For whatever reason – probably because her mother entertained men of the type who might join such a society – she seems to have latched onto this Eldritch Club as the root of her psychosis."

"The Eldritch Club is a very old and very prestigious supper club here on campus," said Vincent Bloomberg. "It's a social group for students, and has never been involved in any occult practices."

"But this is crazy!" I leapt off my chair. "Stop talking about me like I'm not here. I don't have any psychosis. The Eldritch Club is—"

Ms. West kept talking in her creepy soft voice, like I hadn't said anything. "We've seen this before, especially among scholarship students. Miss Waite arrived at this school with no experience of our rigorous curriculum and competitive spirit. She has strained herself mentally striving for unattainable goals and in the process, created this delusion to explain why she has not achieved the high standards we set."

The strange man was nodding vigorously. "It's understandable that given the tragic circumstances of Hazel's past, she's attached herself to the tragedy of Miskatonic Prep."

"There's a reason we don't allow material related to that event in the school," explained Professor Atwood. "It can cause unpredictable trauma in some students, especially those with darker proclivities."

"I don't have darker proclivities!" I screamed. "I've been deliberately brought here as a sacrifice!"

"Vincent thought you might double down on your delusion," Ms. West sighed. "I hate to do this, Hazel, but it's for your own good. Come in, Mr. Demir."

I whirled around. Ayaz stood in the doorway, his dark eyes sweeping over me with a detached hostility that made my hair stand on end. He looked just the way I remembered him when I first saw him across the dining hall – rich brown skin, dark cropped hair that curled a little around his ears, a row of dark stubble across his strong jaw. And his eyes... those dark storms watched me without a trace of kindness, of the Ayaz I'd come to know, to trust.

"Ayaz, what... what's going on?"

Ayaz knelt in front of me, his dark eyes boring into mine. "Please," he whispered, the word clipped and curt. "You need to go with them. You're sick, Hazel. They will get you the help you need."

"No." I shook my head. "You're lying. I'm not sick. You know I'm not. What about everything we've been through together?"

"We haven't been through anything," he said savagely. "We're not friends. I don't even *like* you. You're a pig-ugly piece of trash who doesn't belong at this school."

You're beautiful. His words wrapped around my chest like a vise, squeezing tight. I struggled for breath.

"What about Parris' book? What about that night in my bedroom? What about *this?*"

I pulled my sleeve up to show him the Elder Sign. But when I stared down at my wrist, it wasn't there.

"What?" I rubbed my skin, but apart from the scar, it was perfectly unblemished. "But I had a tattoo. You gave it to me."

Ayaz shook his head. "Tattooing without proper training is dangerous, and that would mean I had to touch you voluntarily. I'd never do that. You've been saying such strange things. I think you're really sick if you think I'd ever be caught dead alone in your room with you."

"What about Zehra?" I demanded. "I didn't imagine her. You held her in your arms. And last night, she didn't show up, and I think—"

"Please," Ayaz closed his eyes. "I wish I'd never told you about my poor, dead sister. You can't keep pretending she's alive and that you spoke to her. It's not true, and every time you do it, it hurts."

Behind Ayaz's violent eyes, I was dimly aware of Vincent Bloomberg moving to the doorway, ushering in two nurses in grey scrubs. They advanced on me, their pleasant smiles sinister. "Please don't worry, Ms. Waite. We're taking you away to a nice, safe place. The Bloomberg Institution will provide you with the care you need to cure you of these hallucinations."

A hand clamped on my wrist. I wrenched my arm free, but Vincent grabbed my hand in midair and yanked it down. Atwood and Dexter fell on me, holding me down in the chair while the nurses unrolled leather restraints and... and...

A straitjacket.

I screamed and howled and bucked and kicked. I gave Vincent a good jab in the instep, but they soon had me overwhelmed.

"Ayaz!" I cried. "Help me!"

But Ayaz wouldn't even meet my eyes. He turned away as the nurses yanked my arms in front of me, tugged on the straitjacket, and tightened it so I couldn't escape. The last thing I saw as they dragged me away was Vincent wrap Ayaz in a warm, fatherly embrace.

TO BE CONTINUED

Secrets. Lies. Sacrifice. Find out what happens next in book 3 of the Kings of Miskatonic Prep, *Possessed*.

Read now:
http://books2read.com/miskatonic3

Or devour the entire Kings of Miskatonic Prep series (with bonus POV scenes) in the boxset:
http://books2read.com/miskatonicbox

Turn the page for a sizzling excerpt.

Get your free copy of *Cabinet of Curiosities*, a Steffanie Holmes compendium of short stories and bonus scenes. To get this collection, all you need to do is sign up for updates with the Steffanie Holmes newsletter.

http://www.steffanieholmes.com/newsletter

FROM THE AUTHOR

She is nine years old. Two girls at her school pretend to be her friends, but mock her and humiliate her behind her back. She confronts them one day, tells them she's sorry if she'd done something to upset them.

"I just want us all to be friends," she says.

Their faces break into smiles. "That's what we want, too!"

One of them says she has something awesome to show the others. "We just found it!" She drags the girl behind the school hall. "You'll love it." She tells the girl to bend down and look under the hall.

As the girl bends over, a hand grabs the back of her neck, forcing her head down. She twists away, but not before her face is pushed into a pile of dog shit.

She stands up and watches her friends double over with laughter, cackling like the witches of Macbeth. She floats outside her body, looking down on herself – this pathetic girl with dog shit all over her face. She runs. She runs from the school, their laughter following her down the road, around the corner, somewhere, anywhere away from them. She doesn't remember how far she runs or how her mum finds her. She just remembers running.

This is a true story. It happened to me.

I have a rare genetic condition called *achromatopsia*. It renders me completely colour-blind and legally blind. I was also a generally imaginative, weird, and introverted child. I was good at art and making up stories and terrible at sports. I wasn't like the other kids, so they ostracized me, called me names, deliberately invented games to humiliate me, locked me in cupboards, told me that I was stupid, useless, pointless, that I should just go away, that I should never have been born.

It took me years to learn to trust people, to let them see the real me. Social situations still make me anxious, and I've struggled with low self-esteem and internalising anger.

In part, this is why I put myself inside Hazel's head to write this book. But it's not the main reason.

I want to tell you a different story.

During my first year at university, I met this girl in my dorm. We bonded over a mutual love of *Stargate SG1* and Terry Pratchett and became fast friends. We moved in together and were flatmates for two years. We had many of the same classes together, we participated in the same clubs and societies, and she inserted herself into my growing circle of friends. She even started dating my BFF.

In my fourth year, the friendship started to unravel. I was doing postgraduate studies in a different subject to her. I'd moved out of our flat. I was making new friends and developing new interests. I started dating a guy she didn't like. She felt like she was losing me – this person who was so important to her life and her sense of self.

She was frightened, I think. And her fear pushed her behaviour to greater extremes. She became obsessive, demanding to know where I was every moment, controlling my life, forbidding me to go out without her. She accused me of lying, of stealing from her. She created elaborate scenarios in her head where I had wronged her and had to make amends. I moved her into my new flat, hoping that some proximity would help her to calm down. Instead, she grew more erratic and obsessive.

My boyfriend at the time saw all this happening. He watched me become fearful of this person who was supposed to be my friend. He noted me trying to appease her, cancelling plans because they'd upset her, choosing her over my schoolwork, retreating into my shell.

He knew I was giving into her because of my past, because I was so grateful to have a friend that I didn't want to lose her. He could see she was taking advantage of my nature to control me.

One day, my friend and I had a particular horrible fight about something. I was staying at his house, and I was terrified to go back to my flat because she was there.

My boyfriend couldn't watch me hurt anymore. He drove me to the flat. He insisted on coming inside with me. Just having him by my side made me feel stronger.

He marched up to her and he told her that she was going to lose me as a friend if she continued what she was doing. He didn't raise his voice. He didn't call her names. He calmly laid out how she was acting and what it was doing to me. He reiterated how much he cared about me and he wouldn't stand by and watch me hurt.

It was the first time in my life I remember someone standing up for me. Listening to him speak to her that day was like hearing him speak to every one of my old bullies.

Reader, I married him.

Time and again in my life my husband has stood up for me, stepping in where I wasn't strong enough. And I've done the same for him – I've been the lighthouse to his ocean when he needed me most. Now, I don't need him to fight for me, because he helped me uncover the strength to fight for myself.

I'm not Hazel, and she isn't me. She's way more badass. She says the things that I think of an hour after a confrontation and *wished* I'd said.

Hazel doesn't need no man to help her find her strength. But I hope as the series progresses, you'll see how Trey, Ayaz, and Quinn can become her lighthouses when she needs them most.

I know this note is insanely long. Bear with me – I just have a few peeps to thank!

To the cantankerous drummer husband, for reading this manuscript in record time and giving me so many ideas to make it better. And for being my lighthouse.

To Kit, Bri, Elaina, Katya, Emma, and Jamie, for all the writerly encouragement and advice. To Meg, for the epically helpful editing job, and to Amanda for the stunning cover. To Sam and Iris, for the daily Facebook shenanigans that help keep me sane while I spend my days stuck at home covered in cats.

To you, the reader, for going on this journey with me, even though it's led to some dark places. Warning: if you thought book 2 was tough, book 3 will leave you reeling. Get it here: http://books2read.com/miskatonic3.

If you're enjoying *Kings of Miskatonic Prep* and want to read more from me, check out my dark reverse harem high school romance series, *Stonehurst Prep* – http://books2read.com/mystolenlife. This series is contemporary romance (no ghosts or vampires), but it's pretty dark and strange and mysterious, with a badass heroine and three guys who will break your heart and melt your panties. You will LOVE it – you'll find a short preview on the next page.

Another series of mine you might enjoy is *Manderley Academy*. Book 1 is *Ghosted* and it's a classic gothic tale of ghosts and betrayal, creepy old houses and three beautifully haunted guys with dark secrets. Plus, a kickass curvy heroine. Check it out: http://books2read.com/manderley1

Every week I send out a newsletter to fans – it features a spooky story about a real-life haunting or strange criminal case that has inspired one of my books, as well as news about upcoming releases and a free book of bonus scenes called *Cabinet of Curiosities*. To get on the mailing list all you gotta do is head to my website: http://www.steffanieholmes.com/newsletter

If you want to hang out and talk about all things *Shunned*, my readers are sharing their theories and discussing the book over in my Facebook group, Books That Bite. Come join the fun.

I'm so happy you enjoyed this story! I'd love it if you wanted to leave a review on Amazon or Goodreads. It will help other readers to find their next read.

Thank you, thank you! I love you heaps! Until next time.

Steff

EXCERPT: POSSESSED

Kings of Miskatonic Prep 3

Enjoy this short teaser from book 3, Possessed.

Two weeks.

That was all the time I had left before they permanently altered my brain and I believed the lies they were trying to force down my throat.

Two weeks until I lose the only weapon I had that could destroy the god and free the students of Miskatonic Prep.

Two weeks until I could no longer remember what was real and what made me who I was. They would take the only beautiful memories I had left and twist them into something ugly. They would erase Trey and Quinn and Ayaz and turn them back into my tormentors.

And that wasn't even the worst thing. Only I knew just how tightly I clung to my last shreds of sanity. Just beneath the surface, I hid something dark, something dangerous. Something I didn't understand and had hoped to banish forever.

But I couldn't hide from myself. Not any longer. Not with everything that was at stake.

The only way out of this institution was to stop trying to

brace myself against the madness. I had to embrace it. I had to become someone I'd always feared, someone I'd locked down deep, because acknowledging her existence meant accepting the monster inside me.

Possessed by fire.

TO BE CONTINUED

Secrets. Lies. Sacrifice. Find out what happens next in book 2 of the Kings of Miskatonic Prep, *Possessed*

Read now:
http://books2read.com/miskatonic3

Or devour the entire Kings of Miskatonic Prep series (with bonus POV scenes) in the boxset:
http://books2read.com/miskatonicbox

MORE FROM THE AUTHOR OF SHUNNED

From the author of *Shunned*, the Amazon top-20 bestselling bully romance readers are calling, "The greatest mindfk of 2019," comes this new dark contemporary high school reverse harem romance.**

Psst. I have a secret.

Are you ready?

I'm Mackenzie Malloy, and everyone thinks they know who I am.

Five years ago, I disappeared.

No one has seen me or my family outside the walls of Malloy Manor since.
But now I'm coming to reclaim my throne:
The Ice Queen of Stonehurst Prep is back.

Standing between me and my everything?
Three things can bring me down:
The sweet guy who wants answers from his former friend.
The rock god who wants to f*ck me.
The king who'll crush me before giving up his crown.

They think they can ruin me, wreck it all, but I won't let them.
I'm not the Mackenzie Eli used to know.
Hot boys and rock gods like Gabriel won't win me over.
And just like Noah, I'll kill to keep my crown.

I'm just a poor little rich girl with the stolen life.
I'm here to tear down three princes,
before they destroy me.

Read now:
http://books2read.com/mystolenlife

EXCERPT: MY STOLEN LIFE

Stonehurst Prep

I roll over in bed and slam against a wall.

Huh? Odd.

My bed isn't pushed against a wall. I must've twisted around in my sleep and hit the headboard. I do thrash around a lot, especially when I have bad dreams, and tonights was particularly gruesome. My mind stretches into the silence, searching for the tendrils of my nightmare. *I'm lying in bed and some dark shadow comes and lifts me up, pinning my arms so they hurt. He drags me downstairs to my mother, slumped in her favorite chair. At first, I think she passed out drunk after a night at the club, but then I see the dark pool expanding around her feet, staining the designer rug.*

I see the knife handle sticking out of her neck.

I see her glassy eyes rolled toward the ceiling.

I see the window behind her head, and my own reflection in the glass, my face streaked with blood, my eyes dark voids of pain and hatred.

But it's okay now. It was just a dream. It's—

OW.

I hit the headboard again. I reach down to rub my elbow, and my hand grazes a solid wall of satin. On my other side.

What the hell?

I open my eyes into a darkness that is oppressive and complete, the kind of darkness I'd never see inside my princess bedroom with its flimsy purple curtains letting in the glittering skyline of the city. The kind of darkness that folds in on me, pressing me against the hard, un-bedlike surface I lie on.

Now the panic hits.

I throw out my arms, kick with my legs. I hit walls. Walls all around me, lined with satin, dense with an immense weight pressing from all sides. Walls so close I can't sit up or bend my knees. I scream, and my scream bounces back at me, hollow and weak.

I'm in a coffin. I'm in a motherfucking coffin, and I'm *still alive*.

I scream and scream and scream. The sound fills my head and stabs at my brain. I know all I'm doing is using up my precious oxygen, but I can't make myself stop. In that scream I lose myself, and every memory of who I am dissolves into a puddle of terror.

When I do stop, finally, I gasp and pant, and I taste blood and stale air on my tongue. A cold fear seeps into my bones. Am I dying? My throat crawls with invisible bugs. Is this what it feels like to die?

I hunt around in my pockets, but I'm wearing purple pajamas, and the only thing inside is a bookmark Daddy gave me. I can't see it of course, but I know it has a quote from Julius Caesar on it. *Alea iacta est. The die is cast.*

Like fuck it is.

I think of Daddy, of everything he taught me – memories too dark to be obliterated by fear. Bile rises in my throat. I swallow, choke it back. Daddy always told me our world is forged in blood. I might be only thirteen, but I know who he is, what he's capable of. I've heard the whispers. I've seen the way people hurry to appease him whenever he enters a room. I've had the lessons from Antony in what to do if I find myself alone with one of Daddy's enemies.

Of course, they never taught me what to do if one of those enemies *buries me alive*.

I can't give up.

I claw at the satin on the lid. It tears under my fingers, and I pull out puffs of stuffing to reach the wood beneath. I claw at the surface, digging splinters under my nails. Cramps arc along my arm from the awkward angle. I know it's hopeless; I know I'll never be able to scratch my way through the wood. Even if I can, I *feel* the weight of several feet of dirt above me. I'd be crushed in moments. But I have to try.

I'm my father's daughter, and this is not how I die.

I claw and scratch and tear. I lose track of how much time passes in the tiny space. My ears buzz. My skin weeps with cold sweat.

A noise reaches my ears. A faint shifting. A scuffle. A scrape and thud above my head. Muffled and far away.

Someone piling the dirt in my grave.

Or maybe...

...maybe someone digging it out again.

Fuck, fuck, please.

"Help." My throat is hoarse from screaming. I bang the lid with my fists, not even feeling the splinters piercing my skin. "Help me!"

THUD. Something hits the lid. The coffin groans. My veins burn with fear and hope and terror.

The wood cracks. The lid is flung away. Dirt rains down on me, but I don't care. I suck in lungfuls of fresh, crisp air. A circle of light blinds me. I fling my body up, up into the unknown. Warm arms catch me, hold me close.

"I found you, Claws." Only Antony calls me by that nickname. Of course, it would be my cousin who saves me. Antony drags me over the lip of the grave, *my* grave, and we fall into crackling leaves and damp grass.

I sob into his shoulder. Antony rolls me over, his fingers

pressing all over my body, checking if I'm hurt. He rests my back against cold stone. "I have to take care of this," he says. I watch through tear-filled eyes as he pushes the dirt back into the hole – into what was supposed to be my grave – and brushes dead leaves on top. When he's done, it's impossible to tell the ground's been disturbed at all.

I tremble all over. I can't make myself stop shaking. Antony comes back to me and wraps me in his arms. He staggers to his feet, holding me like I'm weightless. He's only just turned eighteen, but already he's built like a tank.

I let out a terrified sob. Antony glances over his shoulder, and there's panic in his eyes. "You've got to be quiet, Claws," he whispers. "They might be nearby. I'm going to get you out of here."

I can't speak. My voice is gone, left in the coffin with my screams. Antony hoists me up and darts into the shadows. He runs with ease, ducking between rows of crumbling gravestones and beneath bent and gnarled trees. Dimly, I recognize this place – the old Emerald Beach cemetery, on the edge of Beaumont Hills overlooking the bay, where the original families of Emerald Beach buried their dead.

Where someone tried to bury me.

Antony bursts from the trees onto a narrow road. His car is parked in the shadows. He opens the passenger door and settles me inside before diving behind the wheel and gunning the engine.

We tear off down the road. Antony rips around the deadly corners like he's on a racetrack. Steep cliffs and crumbling old mansions pass by in a blur.

"My parents…" I gasp out. "Where are my parents?"

"I'm sorry, Claws. I didn't get to them in time. I only found you."

I wait for this to sink in, for the fact I'm now an orphan to hit me in a rush of grief. But I'm numb. My body won't stop shaking, and I left my brain and my heart buried in the silence of that coffin.

"Who?" I ask, and I fancy I catch a hint of my dad's cold savagery in my voice. "Who did this?"

"I don't know yet, but if I had to guess, it was Brutus. I warned your dad that he was making alliances and building up to a challenge. I think he's just made his move."

I try to digest this information. Brutus – who was once my father's trusted friend, who'd eaten dinner at our house and played Chutes and Ladders with me – killed my parents and buried me alive. But it bounces off the edge of my skull and doesn't stick. The life I had before, my old life, it's gone, and as I twist and grasp for memories, all I grab is stale coffin air.

"What now?" I ask.

Antony tosses his phone into my lap. "Look at the headlines."

I read the news app he's got open, but the words and images blur together. "This... this doesn't make any sense..."

"They think you're dead, Claws," Antony says. "That means you have to *stay* dead until we're strong enough to move against him. Until then, you have to be a ghost. But don't worry, I'll protect you. I've got a plan. We'll hide you where they'll never think to look."

Keep reading:
www.books2read.com/mystolenlife

OTHER BOOKS BY STEFFANIE HOLMES

Nevermore Bookshop Mysteries

A Dead and Stormy Night

Of Mice and Murder

Pride and Premeditation

How Heathcliff Stole Christmas

Memoirs of a Garroter

Prose and Cons

A Novel Way to Die

Much Ado About Murder

Kings of Miskatonic Prep

Shunned

Initiated

Possessed

Ignited

Stonehurst Prep

My Stolen Life

My Secret Heart

My Broken Crown

My Savage Kingdom

Manderley Academy

Ghosted

Haunted

Spirited

Briarwood Witches

Earth and Embers

Fire and Fable

Water and Woe

Wind and Whispers

Spirit and Sorrow

Crookshollow Gothic Romance

Art of Cunning (Alex & Ryan)

Art of the Hunt (Alex & Ryan)

Art of Temptation (Alex & Ryan)

The Man in Black (Elinor & Eric)

Watcher (Belinda & Cole)

Reaper (Belinda & Cole)

Wolves of Crookshollow

Digging the Wolf (Anna & Luke)

Writing the Wolf (Rosa & Caleb)

Inking the Wolf (Bianca & Robbie)

Wedding the Wolf (Willow & Irvine)

Want to be informed when the next Steffanie Holmes paranormal romance story goes live? Sign up for the newsletter at www.steffanieholmes.com/newsletter to get the scoop, and score a free collection of bonus scenes and stories to enjoy!

ABOUT THE AUTHOR

Steffanie Holmes is the *USA Today* bestselling author of the paranormal, gothic, dark, and fantastical. Her books feature clever, witty heroines, secret societies, creepy old mansions and alpha males who *always* get what they want.

Legally-blind since birth, Steffanie received the 2017 Attitude Award for Artistic Achievement. She was also a finalist for a 2018 Women of Influence award.

Steff is the creator of *Rage Against the Manuscript* – a resource of free content, books, and courses to help writers tell their story, find their readers, and build a badass writing career.

Steffanie lives in New Zealand with her husband, a horde of cantankerous cats, and their medieval sword collection.

STEFFANIE HOLMES NEWSLETTER

Grab a free copy *Cabinet of Curiosities* – a Steffanie Holmes compendium of short stories and bonus scenes – when you sign up for updates with the Steffanie Holmes newsletter.

http://www.steffanieholmes.com/newsletter

Come hang with Steffanie
www.steffanieholmes.com
hello@steffanieholmes.com

Made in the USA
Middletown, DE
12 July 2021

44010615R00196